APR 25 2011

University Branch

Miss

Entropia

and the Adam Bomb

NO LONGER PROPERTY OF
SEATTLE PUBLIC LIBRARY

Also by George Rabasa

The Wonder Singer

The Cleansing

Floating Kingdom

Glass Houses, Stories

Miss

Entropia

and the Adam Bomb

GEORGE RABASA

UNBRIDLED BOOKS

This is a work of fiction. The names, characters, places and incidents are either the product of the author's imagination or are used fictitiously, and any resemblance to actual persons living or dead, business establishments, events, or locales is entirely coincidental.

Unbridled Books

Copyright © 2011 George Rabasa

Library of Congress Cataloging-in-Publication Data

Rabasa, George.
Miss Entropia and the Adam bomb / by George Rabasa.
p.   cm.
ISBN 978-1-60953-035-8
1. Mentally ill—Fiction.   2. Psychological fiction.   I. Title.
PS3568.A213M57 2011
813'.54—dc22
2010040583

1   3   5   7   9   10   8   6   4   2

Book Design by Claire Vaccaro

First Printing

For Juanita

Miss

Entropia

and the Adam Bomb

INSTITUTE LOISEAUX

REALIZING THE WHOLE CHILD

Woodington, MN 55414
520-645-9875
info@loiseaux.com

From the office of

RICHARD GUNDERSON, MD

It has been a dozen years since I last saw Adam Webb. He was then under my care while enrolled in the counseling/college-prep program at Institute Loiseaux, where I am now Director of Counseling Services. Adam entered the Institute at age 13 and in the following four years earned his high school diploma with exemplary grades. He also made remarkable progress in his social readjustment from a moderate personality dysfunction. In the years since Adam left our Institute to rejoin his family and, we hoped, to continue his studies at a first-rank college, I have thought of him often and, in fact, counted his stay here as one of the more persuasive case profiles in the history of this institute.

So it was with great interest that I received from the police department of Two Harbors, Minnesota, which was investigating the circumstances of Adam Webb's untimely death, an e-mail with an attached file containing the document that follows. I couldn't wait to examine Adam's account, which serves as a definitive patient follow-up.

I read Adam's words with a mixture of scientific interest, frank amusement, and, yes, horror at the unfortunate unfolding of events. After all, this was one of our most creative, intelligent, reflective clients, and his narrative engages even the most casual reader with its vivid storytelling, sharp psychological analysis, and emotional insights.

In truth, I am no literary critic, so I forwarded the document to my colleague Dr. Bart Roberts of our English department, who was one of Adam's teachers during his senior year. I am happy to report that my taste has been validated. Dr. Roberts agrees with me regarding the literary merits of Adam's effort. He has suggested some minor editing and the division of the narrative into chapters and principal sections, but otherwise, Adam's words are left to speak in their full candor. It is particularly sad that this emerging talent will not flower to its potential.

While it's not my intention to dispute details of the following account, I do wish to correct some exaggerations in Adam's boasts of "gaming" the system at Institute Loiseaux. Clients do not have the opportunity to barter or sell medications to each other. Prescriptions are closely monitored, and the abuse of psychotropics and painkillers is virtually unheard-of.

Adam's description of the "confessional therapy" developed by our dear founder, Dr. Clara Loiseaux, now retired, is oversimplified. In truth, the process is painstakingly methodical, with careful analysis preceding the medication and counseling protocols.

On a personal note, it was with a mixture of embarrassment and satisfaction that I saw myself portrayed as a character, albeit a minor one, in Adam's story. I am proud to see that I had a strong influence in Adam's therapeutic process through his years here, but I do take issue with his creative characterization of me. I could have deleted or amended some of his more fanciful conceits regarding my person, but I have let them stand in the interest of maintaining the purity and integrity of his memoir. Suffice it to say, with no fear of being contradicted by others here at the institute, that I am not generally known as "Auntie Gunilla." And I rarely wear a cardigan sweater.

One last caveat: while there may be the temptation to enjoy this story for its prurient thrills, or out of curiosity based on the fleeting notoriety of its author, I hope that the following narrative will elicit compassion for the central figures and give us all time to pause and ponder the fine line that divides balance and harmony from the tipping point into dysfunction.

Richard Gunderson, MD
Institute Loiseaux
Woodington, Minnesota

Part One

By the time I emerged onto the porch my well-traveled suitcase had been placed by the front door by either my brother, Ted, or my father, Albert, I clop-clopped to it in my father's shoes, squatted unsteadily, and unsnapped the latches. Everything was there—a worn copy of *Das Kapital*, my collected papers through the ninth grade, a six-pack of Diet Pepsi, and various meds. The only clothes inside were my pajamas. "What a nice gesture! Thanks a zillion." I shouted, in case Cousin Iris was around to appreciate the irony; she was the one who had first introduced me to the sweet sensations of nude 'slumber.

I searched in the pockets of my father's blue blazer that I was wearing and felt the envelope containing the two-page letter from my parents, a kind of report on this latest home leave, which I was supposed to hand to the attendants. I could read it if I wanted to.

The air had grown chilly as I waited, the darkening shadows of a November afternoon, the day after Thanksgiving, blocking out the tentative sunshine of earlier in the day. One by one the windows of neighboring houses lit up. After a while the only dark house on the street was my family's, with all the lights off so as not to give me any ideas about being welcomed back. As if I would willingly return to their stares and smirks. I have my dignity. I imagined them scurrying about in the dark, Father occasionally dialing Loiseaux and asking in a whisper what was keeping the shuttle. Because frankly, there was some urgency here: the client (never "patient") is not to be trusted within spitting range of certain family members. The problem is not just rudeness, though there is certainly enough of that. The fear is that the client in question might resort to violence. That has not happened before, but there are unresolved anger issues that could, if allowed to boil over, erupt into something of a physical nature. Whoa, there, people! Somebody might think the worst about me, that I might be a potentially fratricidal maniac, interfamilial fornicator, self-made orphan.

I knew all this without ripping open Father's envelope or reading the additional letter my mother had pinned to my shirt for the eyes of Dr. Clara. The truth is, the family was scared of me. Every little nutty act, every eccentricity, every non sequitur in the course of family chitchat was seen as a harbinger of mayhem. If I squashed down the yams during Thanksgiving dinner, who was to say I wouldn't pummel Brother Tedious on top of his melon head with something blunt and heavy? If I walked around the house naked with an erection, I was deemed capable of doing something carnal to Cousin Iris. Yesterday I flicked my Bic lighter over and over throughout the day while sitting in the den, holding the phone to my ear, pretending to be in deep conversation, all the time going *flick flick*, until everybody breathed a sigh of relief when the butane ran out. I could go on flicking until my thumb fell off and not generate more than a spark.

I tried to tell everyone, from Dr. Clara to Mother and Father, that I was not in any way dangerous to others. I played with the lighter until it ran out of gas and saw Father sneaking glances at me. I locked into his gaze. "Don't worry, Dad, I'm not going to set anything on fire."

I had to laugh at the scared look he shot me. Like it had not crossed his mind that I was a pyro, but now that I mentioned it, well, that certainly gave them all something to think about. The truth is that I can't deny something if I'm not directly asked. Are you homicidal, my child? No, sir. The world suffers from a lack of communication. Instead of asking me outright, Dr. Clara tries to look into my head through a variety of lenses and mirrors. Dreams, inkblots, free association, automatic writing, regressive hypnosis, and better than all, her own invention—the Confessional.

Dr. Clara, Chief Mistress of the Head Game, does her work in the dark. The patients gather in the parlor with the lights off and the room pitch-black. The slightest sound is magnified. The rustle of our clothes as we shift in our chairs, the bated breath, the whimper, the sigh, all grow into a larger dimension. We take turns confessing, as to a judge, to crimes we have or have not committed. That is the rule: we can admit to something we have actually done, or we can admit to an imagined transgression. What fun.

Harley got out to load my suitcase in back of the van. He is a big fellow, a true Viking Son of Norway, a former WWF Smackdown star with long, flowing curls and a sculpted physique, known in the ring as the Happy Scandihoovian. After he retired from sweat and sadism, he was hired for his firm ways and cool head, and even now that he is off steroids, it's best not to get on his bad side. He has been known to subdue a rowdy passenger with the vise grip of his thumb and forefinger on a shoulder deltoid muscle, all the while smiling and murmuring endearments. Now, now, my precious, settle down and enjoy the ride, or tonight Dr. Clara will withhold milk and cookies. Unprovoked, he is a gentle giant.

"There you are, you little troublefucker."

"And a happy Thanksgiving to you," I muttered.

He went on as if he hadn't heard me. "Aren't you glad to see your old buddy Harley? I drove here quick as I could, on account that your family thinks you're on the verge of doing something really wacko. *Are* you going wacko on us again?" Harley came around the front of the van and slid the door open for me. I resisted going in because I didn't like the backseat being locked from the outside, the passengers strapped in, and a steel-mesh grill caging them in back.

"Let me ride in front?"

"I can't take any chances."

"Hey, this is your buddy, Adam."

"I was told you were going through an episode."

"Who you going to believe, HH? Me or that bizarre family of mine?"

"Good point. I'll believe your family. They're the ones paying the bills."

"Well, I'm not sitting in back of your booby wagon."

"You going to make me work for my pay? On a holiday, yet? I was hoping we'd have a friendly ride back to the 'Tute."

"There's nothing friendly about getting straitjacketed in back." I realized my voice was rising into its distinctive quavery trill, so I took a moment to breathe. No point in sounding shrill when you're trying to get upgraded from dangerous cargo to companionable passenger.

"Relax. I'll play music, take the scenic route, listen to your ramblings."

"How about I ride shotgun and stay quiet?" I did the zippingof-the-lips thing and smiled my best ingratiating smile. Watch out for psychos smiling. We've got the disarming, wouldn't-hurt-a-fly grin down to a fine art. How else do you think serial killers get their victims to stumble into ditches, check into horrible motels, stroll down dark alleys? I grinned until Happy Harley caved.

"Okay. But not a peep out of you for the whole trip."

Oh, but I wanted to peep. It took every bit of resolve not to wheedle, whine, whimper, and weep. As we rolled down Hyacinth Street, where I'd lived off and on since birth, I felt a prick of sadness that only got sharper as we turned down the meandering road, its skeletal elms lit by the yellow glow of faux-historical streetlamps. You can't go home again, and again, and again, without on a given night leaving forever. I was blasted right out of my fantasies by the knowledge that this was potentially the final parting. A death of sorts.

didn't know it at the time, but I was about to make the leap from quirky childhood to fully unleashed adolescence. Out on our porch stoop, waiting for the van, I'd felt the breeze of liberation for the first time in the two months I'd been home. They were coming to take me away, and I was exceedingly glad. Yes, good-bye, Mom, good-bye, Dad, good-bye, Iris, good-bye, Ted, I'm off to Institute Loiseaux. Better known as a home for the cleverly complicated. It's not a place for everybody. The entrance requirements are rigorous. It takes more than being challenged in the conventional ways, reality-warped, emotionally stunted, mentally fevered, attention-deficient. You gotta be cute to get into Loiseaux. No bobbing heads here, no fatties, droolers, spitters, or snifflers. No predators, delinquents, bullies, tweakers, juicers, or tokers allowed, no matter how delightfully odd.

It does help if you're an affluent exotic, a mass of psychic knots, a tangle of phobias and compulsions backed by a trust fund. Then even the suicidal and the homicidal are welcome. Hippies and goons, poets and anorexics, twitchers, Touretters, and the vaguely traumatized are all hugged close to Dr. Clara Loiseaux's pillowy bosom, feeling the warm embrace of the maternal healer, inhaling her distinctive scent of rose petals and licorice.

The first step is the journey in the 'Tute's van, with Happy Harley transporting problem children back from family leave to our true home on the shore of Lake Lucinda, a destination for snowy egrets, geese, mallards, hawks, and loons of various stripes. Except that with winter upon us, I had six months of white tundra to look forward to, the silence of the night broken only by the wind stirring the snowdrifts and the lake's black ice cracking sharp like gunshots into the depths of sleep. Loiseaux is a calm place in winter. New guests are seldom admitted during this dark season; the prospects of six hours of bright sunlight and a night that stretches from 5:00 P.M. to 8:00 A.M. can bring on the kind of melancholia that dries the spirit and rusts the heart.

I rolled down the window, and the whir of tires on the pavement brought back the sound of my trike when I was six, yes, a three-wheeler because I was not blessed with even a minimal sense of balance. After trying training wheels on a regular bike, all geared up with knee and elbow pads and a helmet to protect me in my frequent tumbles, I was given an overgrown child's contraption with balloon tires and heavy-duty hand brakes. No matter. Rocinante, as Mother named my conveyance, flew like the wind, responding to my frantic pedaling on the uphills, then back, feet out, legs splayed like wings, caroming on the downgrades. Swaddled in heavy corduroy pants and a sweatshirt, I could feel the wind blowing on my face and hear the hum of rubber on asphalt singing in my head. In the years since, I've never been able to recapture that sweet momentum, the sensation of rushing so fast that a slight bump on the road would lift me and Rocinante off the ground into a frictionless surface of pure air.

Chapter Two

On that Thanksgiving Day of '01 our house smelled like sweat. Not the musky fragrance of recently exuded aerobic perspiration but the stale, bottom-of-the-clothes-basket kind. It was not the clean sweat that glistened on my father's brow when he was thinking hard or the pearly mustache beading above my mother's upper lip when she puttered in her garden. Certainly not the sweet dancer's moisture that darkened Cousin Iris's leotard along her tight midriff and under her breasts when she did bar work. That day's smell was more like the sweat from my brother Ted's glands, a musty redolence incorporating Giorgio aftershave and hot tar from his road-repair job.

Following my nose, I traced the odor to the kitchen where a fifteen-pound turkey had been in the oven since dawn. I was not going to eat any of it. This presented a problem because food is a contentious thing for my family. The way the day was shaping up, I expected I'd be sent packing once again. This time I was supposed to be home for good, but at thirteen I continued to feel like a visitor.

In the last few years I had undergone periodic banishment via the 'Tute van. This had harsh consequences, considering that I was born to be here among these fine people, ordained by the fates, I'm sure. I don't know that there was anything unusual about my birth; I haven't seen tapes or interviewed witnesses. In any case, my presence at home had been an off-and-on thing. The exact circumstances of my comings and goings were muddled.

Nobody has ever asked my opinion regarding the Webb household. It contains two official parents, one biological brother, and one honorary cousin. But my inclinations toward vegetarianism, Marx, the goddess Kali, alternative fashion, and psychotropic meds were much in conflict with the unambiguous preferences of the family.

On this visit home I carried a thick brown envelope with school transcripts, prescriptions, psychological evaluations, test scores (IQ 173, four As and two Bs, surprisingly excellent for a slacker personality). A second, sealed envelope inside the outer envelope contained a clinical evaluation of my progress that year. If I'd had the nerve to look inside, it would have provided much humorous material; even after years of Confessional Therapy (registered trademark: Institute Loiseaux), my psyche is a closed book to all, including me. An address was pinned to my jacket as if I were some kind of lobotomee who might get confused in the big city: The Webbs, 328 Kimball Street, St. Paul, 651-798-3269.

My suitcase with its scuffed corners and taped handle was crammed to bursting. I had packed a box of raisins for the sugar, sesame sticks for the salt, Diet Pepsi for energy, my prescribed meds for outward equanimity and inner joy. I had some books, including *Das Kapital* bound in black. Also all kinds of clothes because I couldn't decide whether to put on a dress or jeans. Sure, I know what I am; I've got eyes, there are mirrors. Genital considerations aside, from the age of eleven I could go either way, swinging to extremes: either soaking in bubbles under the morning light that flows like honey through the bathroom skylight or rolling in the muddy backyard, a boy-pig in pork heaven.

I started out as a slow reader, but when I finally got around to Marx, I knew he would always be part of my intellectual arsenal. The Big K has, through the years, given theoretical heft to my ideas, from "Communal Order in Wasps" (show and tell, Miss Hanteel's fourth grade biology) to "The Irony of Martyrdom" (honors paper, Mr. Steadman's seventh grade world history). People know better than to argue with me when they realize my theories are solidly grounded. Marx is back in fashion in the better universities, too, now that he doesn't associate with East European bureaucrats with cabbage breath and we have villains with beards and turbans to worry about. Next to those guys, communists are downright quaint.

When life gets prickly, I like to lose myself in reading while the natural order of things takes its course toward more favorable circumstances. That Thanksgiving day I escaped the kitchen smells by burying myself in *Blindness*, a novel about a very scary plague. I've been known to read a whole book without anyone seeing me blink. I used to pull out each page as I read it until the contents were scattered throughout the house, loose leaves slipped behind furniture, under rugs and cushions, in the toilet. I was releasing the story back into the ether. That's what I imagined. It takes courage to let a book go and make room in your head for the next one.

Some people hang on to books and find a permanent place for them, rows upon rows classified by author, title, subject, color, size. My books end up wherever I happen to be when I finish them: a car's backseat, their spines splayed from my trying to hold them steady over the bumps and twists of the road, or water-swollen in a corner of the bathtub, or disappearing into the sand on some beach. They don't stay put for long; other eyes glom on to them. I am only a stop in their journey. Books, like me, are visitors.

Ted, aka Brother Tedious, considered himself a man of action; he did not like books. Or the people who read them. He had not broken the code that separates humans from turnips. He said reading was like being dead to the world, life's experience reduced to black squiggles on white paper. He claimed that even TV is more active than that. His idea of action was Game Boy mayhem—lust, dismemberments and beheadings, explosions and car wrecks. It was a pity he couldn't do anything more significant with his fingers after *Homo sapiens* had mutated through hundreds of thousands of years to the evolutionary peak of opposable thumbs. He also did serious weight lifting, slow, grunting presses that started smoothly and ended with a crash to the floor of his room. He used his strength to get into school fights with numbing regularity.

Tedious is a big, magnificent guy. He's got ape-sized feet with hairy toes and hands like baseball mitts. For this holiday feast he was mashing up various tubers. He took the boiled sweet potatoes and pressed them down with a special utensil that is basically a bunch of small holes with a handle. He took a yam in his hand and showed it to me. At a certain angle, it looked like it had a nose, lips, and chin.

"This is your head," he said. And proceeded to squash it down into the bowl, its features transformed into a dozen squishings wriggling out of the holes in the masher. He looked up and gave me his rascally devil grin.

Tedious was not yet a handsome guy. His face, in fact, was at the culminating point of his pimple-growing career; he may never again have as many pimples at one time as he did that day. His zits were like living organisms with minds of their own. It was as if they had gathered, each with its own consciousness, to colonize his head. As he smiled, an inflamed furuncle by the corner of his mouth got squeezed into exuding a mixture of pus and blood. Scary.

I had planned on mostly eating sweet potatoes with little multicolored marshmallows. In the end I settled on the green beans with slivered almonds and the fruit salad with the same marshmallows as the yams. That, plus not one but two kinds of pie, would make for a balanced meal.

The next biggest person in the family is my father. His name is Al, aka Albert. He's a good guy but hard to get to know. Years ago, before I arrived on the scene, he was reputed to be very fun-loving. A real joker. A ladies' man. He was voted most popular in his graduating class at Edison High School.

His mood changed one day when he said he noticed that his

head kept getting heavier. He sat down at the dinner table, perhaps to a meal of turkey and gravy with giblets like that day's, and his head dropped so low that his glasses got fogged up by the steaming sections of flesh and gravy on his plate. He rolled his bewildered eyes up at my mother. "I don't know what happened," he said. "My head feels like a bowling ball."

"Excedrin might help," She placed her hand on his forehead as if checking for a fever.

Father's head became a persistent concern. For years he had worn a brown fedora. It occurred to him one day that the hat was tighter than he remembered. After that he was able to follow the gradual expansion, a millimeter at a time, of his head, until one day the headband had made a permanent crease along the sides of his skull.

He has become a morose, reticent man who sits at the dinner table or in his favorite La-Z-Boy chair looking tired, his chin resting on the palm of his hand or his fist positioned under his jaw. My mother, who has a flair for words, put it best when she described her Al as a man who was forever carrying the weight of the world on his neck. It was around that time that Albert grew to fear the news in any medium, from the daily paper to the radio traffic report, because he just couldn't stay away from the screen. He found some relief in VCR tapes, watching the planes crashing into the towers over and over, pausing at the moment of impact, then speeding up to the smoke swirling about in a manic conflagration.

His room is strewn with copies of the *New York Times*, the *Washington Post*, the *Nation*, the *Congressional Record*. He is familiar with every nuance of duplicity and disingenuousness on the part of politicians and journalists. He knows details of the budget and can cite examples of federal waste on behalf of obscure subsidies for research into medical sunflower seeds, bridges to nowhere, price supports for bee pollen. He has the radio tuned to 91.1, NPR news around the clock. The more he knows, the more unhappy he becomes. Global warming gives him night sweats. Iran, North Korea, and Israel hoarding enriched uranium fills him with a kind detached hopelessness. On some days, when the news of the day is particularly alarming, he remains unshaven in a plaid bathrobe and fuzzy slippers, brown fedora firmly in place. The family has learned it's best to avoid him or he might clutch an unsuspecting listener by the sleeve and pour out his accumulated chagrin over the course of the war or the latest surveillance of our phone calls, our bank accounts, our hard drives. He can't get enough of the news, and the very subject of his interest makes him sick—the president's voice grates like sandpaper in the twists and turns of his ears. Occasionally Father will write letters to the editor of the *Star Tribune*. These are convoluted essays that drip with anger and sarcasm and are never published.

From time to time I can tell he enjoys looking at Cousin Iris, which I can understand; we all ogle Iris, who is the daughter of Mother and Father's friends, the Fallons, who died when their airplane fell out of the sky. She was six.

Back then we all liked to look at Iris because her every movement was uncannily beautiful from start to finish. It was already clear that, at sixteen, she was a true dancer. The girl's simplest gesture was art, alive in the moment, a singular piece of deliberate grace never to be repeated anywhere in the universe.

On that Thanksgiving quiet tears welled in my eyes as I marveled at how precisely she held her fork while making quick, delicate sawing movements with her knife on a piece of breast meat. It was a brutal act performed with elegance. She then took the morsel to her lips, her long, slender hand seeming to float in midair, fingers poised like flower petals, lips slightly parted. It was a moving thing.

There were already hints of her emerging Christianity, though she was not yet a proselytizing, born-again, rapture-ready zealot. She was best avoided when she felt possessed by the Holy Spirit. She found pleasure mainly in the anticipation of the world's end. I couldn't help thinking that in her estimation, Heaven would be a dull and lonely place.

My mother's name is Marjorie. She was a vastly more interesting person, an artist's model and a poet, in the days before she met my father. Sometimes she was both at the same time: art students sketched her nude while she recited verses to lift their minds from the carnal to the transcendent. She confessed to me once that she had at one time held great expectations of herself. But she came back to earth after she met Albert. There is clearly a pattern here of the members of my family stifling each other's potential.

"I was going to study with Gregorio Hewett," she said. "I was fearless. I wanted to learn the sonnet, the sestina, the Homeric simile.

Then one day, while I was sitting for a life drawing class, your father saw me through a window. He was selling the famous Mightyplate Roof Coating from Fort Worth, Texas, and was on his way to meet with the principal about the school's leaky roof. He had his sample case with him, and he had decided to take a short cut through the school grounds. He stopped and looked up at me."

"Was it love at first sight?" I asked every time I heard the story.

"I thought it was plain voyeurism. There I was without a stitch, twisting myself into a natural-looking pose, when I saw this man outside with his pear-shaped head and wide, amazed eyes. I froze. My heart was beating like crazy, and I was gasping for air. I reached for my clothes.

"It took a while before people realized what was happening. The students were staring and studying my every pore and bump, and Albert was looking puzzled as it started to dawn on him that he may have had something to do with my sudden discomfiture. All he could think of doing was to smile at me kindly and wait for me to get dressed while the kids held their pencils and complained about being left hanging from a breast or stranded in a buttock.

"In the end I scurried out the door. Albert caught up with me, apologizing about a dozen times as he followed me home."

After that Marjorie stopped posing for art classes. The realization that her body held the potential to so unsettle a man made her self-conscious about showing it to anyone other than Albert. By then her grandfather's trust fund had kicked in, and she didn't need the job. In fact, it was Mother's modest wealth that paid for my years of treatment.

Marjorie opened the oven door, and turkey effluvium invaded every corner of the house. She leaned in with a giant dropper and sucked up turkey sweat from the bottom of the pan and squirted it all along the naked bird, which was all scrunched up, vulnerable and seemingly ashamed. Much the way my whole family seems to feel about nudity.

In fact, the one who first inspired me to walk around naked was Iris. Before finding Jesus she would venture forth in the middle of the night, stepping out from her bed and sauntering down the hall to pee. What a free spirit she was then!

I'm the only one who was lucky enough to have seen her. One time we nearly bumped into each other by the bathroom. I had on my pajamas, and she was a vision of moonlit skin. I whispered, "Well, hello, Iris," as we crossed, acting as if the sight of her hadn't taken my breath away.

"You should try sleeping in the nude," she murmured in her haughty ballet-student accent. "It makes the night *très* sensual."

That night I put away my pajamas and haven't worn them since. In my nightly wanderings down the hall I have never again crossed paths with Iris. I have, however, stumbled into Tedious, who said I looked like a turnip, and my father, who told me it was unsanitary to sleep naked, and my mother, who warned that if the house caught fire I would not be properly dressed for the escape.

Sitting around the table that Thanksgiving, I delighted in the secret that Iris and I had something meaningful in common. Our skins shared a nightly experience of smooth sheets, each individual fiber seeming to find a pore to tickle and rub. It meant that when we dreamed we dreamed with our entire bodies. But most important, it meant that we were open to new experiences, courageous enough to be ready for whatever the fates might send us in the night. I never found a chance to tell her this.

Our family likes to dress up for celebrations. Tedious put on a white shirt and a bolo tie with a silver skull clasp. Albert actually removed his hat and slicked his hair back with a dab of old-fashioned brilliantine imported from Argentina to make his hair as glossy as patent leather. Marjorie put on her pearls. Iris wore a black dress that made her white skin positively luminescent.

As for me, I wore one of mother's old Sunday dresses. I liked the style, with the full skirt and the blousy sleeves and the neat row of pearl buttons along the front. The overall effect was capped by a leopard-skin pillbox hat I'd found at a costume shop: the nice lady gone haywire.

White or dark?" Father asked, holding the carving fork in his right hand. He looked me straight in the eye, not letting on if he thought my attire was in any way strange.

"Neither." I smiled throughout the exchange. "I have a contract with turkeys," I said. "We have agreed not to eat each other."

"You're going to die if you don't eat," he said, pointing the carving knife at me.

It sounded like a threat. There are places around the world where people would kill for a slice of turkey. At home convention stands on its ear. I love contradictory logic.

"Okay, I love life," I said. "A bit of white meat, please."

He glanced at the knife, then laughed, as if it had just explained the joke to him. "I meant that you need the protein." Still chuckling, he looked to his right and his left, and Mother smiled along with him, and Tedious shook his head with exaggerated incredulity. Even Iris rolled her eyes and quickly darted her tongue out at me. What a traitor. I loved her anyway; her tongue made the moment for me.

I held out my plate graciously because I knew how much love and enthusiasm the family had put into this meal. Still, even if Father hadn't meant he would personally kill me for not eating turkey, the thought had wormed its way into my subconscious.

My plate was piled high with slices of meat drowned in gravy with bits of the bird's most private organs floating about. Tedious had loaded on his potatoes and yams, and Iris had served me a huge helping of green beans with slivered almonds. The plate weighed a ton. I looked around the table and decided that I had more food in front of me than the four of them put together. Mountains of it sat there steaming, sending up to me a sweaty fragrance.

Suddenly out came a camera, and the flash went *pop! pop!* in front of my eyes. I got it: a family joke. I didn't let on that anything was even slightly strange. I didn't ask what the hell was so interesting about me that day that they needed to record it for posterity. Was it the clothes? They'd seen them before. Might it be the last time in my life that I would ingest turkey? Big deal. The frightened look in my eyes as I ate for my life? Yes, and how cruel. The old eat-to-live adage in living color. I straightened out the leopard-skin pillbox hat, which was about to teeter off, and proceeded to dig in.

Ah, how I dug. In contrast to Iris's delicate ballet of knife and fork, I was spearing large chunks of turkey, then driving the meat into the hills and mounds of yam and beans and sending it flying into my wide open mouth. *Pop!* went the flash. Ha, this was fun. Even as I attempted to masticate one clump down to size, I was already angling the fork into a dive for the next bite.

It occurred to me that I'd lived this moment before. That I was only repeating a ritual that can't be exhausted, which must be relived time after time with undiminished intensity. A fork dives and soars like an airplane doing acrobatics. The engines roar and whine as the payload is lifted into the sky and brought down with ballistic precision into the open cavern of my mouth. Watch it, here it goes! *Hmmm, munch munch, yummy.*

After a couple of passes I looked around the table. Nobody was laughing; they were doing their best to ignore me. I glanced from Tedious, who was staring blankly at some point in space above my head, to Iris, who was picking the almonds out of her green beans, to Albert, who was staring at my mother at the other end of the table in a silent appeal for help. I flashed Mother a grin.

She seemed about to cry. Carefully she leaned toward me and spooned off the remnants of turkey gravy on my chin, then handed me a napkin, which I put down on the table. Undistracted, I counted out ten green beans to spear on my fork.

"Every year it's the same disgusting thing," Tedious muttered under his breath.

He had no right to say this. Bits of pink-and-white marshmallow formed a mustache along his lip. He was wrong, of course; it's not the same thing every year, but as I opened my mouth to speak only a couple of muffled grunts emerged.

"I've lost my appetite." Ted pushed back his chair and crumpled his napkin on the table.

"For Christ's sake," Father said. "Can't we all be in harmony as a family for one meal?" He looked at Mother as if his question hadn't been rhetorical.

"Of course," she might have said. "We're together as a family, a wonderfully extended family if you take Iris into account, and we're together every moment of our lives, whether we are sitting at the table or not."

But this was not what Mother said. What she did say was, "I'm so sorry."

"Sorry for what?" I asked, but nobody understood what I said because my mouth was still full. "You wanted me to eat, right?" My mouth went *hlumph, hlumph*.

Albert got up from the table and took his plate to the La-Z-Boy in front of the TV. He settled down to watch a replay of the famous 1966 Super Bowl.

"Eat up before it gets cold," Mother said to the ones left at the table, namely Iris and me.

"It's still warm." I pressed my palm onto the heaping plate, as if to check its temperature, and let the warm ooze of stuffing and potatoes and gravy-soaked turkey seep between my fingers. It felt nice. It felt better than it tasted. I had visions of the different flavors and textures getting into my body through the skin, finding their way into the capillary network, entering the bloodstream, swimming around the system putting a little sweetness here, a little salt there, making the blood redder and richer. I bypassed the middle organs and got right to the heart of the matter.

I looked up at Iris and thought she could really understand this tactile stuff, the old touchy-feely, as they say, a naked kind of thing with nothing in the way between the brain and the food. Talk about sensuous. No, don't talk about it; do it. "Hey, Iris. Put your hand on it. It's like eating naked."

"That is something strictly between us," she said. For a moment I thought she was going to give me that sly grin of hers. But no, her lips were pressed tight, her eyes squinting mean thoughts at me. She put down her knife and fork, lining them up alongside each other on the edge of the plate. She stood up, smoothed down the back of her pretty dress, and said, "Excuse me," to my mother. "I need to make a call." To me she said nothing.

Then, it was just Mother and me. Like in the old days. And like other rough times, it looked as if we were about to have A Talk. She took her chair and pulled it around the table to sit beside me. She dipped a napkin into a water glass, lifted my hand off the plate, and wiped it clean. I started to put my other hand down on the mass of holiday victuals, but she gripped it by the wrist and bent it back until I cried out. She pushed the plate beyond my reach.

"I think I should go back," I said.

"Are you happier there than at home?"

"They eat what I do."

"All the residents are vegetarian?" She was not taking me seriously.

"They range from macrovegan to fishoterian. I fit right in the middle."

"After all these years." She started to weep. "Back and forth, back and forth."

"Not always my idea."

"We never should have sent you away in the first place," she sniffed.

"Terrible things could've happened, Mom." I gave her a little jab on the shoulder. "I have considered castrating Tedious, assaulting Iris."

I didn't qualify for the Clean Plate Club that year. An hour from the time I sat down at the table, the mountain of sliced bird and mashed tubers sat lumpily before me under a translucent sheath of congealing gravy. Mother gave up and left, stifling a sob. Brother Tedious returned and picked up around me, gathering silverware, the big platter with the dismembered bird, the sloshing gravy boat. I remained alone, knowing I wouldn't eat any more but afraid to cross the living room, where I knew I would have to face my destiny, again.

Finally, unwilling to consider the lifeless remnants of my friend the turkey any longer, I rose from the table and edged out of the dining room, hugging the wall along the stairs to my room. I kept my head from turning, even though out of the corner of my eye I could see Albert, Ted, Iris, and Mother all sitting next to each other on the blue couch. They appeared primed for intervention.

"Come here, kid," Albert said softly. "We need to have a talk."

Well, it just about cracked me up to hear him call me over so tenderly, so sadly, knowing I had let him down in the worst way.

"Now?" I hoped he would say, No, not now, not this minute, a little later maybe. "Yes, now," he said. "But it can wait while you change out of that getup."

"I'll be right back." I gathered the skirt hem in one fist and, hanging on to the banister for balance with the other hand, continued up the stairs two steps at a time.

I went straight into my parents' bedroom and rummaged through their closet. I pulled out, hastily, a pair of Albert's plaid golf pants (very St. Paul, ca. 1978), a gray silk shirt with French cuffs, a double-breasted blazer with a nautical insignia. The ensemble really came together with a wide tie of petunias on steroids. The dresser mirror told me that the getup still needed work. But give me an A for effort.

"Who the hell do you think you are?" Albert said when I entered the living room to face the tribunal.

"I am my cousin's cousin," I answered. "And my brother's sibling," I added, meeting my mom's tear-filled eyes. "My mother's daughter and my father's son. I am part of this family."

Chapter Three

The van braked at an intersection and I was back in the moment, debouching from Hyacinth onto Snelling Avenue, the previous serenity of the residential street blown apart by the grinding truck and bus traffic heading toward the corner with University, easily the most polluted intersection in Minnesota. I wanted to remember everything: the peaceful vision of darkened houses, their windows lit by TV sets, was overwhelmed by the gas station, the liquor store, the incongruously green-tiled commercial building, further west the Turf Club bar, where I hoped one day to party, and the Keys Café, where I hoped one day to die with one of their sticky buns in my hand. But then, instead of heading north on the freeway, Harley exited toward the northern burbs.

"Are we picking up any other patients?"

"Clients," he corrected me automatically.

"*Pardonez-moi*, a client!" The trip would be more interesting than usual.

The term, preferred at many modern treatment facilities, was supposed to protect our dignity, which becomes a precious thing indeed when you lose your mind. It means not getting laughed at when you confess to a desire to eat poop. Or insulted when you admit to lusting for your sibling. Or derided when you refuse to acknowledge the existence of a Higher Power. As if the Big HP's main occupation was the creation of twelve-step deals to dry up alcoholics, clean up addicts, slim down fatties. What a drag it must be supervising all those meetings every day of the week and twice on Sundays. Loiseaux thinks we all have a direct line to the HP if we're willing to dial up. Blah, blah, blah, my name is Adam Webb and I'm ambiguous, ambidextrous, ambivalent, ambipamby.

As a Marxist, for me to accept the existence of the HP would be intellectual sacrilege. I said as much during my first Confession. I considered the HP little more than a dope dealer, a pimp, a grifter. It was my goal to kill him one day. I would be the great liberator, the big bogeyman slayer, the universal unshackler. Oh, man! What a job. My weapons would be the blinding light of my intellect, the purveying of truth, the laser beam that would shoot all the way to the center of the universe.

When asked years later in a questionnaire what I hoped to accomplish during my stay at Loiseaux's, I answered, "To kill the Higher Power." That got the good doctor's attention. I was thirteen and already considered a kind of prodigy in the mental arena. Surrounded by autistic, thumb-sucking, stuttering, hallucinating, drooling misfits, I was a beacon of rational eccentricity. Star of the show, role model, a case for the textbooks. None of that went to my head. I conducted myself with modesty and self-control and the dignity befitting a client.

Dr. Clara was crazy about me. I was coddled and humored, allowed to read Marx, worship Kali, dress up, eat raw vegan. Once, in a rare candid moment, the good doctor revealed that my mother and father did not realize what a gem they had in me. I agreed, happily.

W e do have one stop before heading out," Harley admitted as he bypassed the ramp and stayed on Snelling toward New Canaan.

"What's his name?"

"She goes by Miss Entropia."

"How cute," I exclaimed, already picturing a creature of chaos and destruction. "What's her real name?"

Harley shrugged because such details are none of my business. Still, the man has a need to talk. "Francine, but she won't answer to anything but Miss Entropia. Can you believe that? Her parents are Felicia and Harold Haggard. I know this much because I'm supposed to check ID to match their names to the court's commitment order."

"Ah, an involuntary. Maybe a spitter, a scratcher, a kicker," I speculated. "Are you going to strap her down?" I love the idea of watching a client resist. They show a spirit and a sense of justice that I don't have. From the beginning, I had been a passive case. Take me away, bring me home, take me away, bring me home. This was my fourth trip back to Loiseaux's. I knew the way so well that, once I got my license, I could get a job driving the van. I knew I would provide a better ride than Happy Harley does. Stimulating conversation. Better music. A scenic route. The only thing lacking would be Happy's irrepressible good cheer.

We stopped in front of the Haggards', a pillared and porticoed faux colonial set back from the street and approached through an ornamental gate into a circular driveway. Outside, a Benz and a monstrous Land Rover stood ready to rumble. It was obvious, from his choice of vehicles, that Mr. Haggard suffered from small-penis syndrome. Nothing like raw horsepower to bolster the self-esteem of the limp-dicked. The covered portico was ringed with lights, blinking cheerfully as if announcing to the world that sanity and good cheer dwelled within. What a hoax. I pictured the Haggards as a family of psychic mutants, incestuous, abusive, Republican. Within dwelled violence and mendacity.

I like rich people, actually. Their children have interesting mental conditions. Not your standard ADDs or ADHDs that are easily medicated with the usual household drugs but disturbances in a more sociopathic vein. Anger issues. Sex issues. Authority issues. Mainly, my kind of issues. Issues that make you a person of some depth. Issues that make you an astute observer of the human world, a provocative conversationalist, a skilled manipulator of the powers that be. Beats knee jerking and head banging. I couldn't wait to meet Miss Entropia.

Harley parked the van in front of the covered portico, but, true to procedure, he stayed inside. He turned on the CB and announced, "Pickup to Base, Pickup to Base. I'm at the site. Over."

"Base to Pickup. We're calling the client's parents. Over."

"I'm on it. Over and out."

I loved those old-fashioned CB radios. They made everything sound so military.

Harley signaled his presence with three taps on the horn, as was the usual first step when doing an involuntary. The porch lights came on, the house suddenly awakening. Following the established procedure, someone would appear at the entrance, give the go-ahead nod, and then leave the door unlocked. The family would try to reason with their kid, who might have locked herself inside a bathroom with a medicine cabinet full of downers, or held a gun to her head, or shackled herself to a bedpost. Much conversation might ensue before Happy Harley was brought into the scene.

Once they decided they needed him, the lights would blink three times. Harley would rush in with a blanket that he would place over the involuntary's head and shoulders to confuse and disorient her. Then, he'd quickly lead her out of the house and push her inside the van. He'd strap her to the backseat and then slide the side door closed with a bang. Sometimes, if the involuntary was a young kid, he'd wrap him up in his wrestler's bear hug and bodily lift him into the vehicle, all the time cooing endearments and positive thoughts. The whole maneuver would take less than sixty seconds. I'd seen it happen. This guy was a paragon of fluid coordination, a graceful thing to see.

Meanwhile, he warned me to stay put and not get in the way. "This will be easy," he said, "if you don't try to be helpful."

The lights in a front window blinked three times, and the race was on. Harley was out of the van, a folded blanket tucked under his arm. Somebody opened the front door for him, and he didn't slow his stride; moments later he emerged with his massive arms hugging a slight figure who, under the blanket that covered her head and chest, was wearing a shapeless black dress, ripped stockings, and pointy black ankle boots. I notice fashion touches.

The girl, I was glad to see, was putting up some resistance. She almost wriggled out of Happy's embrace, and even as he used both arms to hold her, her feet inside their sharp-toed boots were kicking a quick beat on his shins. From inside the blanket I could make out a muffled stream of colorful complaining. He strapped her in with a yank on the seatbelt and slid the van door shut.

In a moment of inspiration, one of those impulses that rise like jewels from the brain's primal core, I clicked shut all the door locks as Hansen was going around the van to the driver's side. It was the loudest click I had ever made. Harley heard it, too. He tested the handle on the door, patted his pockets, then found himself peering in dismay at the keys dangling from the ignition slot. He met my eyes through the windshield with a cold stare.

The locking of the doors impressed Miss Entropia, who had shaken off the blanket to reveal a pale face crowned by a mop of black hair. She stared at me curiously out of her raccoon eyes. Our first meeting, and already there was a surge of energy between us. In an instant the three of us, Happy, Miss Entropia and I, understood that the power balance among us had shifted with a single click.

"You are so crazy," she said, more in wonder than in praise.

"You were expecting someone normal?"

"I wasn't expecting another patient."

"We're clients, actually."

"Right. And that guy is not a goon, and Institute Loiseaux is not an insanitarium."

"It's not so bad. Most of us are really, really functional. ADD, ADHD, OCD. Take your pick," I said, enjoying the status that came from experience. "The hardest period is the first ten weeks. No phone, no online, no TV, no games, no chats, no free time. They schedule you down to your toilet trips. Then you get used to having your life nicely arranged. Some of us are not good with decisions. I've been there off and on for a couple years."

"And you're glad to be going back, right?"

I hadn't quite figured out *glad*, I wanted to tell her. I was not happy at home, certainly not with Tedious tormenting me, Iris betraying me, Dad retreating into his brown fedora, and Mother sweet but clueless. "Going back? That's okay."

Harley was pounding on the sides of the van, shaking it, jerking at door handles, as if his wrestler's grip could intimidate the doors into opening.

"You are in so much trouble." His shouting was muffled by the closed windows.

I shrugged and gave him a disarming smile, the one I use when I can't explain myself and hope that circumstances will excuse me. In this case, I could just surrender and open the van and cut the damage. Ha, ha, just kidding.

Miss Entropia in the backseat had wriggled out of the belts and was trying to pry open the grill that separated the front from the back. "I don't like it back here," she said. "It feels like I'm in a cage already."

Happy had stopped his yelling and pounding and was marching toward the house. He had clearly come up with an idea, and while I waited for the results of his brainstorm, I devoted my whole attention to Miss Entropia. Her eyes were squinting, her lips pressed tightly, tears streaming down her cheeks. Her fury was downright cosmic.

I told her to stop pounding on the grill while I figured out a way to take it off. The panel was latched to the door posts, and it was easy to unfasten them and then lower the grill to the floor.

"See?" I held out my hands to show how simple the operation was when you put mind over brawn.

"You are smug," she said, her expression softening.

I moved over to the driver's seat so the girl could clamber over the back and sit next to me. Placing my hands on the steering wheel, I could barely see out the windshield, but I thought it would be fun to drive the van, even if just around the circle.

"People really call you Miss Entropia?"

"Pia is fine," she said. "Ms. Entropia is a formal name. I let some people call me Pia."

"So I should be flattered?"

"Yeah. But don't be a bonehead about it."

"What does your family call you?"

"Francine."

"You don't look like a Francine."

"Thanks. I don't answer to it."

39

"My name is Adam Webb." I used a confidential tone of voice, as if afraid to be overheard. It was all for show because everyone knows my name is Adam. But since Pia and I were exchanging confidences, I wanted her to believe she was getting privileged info.

"Most people," I added, "call me something else. Like my older brother, Ted, calls me Jerk-off. Iris, a kind of cousin, calls me Shorty. Mother and Father call me Problem Child." It's about then that I noticed that with her black look, from lip gloss and mascara to spiky black hair, Pia was as close to a living manifestation of the Goddess Kali as I had ever encountered. After all those nights praying to the deity, with her multiple arms, her earrings made of skulls, her belt of severed hands, here we were actually chatting.

Even as I pictured the goddess sowing chaos, a look of sadness clouded Pia's features. The goddess was showing her vulnerable side. Nobody could be a full-time deity and still function in the world.

"What's the matter?" I asked.

"I can't believe my parents would send me to a facility for nut-cases."

"That's parents for you."

"Honestly, I didn't think I was ready to be institutionalized. If that's the word."

"It is," I said. "The very word." Still, I wanted to reassure her that things at the 'Tute wouldn't be as bad as she feared. "Some of us get treated better than at home. The food is varied, the company is interesting, the schooling is good. You learn useful skills like how to shake hands without breaking someone's bones, how to keep from screaming when that's what you hear inside your head, how to talk without spitting, chew without smacking, sneeze without spraying."

"I really, really don't want to go."

I started to tell her again that things would be better than she expected, that she might even grow to like the place, as some of us do, when I was startled by insistent pounding on the passenger-side door.

"Are you just going to ignore him?" asked Pia as Harley's pummeling shook the van.

"I don't think it's for us."

"Ha!" She had a way of succinctly reacting to apparent absurdity. "Of course it's for us. Or rather for you ... Adam." The sound of my name sent a shiver to the back of my neck.

Harley walked to the front of the van and held up a plaid coat for Pia to see.

"He brought your coat out," I said. "That was thoughtful."

"I hate that coat. My parents know that."

He turned his back to us, but I could see that he was talking on a cell phone. I imagined he was calling the 'Tute for a second set of keys. That gave us at least an hour of fun inside the van. Good luck, Happy, I thought. Try to explain that the inmates have taken over the asylum's wheels. "So," I said, as if continuing a conversation that had been interrupted, "are you into entropy or misanthropy?"

She seemed amused for the first time. "You'll figure it out eventually."

"How about both? Chaos and hatred simultaneously."

"Not so simple," she said. "The Pia part of Entropia connotes devotion, piety. So go figure, Geniusboy."

"My name's Adam." I did not need another moniker.

Pia grabbed the microphone from the CB radio, "Calling Adam, calling Adam."

"Roger and out." I clicked off.

"Are you old enough to drive?" she asked.

"I know how to drive," I said. "Where do you want to go?"

This struck Pia as being unbearably funny. "Oh, my! Hardy-hardy-har." Even if she was mocking me, I enjoyed the attention.

"How about California?" she added. "We'd better do something before the driver calls the cops."

"I don't think the Institute would like the publicity," I said. "We'd be on Channel 11 in minutes. But it will take them an hour to send someone with an extra key."

Happy sounded tired as he shouted toward the windshield, "Hey, Mr. Problem." He added another name to my collection. "Unlock the door or I'm calling the cops."

"Great. I'll call the media." I waved the CB mike for him to see through the windshield. There was not even a wave as he shuffled off. "Later, alligator!" I sang.

This time Pia cracked up. "After a while . . ." Her laugh, a clear peal of delight, emboldened me. I sat up and clutched the wheel with both hands, assuming control of our hijacked vehicle.

"You don't look like you know what to do," she said as mockery edged back into her voice.

"Watch." I turned the key, and the van came to life with a pleasing rumble. I pulled the seat closer to the steering wheel until I could reach the pedals with the tip of my foot. I stretched as high as I could to get a better view out the windshield, shifted to D, and we were off, rolling slowly on the gravel driveway.

Chapter Four

At this point I hadn't yet decided we were going anywhere. It was enough to be moving around the circular driveway, steering the van as big as a truck, while Pia hooted with delight. When we passed the front door, Happy Harley and the Haggards were standing in our way waving for us to stop. Obediently I stretched for the brake pedal but pushed the accelerator instead, lurching forward and causing the three to scramble to safety. I jerked my foot back, and the van slowed down. Just as we were about to hit a tree, I stomped on the brake pedal and the van slid to a stop. When I saw Happy Harley in the rearview mirror, running toward us, I nudged the van forward, waited for him to come closer, then hit the gas, and so on. It had started to snow big, fat flakes. After three cycles of this routine, Harley retreated to the front door. Not funny, he mouthed as we passed by one more time. Sorry, I mouthed back with an abashed shrug, as if to communicate that this thing was sliding and twisting on the slippery pavement beyond my control. Big fun.

"Watch out for the circle jerk!" cried Pia.

I gained confidence and sped up. By the tenth circle I was swerving and fishtailing on the loose gravel. I loved peeling out and then slamming on the brakes and skidding to a stop. There was a smell of burning rubber and gasoline. I turned on the headlights, and the high beams swept ahead, lighting up the road, the fountain, the front door, and the three jumpy adults waving at us to stop.

I tuned the radio to KPNK and turned the volume way up. Slipknot screeched from speakers all around us. Pia and I bounced on our seats. I liked the domestic picture we made, a nice couple out to view the neighborhood's Christmas lights, glowing since before Thanksgiving. Happy kept running after us as if he expected to catch up. I eased the van out the gate and onto the street. We were free.

Time to get serious, I decided as I concentrated on staying on the right side of the street and easing to a stop at the first intersection. I looked right and left and broke loose from the pull of the big house behind us. Pia's earlier rowdy mood was replaced by a pensive quiet. She pulled the seatbelt across her chest and clasped it securely, as if preparing for a long ride. "Take a right at the next corner," she instructed. "We'll get on Snelling and then it's a straight shot all the way to Rosedale. We'll be there in less than fifteen minutes. We can park in one of the mall lots, and nobody will find us for days. I always go to the mall when I want to be alone. I like the trees and planters, the fountains, the food court, and the Sticks and Wicks store. The mall is my favorite place for solitude and reflection."

I didn't admit that I'd never driven on a street before. On that snowy night, I felt squeezed in by trucks and buses bearing down on me with their blinding headlights.

"The police will come after us," I said.

Pia shut off the CB. "No radio signal for them to track," she said, and I was again impressed by her sophistication. "We'll be safe once we get to the parking lot," she insisted. "It's going to be packed for the biggest shopping weekend of the year. People camp out to get their first crack at the bargains. Some stores are opening at midnight. It's a great time for shoplifting."

"You are evil." I couldn't contain my admiration.

"Let me know what you'd like for Christmas."

I could tell she was starting to like me. "You'll get me a present?"

"Better, I'll show you how to steal it. If you can carry it, wear it, or swallow it, you can own it."

I realized I was in love for the first time in my life, if you didn't count Cousin Iris, whom I loved only theoretically because she was unreachable. With Pia, my lust might be satisfied one day. I wondered what it would be like to taste her tongue, feel her budding chest, wear her clothes. I was looking at her with adoration when a chorus of honks and beeps alerted me to the van swerving and sliding away from me.

"What we don't want to do right now," Pia said coolly, once I'd regained my place in the middle lane, "is to get noticed because of your stupid driving."

"I got distracted."

"I'll let you know when you may gaze upon my bosom," she said. "For now, keep your mind on the road as if our lives depended on it."

"What made you think I was looking at your tits?" My attempted sneer turned into a stupid grin.

"That's a very disrespectful term. You are to refer to them as 'breasts,' or you can believe you'll never get to see them."

"Yes, breasts!" I nodded but didn't dare look away from the road. The entrance to Rosedale Mall was right ahead. And so far no sign of cops.

"Look for the Alligator signs," she said as we circled the parking area. The lots are marked with cute animals to help people remember where they left their car. Zebra lot, Lion lot, Hippo lot.

"Why Alligator?"

"It's near Marshall Field's. Easier to be invisible if we're jammed in by cars."

I found a space between two fuck-you-vees, proud that I did not scrape their sides. Pia covered our license plates with handfuls of snow, then climbed back inside the warm van. I think she had done this sort of thing before. Fortunately, Loiseaux had avoided putting any identification on the sides of the van to protect the passengers' privacy on their way to the madhouse. Very thoughtful. A Megan Alert APB for missing children likely had patrol cars cruising the freeways, our names flashing on LED screens. Help find the joyriding children in their stolen van, which looks just like a million other vans on the road. Soon our pictures would be out there on TV screens and milk cartons. But for now we had happily vanished into the frenzy of the big shopping night.

As we burrowed in the backseat, scrunching down below the window line, laughter poured out of us, a cascading mix of triumph and relief. To be in love and driving at the same time is a giant leap, a rite of passage rivaling the second birth of the Christian, the satori of the Buddhist, the transformation of the alchemist. Eureka! I drive, I love. I was way ahead of myself, becoming the prodigy I knew I was.

"When do you think they'll find us?" said Pia, suddenly rational.

"Never, I hope."

"I'd say three days. One day to give up on the highways. Another day to check out hospitals and shelters and friends' houses."

"Lots of luck." I smirked. "I don't have any friends."

"Me, neither."

Pia was so cool, so beautiful, I didn't see how she could be friendless. We were now each other's best buddy.

"Three days," she repeated. "And they'll say, '*The mall!* How come we didn't think of it sooner? Kids *love* the mall.' They will have a dozen malls to check out."

Three days sounded like forever to me. "We're going to need money." I pulled out the envelope Mother had pinned to my shirt, and sure enough, there was a ten tucked into the folds of her sad letter to Loiseaux.

Pia dug out some crumpled bills and change from a beaded coin purse she carried around her neck. We were rich. I counted $16.83. "That's about five bucks a day—for popcorn, french fries, Mountain Dew, frozen yogurt, Cinnabons, pizza slices, Gummi Bears," I said.

"Plus what we can serve ourselves from trash-can foraging." Pia was way ahead of me in the food department.

I must've looked skeptical. "You wait until closing time because they get weird about people eating trash. I once made a whole meal out of pizza crusts. When I bragged to my parents, the thought of their child eating garbage appalled them. Right there in the same class as my tattoo."

"You have ink?" I didn't know any kids who had real tattoos. "I thought you needed a parent's permission to get one."

"Theoretically." She pulled down her blouse to the top of her breast to show me a black rose dripping red blood. I hardly got a glimpse before she covered up.

"We could live off the mall for a long time," she went on. "Hunting and gathering. Begging works, too. Only you have to phrase it so it sounds like an emergency. Clutch a bunch of coins in your hand and ask for fifty cents to complete bus fare. It helps to be in the right place. Stand by the pay phones and ask for a quarter to call Mom. Once, outside the women's restroom, I got some ogling old dude to give me a whole dollar to buy my poopy baby a diaper. He couldn't wait to get away from me, the scruffy teen mom."

Cool as she was, my Marxist righteousness raised its uncompromising head. "It is stealing. Right?"

"Actually, they end up feeling good about themselves. People usually give to a beggar out of guilt. 'Here's a dollar, now please go away.' I let them help a child who could be their own."

From inside the car, I gazed at the falling snow glistening under the lights on the cute animal posts. I was suffused with well-being, sheltered inside the warm car, invisible behind the fogged windows. There was a sense of inevitability to our adventure so that however things turned out, these moments were a gift.

"Pia," I sighed happily as my hand inched across the seat to press, very slightly, my pinkie against hers. That first touch, a signal event in the history of the communion of our skins, quickened my breath. "You're a deep thinker."

She took her hand back. "We can fool around later. Right now we need monster coats. It's going to be a cold night. And more snow will make the white van even more invisible."

The hint at future intimacies strengthened my resolve to follow Pia in the ways of survival. She wanted a beggar? I'd beg. She wanted to flee to California? I'd drive. She wanted me to dive into the trash? Watch me go headfirst. Right then she wanted me to steal.

Pia had shoplifting down to an art. "Inside the store turn down your energy so security won't notice you. Hold your breath as you pass close to somebody. And don't touch stuff; it betrays your lust. Look lost, as if you were searching for your parents. People will stay out of your way. If you have a problem, they don't want to end up with it." She paused to check if I was absorbing her lesson.

"Ready?"

I nodded uncertainly.

"Do what I tell you."

"Okay!" I nodded more decisively this time.

"We'll leave the van separately and go into the mall through different doors. We'll end up at the coat department at Penney's. We won't talk to each other. I'll stand around looking suspicious to draw attention. You will pick out a coat from the clearance rack. Nobody, but nobody, bothers to shoplift from Penney's clearance rack. Just stroll to it and grab anything that looks big and warm. Don't worry about color or style; just pull it off the hanger confidently, as if you were going to take it to a cashier, but instead, saunter out the door with it. Don't worry about the beeping you'll set off. Nobody ever thinks there's an actual theft going on."

Pia jumped down from the backseat and jogged ahead, weaving her way between the rows of cars to the nearest mall entrance. I knew I should follow suit and head around the building to another entrance, but, once alone, the full weight of what I was doing landed on me. I was filled with courage and self-confidence only when Pia was near.

I realized I didn't have much aptitude for even the most trivial delinquency. I had to force myself to leave the van and trudge diagonally, dodging the cars circling about looking for a parking space, across the Alligator to the Crocodile lot and on toward the north entrance. My resolve not to let Pia down thrust me onward.

Chapter Five

On the biggest shopping night of the year, the mall welcomed me from the grim night into a feast of light and scents of evergreen and cinnamon; the sounds of familiar ditties surrounded me like a giant music box tinkling and chiming. I found myself humming along to "The Little Drummer Boy" as I wandered past the Candle Shoppe, Grandma's Fudge 'n' Taffy, the Baubles, Bangles. and Beads Emporium. The massed generations, the kids tugging at frenzied parents, the trailing grannies and grandpas, and the weaving strollers made me yearn for a kind of normalcy that my family, with its eccentricities and small cruelties, could not give me. Shopping bags were filled to overflowing with wrapped packages, their bows and tinsel promising the sweater to end all sweaters, mittens to warm the heart, dolls to awaken the maternal urge, stuffed bears to comfort toddlers, games to screech and buzz their way into adolescent brains. Me, I'd be getting a good warm coat.

I bypassed Field's to head toward JCPenney at the end of a wide concourse. No classy couture for me, the apprentice shoplifter, but the tired pickings of the suburban lumpen. The crowds were thicker here than at the fancier shops, mostly with adults who make do with knockoffs of last year's cool stuff so their children can keep up with brand peer pressure. The store felt overheated, the air stale, as if the scents of the season had been lingering since last year. Here the evergreen smells from an aerosol can collided with the perfume ladies in ambush, spritzers poised. I saw one around the bend of the cosmetics counter, and, holding my hands in front of my face, I fled in mock horror: "No, no, please no!" Several people turned to stare, the perfume lady rolled her eyes, I got no laughs.

I did get a seriously dirty look from Pia, who had been waiting, obviously impatiently, for me to show up in the coat department. I know, I know. I shouldn't have been attracting attention. But when confronted with the opportunity for a little public theater, I couldn't resist. I flashed her my most endearing grin, but she had become impervious to my charms. She nodded toward the clearance coat rack. "*Hurry!*" she mouthed. She went back to fingering blouses, acting suspicious, so I could have a free ride out of there. There was no time for hesitating. If I looked around to see if I was being watched, I'd be spotted by security. I would have to make my move, take my chances, claim my prize. The stroll, the turn, the grab, the flight would happen in seconds: one fluid motion, so smooth it'd be over before anyone noticed.

With no possibility of changing my mind, no hesitation or meandering allowed, I wondered that the thumping of my heart did not attract attention. Then, off I was. To the coat rack in four strides, and even before I knew what I was reaching for, my hands flew to a size 14 in violet, an overstuffed poly thing with Michelin Man concentric doughnuts going from hood to hem. Unwieldy and voluminous under my arm, it trailed the ground as I headed for the exit. I couldn't resist the temptation to turn and look back at Pia to see her reaction, but she was having an animated conversation with a blond woman in a pink cardigan sweater and beige slacks who looked all sunny and cheerful in the midst of this storm, as if life in the suburbs was conducted in perpetual springtime. A neighbor? A teacher from her high school? A predatory lesbian? My mind was brought to the present moment as the clunky antitheft tags elicited screaming beeps from the security posts at the exit. Their sound blared inside my head, its rhythm syncopating with the drumming in my chest. This was easily the most exciting thing I had ever done. A sharp, metallic taste rose at the back of my throat. What a rush. I owed it all to Pia.

I paused outside, on the edge of the vast parking tundra, and realized I had little notion of the van's location. As far as I could see, vehicles in every direction were jammed together in the dark, their soft forms only hinting at the SUV, the minivan, the Lexus. The wind blew in sudden gusts, and I put on the big violet coat. Its majestic heft and length to my ankles clearly signaled its questionable origins. I began weaving through the parking slots, my earlier agility replaced by a slow, erratic muddle. People brushed by me, some actually shoving me out of their way, anxious to get beyond my presence. The weird kid in a woman's fat coat without a clue as to where his car was parked was too pathetic to be funny. Who hasn't been in that situation, searching the Alligator lot for another generic automobile? Laugh at your own peril; boomerang karma has been known to bite the ass within seconds of the mean thought, the insult, the mockery. I buried my head inside the coat's ample hood, a poofy apparition damned to wander the vast wastes of the Rosedale tundra.

I was lost.

Chapter Six

I wandered for about an hour, trying to keep a level head in spite of the confusion, my eyes smarting with tears of frustration. As it grew late, the cars thinned out. I must've traversed the Alligator lot several times when I saw in the distance the yellow-and-black markings of an approaching wild feline, oddly out of context, as if it had somehow teleported itself from some tropical jungle to this frigid wasteland, perhaps to rescue me from certain death by freezing and starvation. The leopard before me could only mean Pia, in *her* new coat.

"What a sweet bonehead!" she said, holding me in a warm embrace for several moments. She then turned me around and pushed me ahead so that I was trudging still blindly but guided by her sharp pokes.

Magic aside, I do know a miracle when I'm found in the middle of the tundra. Ahead of me now, our van awaited. I slid the door open, cracking its frozen track, clambered onto the front seat with

Pia, and started the engine. The car was an icebox, but I managed to stay warm inside my new coat until the heater kicked in.

We clambered over the front seats and settled snugly in back, ducking below window level. A soft glow from the parking-lot lamp shone in through the steamed windows. It was enough light to study Pia's coat, an extravagant faux-fur item to midthigh, reminiscent of a Hollywood streetwalker. Though I'd never seen one, prostitution as a lifestyle and an avocation was one of my interests. I took to whores intuitively, finding common ground with their subversion of the established order, their pursuit of style, their lack of ambition.

"Great look," I said. The yellow was a nice relief from her goth palette.

"Thank you," she said. She poked me again, this time on the chest. "Yours is a fine choice as well. Purple suits you."

"It's violet, actually."

"Why, yes, it is!"

Then, out of her coat's deep pockets, she pulled handfuls of goodies. "I went foraging while you tried to gather your wits." She laid out some favorites on the seat: Reese's Pieces, Gummi Bears, Cracker Jack. And that was just dessert. Pia had found us a half-consumed tub of fries with two ketchup packets, the remains of a Domino's pizza, a nearly full tray of nachos generously topped with cheese goop. She even had a handful of paper napkins, which she spread on the seat as place mats. To drink, we were to share a gigantic cherry slushy. In the presence of such abundance, warmed now by the van's engine, it was easy to forget that out there on the freeways, our names were crackling through the airwaves.

"Well, are you going to eat or what?" she said.

"You first," I offered.

"Too disgusting for you?" she sneered. "It's all fresh leftovers."

I ate happily. Candy, pizza rinds, nachos. I skipped the fries, which had grown cold and limp. All in all, it was a more successful Thanksgiving meal than what had been attempted at home.

Contented as we slurped the last of our slushy, Pia and I spread out, resting our backs at either end of the backseat, our legs stretched along the length of the cushion. I reached over the front seat and turned off the ignition. Once the mall closed, the blowing exhaust would attract attention. Unoccupied, the van was one more vehicle stranded in a parking lot. It could be days before anyone decided to investigate and call the tow truck. Meanwhile, I imagined the search continuing unabated on the roads. Our parents were not likely to give up on their vanished children. Or the 'Tute on its missing patients. Of course they would find us. The suspense was all about when. And how.

I scanned the radio for news until I hit KTOK. We got Fred Heller, but there was no mention of runaway kids. I never thought Fred knew much of anything.

"The sounds of home," Pia said. "Dad's a Heller kind of guy, and Mom's a Martha Stewart gal. Can you believe that in this day and age they get their sense of the world from a wing nut? Heller parrots that shit all the time. Conspiracies, acts of treason, porn, teens amok, God endangered, gays ganging up, guns going going gone. If you're really desperate over the state of the world, you make Christmas cookies in the shapes of angels and stars. And they think *I've* fallen in with the wrong crowd."

"That would be me?"

"Nah, I am everybody else's parents' idea of bad company."

"If your thoughts could be seen . . ."

"They'd put my head in a guillotine." Pia was suddenly grave. "Can they read your mind?"

"At Loiseaux's?"

"Yeah."

"Nobody can see inside your head, Miss Entropia."

"I thought they had some techniques that make you blurt things out."

"They do," I said. "But you can fool them. You can make stuff up. They look at your brain-wave patterns and they know something's up. The squiggles and spikes show you're disturbed. Then you get some fine pills."

"You like it there."

"You adjust," I tried to reassure her. "You work the system. Special dietary considerations. Extra meds. Late-night parties in your room."

"You'll be expelled for stealing the van."

"Probably not. Our little adventure makes us a fascinating challenge. Plus, they wouldn't want to give up the fees."

"We're lucky our parents are rich."

True. My only exposure to the misery of the world had been as a spectator.

"Have you ever thought you might be one happy kid if they died?" Pia's voice had softened to a whisper.

"I love my parents."

"I could probably kill mine."

"For money?"

"For air." She snapped her fingers. "Just like that, as soon as they stopped breathing the house would fill with oxygen. Whoosh. When they're both around, I can hardly breathe. They watch my every move, listen in on my conversations, tap my phone, my computer, my closet. They took everything away when they called Loiseaux. I'm totally adrift. But at least I can breathe." She opened a window and an icy blast swooshed into the van. "I can't even imagine loving my parents. I'd probably love a brother or a sister, if I had one. Also my uncles or aunts or grandparents, if I knew any." She closed the window and slouched down into her coat. "I'm not sure killing them would solve the problem. I'd have to burn the whole house down, blow up the Benz and the Rover. The heat would melt down their photo albums, the family souvenirs, their passports and birth records and marriage certificates and driver's licenses and school diplomas. Poof! The flesh would drip off their bones, hair turn to ashes, eyeballs bubble inside their sockets. I'd watch the whole of their lives go up in smoke."

I tried to make out Pia's face as her features were illuminated intermittently by the passing headlights of cars circling the parking lot. Her eyes, focused on some distant point, revealed nothing. Her voice had gone into a drone as she reveled in her thoughts of familial violence. Then the passing headlights swooped away, and there was just her voice in the dark, deep and so close I could feel her breath on my cheek as she went on lulling me with her visions of normal life turned upside down. Her visions of carnage and destruction would be a big hit at the 'Tute during Confession.

"They'll love you."

"I'm just making shit up."

"You wouldn't really set your parents on fire?" I hoped I didn't sound disappointed.

"Would you?" Even in the dark, I knew she was shaking her head in disbelief. Of course, she meant to say, the leap from the thought to the deed is a short one.

"No." I was growing impatient with her games. "The question is about you. I haven't thought of doing evil to my family."

"Try thinking it. It feels good."

I wasn't at all like Pia. I didn't hate Mother and Father. I didn't resent their sending me away for the fourth time. In fact, I didn't blame them. I would get rid of me, too, if I thought I was going to be stuck with me for a long time. I don't make myself happy enough to want to spend the rest of my life with me. I'm schizoid by definition, a union of opposites by luck, two sides in perpetual conflict. I was scared of Pia. I was drawn to Pia. And I wanted to please Pia.

"I have a brother," I began. "His name is Ted. I call him Tedious. He has a face full of zits. He has a voice like a buzz saw. He has the brain of a turnip. He shakes the dandruff out of his hair all over the dining table. He is full of gas, which bursts out in farts and belches just when you're sitting close to him. His feet smell like skunk. He's always eager to beat someone up. His eyes give him away."

Pia said nothing, waiting for me to continue. She would be silent for as long as it took until I spoke again. It was no way to have a conversation. I went on, "What I mean is that no matter what he says, you can tell what he really thinks. Even when he doesn't say anything, just looks at you, his eyes are like crystal balls. If you can get near him, if you can stand the smell or the possibility that he will pummel you with his ham fists, then you can see the inside of his head. He knows this. Look all you want, he says. I know what you see, and I don't give a shit."

"You want to poke his eyes out?" Pia finally spoke, and her voice, now low and barely audible, chilled me.

"I haven't said that."

"You just thought it." Then she laughed. "Relax, we're just playing here. God, you're a serious boy."

"Saying stuff is okay, I guess," I felt myself surrendering. "It's not the same as doing."

"Almost."

Chapter Seven

We must've talked for an hour before we finally fell silent, vaguely attentive to the chance of news about our adventure while KTOK buzzed on. Outside, the night grew colder, yet we were cozy in our new coats, and after a while Pia nestled closer to me and pulled my arm around her shoulders so that I was taking care of her instead of the other way around. There we were, Pia and I, together on the backseat, our intertwined legs stretching out through the gap between the two front seats. I couldn't believe my good fortune.

I slipped out of the van around two A.M. under the pressure of the giant slushy. I pulled out my pud and felt it start to numb in the blowing wind, so I pushed out the stream to piss as fast as I could. I couldn't wait to get back inside the warm van.

"Where did you go?" Pia's voice was thick with sleep. "Man, you're freezing." She rubbed my chest and shoulders to warm me.

"I had to go to the bathroom."

"What bathroom?" she asked, suddenly awake.

"I went outside, under the stars."

"Well, you're lucky to be a boy. You can just stand and squirt."

"Yeah, I didn't have any choice in the matter."

"I wish I had a penis," she said. "Much more practical than having to squat."

"It was freezing out there." Pia and I were talking about stuff that was way beyond anything Cousin Iris and I had discussed during our nighttime encounters.

She snuggled closer to me. "Oh, you poor, poor boy." Her breath was moist in my ear as her hand inched up between my legs. "Did your dickie get cold?"

I knew then that the communion between us would endure forever. Her touch was a gift, and I didn't dare ask for more than she would give. A gust shook the van.

"Whoa," I said. "Listen to that wind howl."

"Just shut up," she whispered. "And close your eyes. I can't stand you looking at me like that."

"Like what?" I groaned.

"Like you're about to have a seizure."

After that I didn't speak or move. I even managed to keep from thrusting myself into her grip. I was sure that if I expressed too much enthusiasm she would stop. She tugged at my fly and told me to help. I unzipped, I was putty in Pia's hands. She went about her manipulations with a kind of clinical concentration, sensitive to my reactions, first running her nails gently up and down, then gripping, kneading, twisting until she held me in a loose fist and jerked it rapidly. I tried by turns to twist out of her grip and to hump into it. Then, in a matter of seconds, a shudder seized me from the base of my spine to my groin and I was melting into her hand. She pulled back and lightly rubbed her moist fingers on my lips. "It's better than Chapstick," she said. "I like milking boys. It turns them into puppies."

"I love you," I said as I tried to catch my breath.

"Don't be a bonehead," she said. "And don't tell anybody. I could go to sex offenders' prison, being that you're barely in middle school, and I'm fifteen."

Of course I loved Pia, especially in light of the risk she had taken on my behalf. I had never experienced such pleasure, though I'd known from the way my penis stirred at unpredictable times that I was on the threshold of a mystery. Dreams in the night had left the gummy evidence of pleasures hidden by the veil of sleep. Talk from older kids hinted that bliss was within reach, with little risk beyond hairy palms, warts, or mental retardation. That my first orgasm had come at her hands filled me with gratitude to Pia, Pia my initiator, Pia my tutor, Pia my priestess. And why not? My goddess.

Chapter Eight

They found us sooner than I had expected. Pia was not surprised; the woman I'd seen her speaking with in the store turned out to be a neighbor who busted us when she saw our photos on the early-morning news shows. It was still dark when the cops reached the parking lot; it took them about a minute to locate us. The search party spotted the frozen yellow stain where I had pissed like a donkey under the watchful eyes of the Alligator. Now, with all the banging and pounding on doors and windows, we were under assault by an army.

They kept shouting our names. "Come out, Adam, come out, Francine. Be good kids, now." It took a while for me to remember that Pia's name was not really Pia. For a moment I thought they had the wrong girl.

We hadn't made a sound, and for all they knew, we had frozen to death in the night. They tried scraping off the ice and shining lights through the windows, but our breath had frozen on the inside of the glass.

"They'll take us out for pancakes," I predicted.

"Yummy," Pia said. "They will be so relieved we're alive."

It took them just a few minutes to use a master key to unlock the van, all the locks snapping open at once so that Pia and I were cowering in a corner under the sudden rush of frigid air and the crossed flashlight beams on our faces. A regular SWAT team had come for us, complete with helmets and armor vests. They were followed by one of Loiseaux's shrinks, Dr. Gunderson, the one we called "Auntie Gunilla." He wore a cardigan, always the same green one, and he usually offered his clients a cup of tea during sessions in his study. Hence the "Auntie." Once I caught a glimpse of him hovering behind the cops, I was relieved that I wouldn't be going to some juvey joint. Loiseaux was home.

Still, I wasn't about to go quietly. I went limp, sprawled across the width of the seat, my hands clutching the armrests. A policeman grabbed me from behind, digging his mitts into my armpits, dragging me ass-backward out the door. By then I was twisting and kicking away from my cop, hoping Pia would admire my feisty resolve.

A female officer peered in once I was out and spoke in Pia's ear. She slowly emerged from the van. She stood for a moment listening to the policewoman, seemed to give the words some thought, then surrendered. The policewoman guided her into the patrol car, pressing down her head so she wouldn't bump it, and slammed the door before I could have one last word with my new girlfriend.

"Hang in there, Miss Entropia," I called. "See you at the 'Tute." I pictured us as buddies at Institute Loiseaux. We would eat together in the cafeteria, watch TV in the lounge, and maybe sneak into each other's rooms for some late-night subversions of the system. I don't know that she heard me.

As she sped away in the patrol car, I finally stopped wrestling against the cop's grip and allowed him to lead me to everybody's favorite counselor. Auntie Gunilla opened the passenger door to his big BMW, and I sank into the leather seat. I liked it that he could afford a nice ride; it said something about his professional abilities, even if the Beemer did not match the ratty cardigan. In any case, he had a smile that made you trust him. I was about to ask him if he had brought tea when he pulled out a thermos and poured us two cups.

A warm sensation at the center of my chest pulsed as I thought of Pia and this the most amazing night of my life. Actually, I was relieved we'd been found. I didn't have it in me to be a runaway. I was too fond of the comforts at Loiseaux's.

"Where's Pia going?" I sipped the nice Earl Grey, feeling its warmth spread into my belly.

He looked momentarily bewildered. "You must mean Miss Haggard. Francine, right?"

"And you must mean Miss Entropia."

Auntie sighed unhappily. He got someone at the Institute on his phone. "The boy is fine. He got a little chilled, but he's sitting right here next to me enjoying a cup. No, he did not freeze. In fact, he's wearing a very large warm coat. Violet." He turned to me and added, "You are all right, aren't you?"

I nodded.

"Yes, he's fine."

"Ask about Pia," I broke in, but Auntie ignored me. "Where the fuck is Pia?" I shouted.

Auntie moved the phone out of my reach and signaled that I should be patient. After years at the 'Tute they thought they had stopped my tendency to scream whenever I got frustrated. "Pia. That's what he calls the Haggard girl. What can I tell him?" he asked. "They've become friends."

I was not encouraged by the way he sighed and kept muttering, "Hmmm, yes. I understand. I can handle it," adding various mumblings people use to avoid unpleasantness. Still, I didn't think it was serious. I figured they'd recruited another staff shrink in the middle of the night to deal with Pia before admitting her. As a reluctant newbie she presented a challenge.

"So," I said after he disconnected and sat back with a sigh to sip his tea, "are you going to tell me what's going on with Pia?" I tried to keep my voice calm because cursing and yelling were not the Loiseaux style. Signs of passion or anger would hit a wall. Some of the kids who went around moaning and wailing obscenities were isolated to keep the rest of us, more functional types, from getting infected. I had always looked down on these exhibitionists. Now I was on the verge of becoming one of them. If I didn't get some idea of what was happening with Pia I was ready to cross the line from Borderline to Acute. Fuck knows, it could be fun. There I went, effing this and effing that. I was definitely backsliding. Auntie sighed; he always sighed as if his existence required unending endurance. "Ms Haggard's parents are reconsidering Institute Loiseaux as the most suitable place for their daughter's development."

"She's not going to be at the 'Tute?"

"Not right away." He breathed that pained sigh of his. "It seems they are disappointed that we lost control of her safety."

"So it was my fault?"

"We prefer to think she's the one who provoked your little adventure. She may be too disruptive for our Institute."

"If she's not going, I'm not, either," I said as firmly as I could. "I'd like to go home now." I was wondering if Auntie would fall for it.

He didn't.

"You'll have to work that out with your parents, won't you?"

"Fine," I said with more confidence than I felt. "Take me by my house."

"Actually," Auntie began, "they don't want to talk to you. Everyone thinks you're too hyper right now for normal conversation. Your father says he'll come see you next week, once you've had a chance to settle down."

"Hyper!" I heard myself scream in spite of my resolve to stay on the cool side of the emotional spectrum. They would see hyper, all right. I could drool and gnash and spasm with the worst. Nothing would chill me—not Ritalin, Luxor, Zoloft. Only Pia. But when Auntie said he'd been hoping I would settle down because Loiseaux wanted to strap me in the van for the ride to the 'Tute, I became as meek as a lobotomee.

"Okay," I said. "How about pancakes? I'll go quietly if you take me to Al's Breakfast for whole-wheat-wally-blues."

Auntie nodded amiably and started the car. "You'll be nice and not bring up Miss Haggard or the night's adventure or your feelings about the Institute?"

"I said . . . I'd be . . . fucking quiet." I heard myself shouting before I could rein in the volume. It happens like that sometimes, I lose myself in the stress of a situation. I know better. I've learned to separate myself, to observe the moment, to take responsibility. I can be a model client. I wanted pancakes that morning.

"Sorry, Dr. Gunderson." I regaled him with my earnest voice and my winning grin. "It's been a while since I've been to Al's. The last time was with you when I went to the U for some testing. I scored 178, and you said a genius could have anything he wants for breakfast. You'd been going to Al's since your student days and claimed it was the best breakfast in the world."

I could tell I'd made Auntie Gunilla nervous. I'd already proven to be unpredictable that day, swinging from more moods than a monkey on trees. We sat at the counter at Al's, where Auntie cleverly maneuvered me into the end seat of the fifteen, so I had the wall to my left and Auntie to my right. Little danger here of me freaking out some innocent bystander. He ordered for both of us. Tall stacks of whole-wheat-wally-blues, Al's signature pancakes with walnuts and blueberries.

I waited as calmly as I could, hands folded primly on the laminate counter, my butt poised on the red vinyl stool, my eyes staring ahead at the meal-coupon books lined up on a shelf, a hundred of them with customers' names, some new, others yellowed as if forgotten by their owners years ago but still on hand to provide a fantastic breakfast, already paid, so that it would feel free. I recognized the photo of the original Al in his tall chef's hat and the reminder sign that read, "Tipping Is Not a City in China." This was only my second time at Al's, and already I felt like part of the tradition.

Behind the counter Al's spiritual heir, Doug, ruled over the grill. He'd taken over the place and had quickly become an archetypal breakfast wizard in his own right. "Hey, you squirt down at the end, ask the good Dr. Gunderson if he'll pop a dollar for real maple."

"Okay, real maple," Auntie Gunilla voiced.

"Coming up! Whole-wheat-wally-blues with real maple for the big spenders on the end."

"Hold the butter on mine," shouted Auntie.

"Gotta watch that girlish figure!" sneered Doug.

Soon he was standing in front of us, proudly holding the two plates and motioning for us to lift our hands off the counter. "Hands clear, cakes coming down!"

I was hungry after my night in the van and was about to slide the ball of melting butter around the top pancake when I suddenly pushed it back to the edge of the plate. There, in the markings of the scorching grill, contrasting charred black against the surrounding golden cake, blueberries poking up strategically, walnuts providing depth and texture, was a figure, a dancing silhouette, one foot off the floor, two arms up high, two other arms bent at the waist, head tilted toward me.

Kali.

I don't know how long I stared at that pancake before I was startled out of my reverie by Auntie elbowing me. Perhaps the image was something my brain had concocted for reasons of its own, a fancy that would vanish at the first blink.

I blinked again and again, and Kali was still there. The black goddess was actually moving over the surface of the pancake, and I could faintly hear the slap of her bare feet and the jingle of her ankle bracelets, sounds so tiny that they seemed to have wormed their way inside my ear. I don't know how long I sat there, my head hanging over the plate, but judging from Auntie's alarmed rasp, it might have been a minute or two.

"I can't eat this," I whispered, hoping only Auntie would hear.

"Something wrong with the pancakes?"

"No, not wrong," I said, moving the plate in his direction so he might also see the goddess. "See?"

"See what?"

He stared at the pancake, as if the reason for my reaction might reveal itself spontaneously. He didn't get it, but the message was there, as clear as an eye chart.

"It's Kali. See? These are her four arms." I pointed with the fork. "And her three eyes, her belt of skulls, the severed head of ignorance in her hand, and the dwarf under her dancing feet."

"Of course," said Auntie. "I see."

I'm not sure he saw. I lifted the top cake from the stack, holding it gingerly between my fingers, and held it out to the others in the diner. "It's the goddess Kali." There were some nods and smiles and frowns, but most seemed uncomfortable with being confronted by a really fierce deity so early in the morning. Finally I asked Doug to wrap that particular flapjack in foil so I could take it with me.

I then attacked the remaining stack of wally-blues, all the time keeping an eye out for scorch marks that might hold additional revelations. I poured on the real maple syrup until the stack was sopping up a lake of nectar. Next I dug out the blueberries buried in the world's most perfect pancake until there were a few on each of the tines of my fork. I then picked out the walnut chunks to crunch on one at a time. I saved the best for last, taking in huge bites of pancake until I could taste their salty-mealy-sweet-buttermilky wonder with the whole of my mouth. Ah, bliss!

I was so wrapped up in the experience that I was unaware of anything except my own sensations. I have to give Auntie Gunderson credit for just munching on his own breakfast without giving me another look. I shouldn't be surprised; he's used to eating with psychos and delinquents. Not that I qualify as either. But at the 'Tute we are all oddballs; some of us are better at passing for normal than others. Except in our dreams.

Dreams are the best way to get the attention of the staff at the 'Tute Loiseaux. Reveal an inner life plagued by beheadings and castrations, floods and quakes, cannibalism and necrophilia, and you will be taken seriously when you ask for an extra helping of ice cream or a little something to keep the devils at bay. What devils? You might ask. Any devils will do; devils can be your best friends inside the 'Tute, though a nuisance when out in the real world of families and jobs. You don't have devils? Borrow one. Any client at the 'Tute will be glad to describe the Eye-Ball-Pecking Bird of the Night. Or the Formless

Incubus in the Bloodstream. Or Lady Susurrus, the Bug in the Ear. Earle, the Talking Dog (G-o-d backward) is still very popular.

After breakfast I got Auntie to take me to an art shop where I could get the Kali pancake laminated. Otherwise it might be found and eaten by one of the 'Tute's bulimics. I couldn't begin to think of the consequences of, even inadvertently, ingesting the goddess. Humans can handle only so much divinity before they crack.

Auntie was out to humor me that day. At Dinkytown Arts, the pancake was sandwiched in plastic and pressed in something like a waffle iron. The result was that the pancake was now a rigid flat disk, about seven inches in diameter, the scorched silhouette of the goddess clearly discernible. Short of having a photograph of Miss Entropia, the Kali-cake would serve as a reminder of her compelling presence. But just in case any mental health professionals read this: no, I do not think Pia *is* Kali!!!! (I cannot put enough exclamation points to emphasize this.) Pia is a human representation, not a manifestation—I'm not deluded—of the goddess, and as such, she is the bearer of piety, a translator, a channel, not to be confused with the object of devotion.

On the other hand, Pia embodied enough tangible qualities of the goddess that to be touched by her, to hear her voice and feel her breath, was no small gift. The pancake was a tangible representation of her presence. I could attach a hook and chain in back to wear it as a medallion during meditation. After a taste of her presence, I would do what I could to keep her close.

"So did her parents say where they were going to send Francine?"

Auntie sighed. "Do you think her parents would want me to tell you where she would be?"

"I mean, it's not like it was the 'Tute's fault that I hijacked the van."

"Yes, it was." Auntie sighed again. "Harley lost control of the transportation mission. He let you ride in front, left the keys in the ignition, picked up a difficult client without backup. I'll be surprised if he keeps his job. How does that make you feel?"

"Like a toad."

"There may be hope for you yet."

Chapter Nine

'm not sure they were happy to see me at the 'Tute. Dr. Clara did not greet me personally. Even Happy Harley, a once reliable buddy, was evasive, hardly giving me a glance from his paperwork. Auntie himself led me to my room. He opened the door, and for a moment I refused to step inside. It was not the room I was used to; it was one of the secure rooms reserved for challenging clients. My one small prank, a small detour on the way to my eventual emotional balancing, had moved me from client to inmate. This room had a grill on the window, an overhead fluorescent fixture, and a slit in the door with a view of the bed. I was to be subject to searches and inspections, watched, scrutinized, analyzed to the core. I resolved to be on good behavior for the next few days.

I know Auntie didn't approve of obsessions with hopeless objects of desire, but I couldn't stop thinking of Pia, even as I lay in bed, eyes closed, trying to conjure the image of her face, her voice, her skin. I turned to books for hiding. Even then my reading was censored for its potential for brain rot. My copies of *Das Kapital*, the *Bhagavad Gita*, and *La Philosophie dans le boudoir* were confiscated. In their place I was allowed to browse pabulum from the 'Tute's shelves—Proust, Robbe-Grillet, Sackville-West. Where did they get these literary Nembutals, anyway?

Still, the 'Tute likes to make things homey for clients. The pattern of red-and-black art-deco geometrics in the curtains was repeated in the bedspread and reinforced in the carpeting. The walls were a sunset shade of rust and the armchair a comfy tan corduroy. I couldn't wait to ruin the overall design of the room with my posters of Karl Marx and Joe Strummer. And the laminated Kali pancake on the nightstand.

Things stayed awkward for several days. I kept hanging on to the familiar routines, but somehow the place was full of ghostly threats. I complained that my room had been "possessed." I left it at that. Possession is within the range of symptoms the medical committee routinely deals with. Dr. Auntie and Dr. Clara graced me with their tolerant smiles and helpful nods during my therapy sessions, even when I mentioned that the possessors I was talking about were more human than supernatural.

I explained patiently that as recently as last night my room had been penetrated by parties unknown. To the untrained eye nothing was disturbed; the pillow was as I'd left it, the folds of the blanket exactly so, the telltale hair under the shoe-box lid at the rear of the closet in place. I had opened the door but not yet stepped inside when I felt on my face a warm rush of moist breath as if from the walls themselves. The variety of smells left behind by the snoopers was overpowering. There was in the air a mixture of peanuts and caramel, possibly from a Snickers bar. There was the hint of a newly ironed white shirt. One of the advantages of the disturbed is that we develop enhanced sensory perception. A nuisance in some situations to have us sniffing about like hounds.

I worked out in my mind the exact words I would use to confront Auntie, Dr. Clara, and their minions. I would keep cool and steady and low-key. "Good afternoon," I would begin pleasantly. "I realize that it is your declared policy not to search rooms, yet there is no doubt in my mind that some officious little voyeur (perhaps Dr. Liester) has searched mine.

"Certainly the Institute Loiseaux has a clear position on the matter of my hallucination, as you disrespectfully refer to the goddess, but to search my room looking for an imaginary goddess compromises your scientific position in the matter. Especially since, as recently as last week, Dr. Meloche reiterated the official line that there had never been a goddess, that I created her and therefore it was up to me to drive her away. If that's true, what where you expecting to find in my room?

"At any rate, I know there is a gap between what science says it believes and what its practitioners, namely you distinguished professionals, can give credence to. After all, from the start I've considered us a team. Together we would try various strategies to drive away the intrusive presence that has so thoroughly screwed up my life, even if our respective versions of reality are at odds. You're coy about the names of the drugs you prescribe, so I have my own names for them: Equilox (those lovely azure capsules with a yellow band) and Serene Seven (aquamarine tablets with the big Roman VII etched into the sweet shell). I've swallowed them cheerfully, even with the understanding that they would turn me into such a sodden, torpid fool that my goddess friend, all my friends for that matter, will soon grow bored with me.

"I still remember the week you had me on triple dosage. I had on the pink pajamas with a print of letter blocks that I now wear at night, since sleeping nude, as has been my preference, makes me way more vulnerable than I would like. When my mom sent them as a joke, neither of us expected I'd be wearing them in such grim circumstances.

"At any rate, you took me to the dayroom, and when I say 'took,' I mean you *rolled* me there in a wheelchair. My muscles had turned to mush under all that chemical persuasion; it was a struggle just to get my head above my shoulders and keep it from swiveling on my neck, tilting first one way, then the other. When you sat me down at one of the card tables near a sunny window with a view of the wisteria with its nice clumps of purple flowers and you gave me a blank tablet and some crayons to occupy myself, all I recall is a thread of spittle dribbling down my lip and then hanging on the edge like a climber on a precipice before finally landing with a loud PLOP (which I assure you *I* heard) on the lap of my pajama pants. Everything around me was blurred except for the growing wet circle on my lap.

And, of course, the goddess dancing at my feet, looking up at me with her big black eyes wide open and feverish with anxiety. She was saying nervous, agitated things that I couldn't make out because I kept drifting off. Occasionally I'd feel her tugging at the cuff of my pajama pants, and that would startle me back into the present moment. I spent most of the afternoon filling in a single sheet of paper with spirals. You say I spent a week drawing spirals? My, but time does fly. You have a copy of this artwork in my case folder."

The goddess stayed. Dr. Loiseaux decided that the way to drive her away was to stampede my brain cells into firing a steady stream of big, spectacular visions. You know, the Big Bang, Black Holes, the Furies. I still don't know exactly what was inside those capsules marked EX-D23. But it's clear that the '60s made a significant contribution to science after all. The whole idea behind the hallucinations was to keep me too busy fending off the chemical illusions to pay much attention to the vision that had become such a part of my life. Inevitably, when the little goddess joined in, it was like turning a kid loose in a candy store. There she was, dancing along the ring of fire into the crater of Krakatoa, trading air kisses with Auntie, chasing dwarves. She was right in her element. I was so proud of her.

In the end reason prevailed after a vibrant counterpoint of chemicals and counseling. I asked Auntie to get me off medication for three days so I could straighten things out. Once I was thinking clearly again I simply sat down with my troublesome deity and we had a conversation. I remember the day well. I had wanted to sit on one of the benches outside, under the big oak, but it had been raining and the ground was muddy. Auntie said I shouldn't go out there in my pajamas, that I could come down with something. I appreciated everyone's concern. We ended up back in the recreation room at a nice table off in a corner by ourselves. I sat on one end, and my visitor stood on the opposite chair, her little head just barely peeking over the edge, black eyes twinkling, looking at me curiously.

"Dear Kali," I said to her.

She gazed at me expectantly, still for once, her multiple arms aloft, her little feet firmly planted.

"Much as I value our relationship, your presence in my life is causing me some difficulties." That was the nut of it. We simply hashed out a trial separation. I made sure she understood I did not hold her personally responsible for the problems I was facing. In fact I would rather have her friendship, with all the challenges this entailed, than a quieter existence without her. Still, since she was my friend, I knew she would be interested in the current state of my life, and would then act according to the dictates of her heart. I always said that if the goddess were allowed to make her own decisions, there would be no goddess problem. There has been no contact between us since that day.

K ali was never again within reach. Pia awaited. I would openly let go of the delusion and secretly embrace the obsession. This great step toward regaining mental stability was not lost on the Loiseaux team. I was returned to privileges, enrolled again in literature, history, and philosophy, and allowed to postpone math and biology for a semester. And my journal was returned to me after the shrinks had scrutinized it for any clues to impending self-mutilation and sociopathic mayhem.

Auntie was the first to welcome me back, ready to iron out what few kinks still clouded my psyche before I could graduate from the 'Tute and be sent home on the van's return trip. I was eager for that because it would enable me to track down Pia. Not easily, since I did not know her phone number or e-mail address and barely recalled her house in the general neighborhood of Sylvan Heights. The people at the 'Tute who could be helpful were not talking. Happy Harley was still pissed off at me. Auntie was more interested in *why* I wanted to know about Pia than in giving me even a clue as to how to contact her.

"What would you say to Pia," he asked, "if she were sitting here with us?"

"We would speak of Hansel and Gretel, of Oliver Twist and Mowgli, of Baudelaire and Rimbaud, and all the world's lost children."

"You are losing me." Auntie sighed.

"You asked." I clammed up, feeling I had already revealed too much of Pia's special place in my heart. I tried to visualize Miss Entropia, all in black from her head to her pointy boots, dark eyes fixed on mine, all the time Auntie smiling kindly in his pilly cardigan, eyes twinkling behind his gold-rimmed glasses. He slouches like such a marshmallow that it's easy to underestimate his clever ways. He's a cat curled up on a couch, apparently asleep until he catches the sight and scent of prey.

"Let's have tea," he said. He took the thermos from his desk and poured two cups. Then he placed another cup on the table between us. "We'll pretend that one of these cups is for Pia and that she is also having tea here. It will be just us three, and we can talk amongst ourselves, and everything we say will be private."

I stared at the cup that would sit untouched at one end of the table. And then at Auntie in disbelief. It happened often at the 'Tute that the keepers and the kept seemed to be cut from the same disturbed cloth. Uncertain as to how playing along might affect later evaluations of my behavior, I waited for Auntie to start things.

"Milk or lemon?" He directed his question to the empty chair, where I could now picture Pia sitting demurely. I glanced at Pia, then at Auntie, then back at Pia. And waited.

Auntie sighed. "For this to work, considering that you and I know Pia is not going to talk to us about her tea, much less drink it, you will speak for her."

"You want me to tell you how Pia would like her tea? Milk, lemon, sugar, whatever?"

"That would be an easy way to start this exercise."

"Psychodrama."

"More of a psychoskit."

"I don't even know if Pia likes tea," I said. "She's more the espresso type."

"Humor me on this, Adam." Auntie sighed for the nth time. "You might find it interesting to see where we go."

"Lemon," I said after tilting my head and cupping my ear in the direction of the empty chair.

"Lemon it is." Auntie squeezed a few drops into Pia's cup. "And for you, Mr. Webb?"

"Black."

"Sugar?"

"No."

"For Pia?"

"No."

Auntie went on, fully into the scene now, "Does Pia know you're in love with her?"

"Did I say I was in love?"

"No. But I'm guessing you are," Auntie said. "More to the point, what does *Pia* think?"

"This is stupid."

"What is Pia saying?"

"You don't want to know." I was getting into this routine.

"But *you* would want me to know, right?"

He had me there. "Pia says you're not as harmless as you make yourself out to be. She's warning me to be careful around you."

"Doesn't she want you to get well? Adjust to your family? Be happy in the real world?"

"Apparently not." I leaned toward the empty chair and made a big thing about cocking my head to hear better. I pitched my voice lower to Miss Entropia's throaty register. "Some odd people are not meant to fit into the world but to make the world fit us. We are sane only when we embrace our weirdness. We free ourselves to be artists and teachers and preachers. When we refuse to be straightened out, the world bends by small degrees in our direction." It gave me great satisfaction that Miss Entropia would speak through me.

Auntie tried his best to put on a tolerant smile. "Sounds like a real megalomaniac, your friend Pia. I don't think she would have been a good fit in our little family here."

"I would have been running amok," I said as Pia.

"She sounds as if she were proud of it," said Auntie.

I waited for Pia to respond, but she had grown silent. "No," I ventured. "Pia would be self-accepting. Not proud. She knows who she is."

"She needs help." He did his Auntie sigh. "And she doesn't know it."

Of course he was right. And I would be the one to help her. The hows and wheres and whens would remain undetermined. But somehow I was convinced that coming to the aid of Miss Entropia would be a determining mission in my life, perhaps even my greatest accomplishment. It was a bold resolution since I didn't know what exactly Miss Entropia needed help with, or where she lived, or how to contact her.

"Maybe her parents will change their minds and send her to the 'Tute after all," I ventured.

"No chance. You trashed our image with them forever."

"I could call them. I'd apologize and take responsibility." I tried to smile cheerfully under Auntie's bemused gaze. I said I needed Pia's phone number or her address. Auntie was not cooperative.

"You will find her eventually," he pronounced in the style of a fortune-teller. "But for now, you're not getting any help from me." Our conversation was over. "Finish your tea," he said. "Time is up."

Part Two

Chapter Ten

What a difference three years make. I had served my time at the 'Tute, shown a steady, med-free composure after much therapy with Auntie and the others, and earned my high school diploma after a final summer session, ahead of my age level, with an A average. Instead of the van bringing me home, Brother Ted came to get me in his trusty Corolla. The fact that I was not in the 'Tute's custody for the ride home, with Happy Harley at the wheel, signaled my conclusive emancipation.

I was the showcase client, a success story, a thoroughly rehabilitated problem kid; the adventure with Pia in the getaway van had been erased from my files, though not from memory. That moment of freedom had been a transformative event in my life, the leap from childhood to adolescence. After that night came pimples, sore nipples, a crackling voice, peach fuzz, and a rare talent for masturbation in a variety of circumstances. A dozen surreptitious strokes would have me deliquescing in the middle of math class, at chapel services, even while waiting for a therapy session with Auntie. I turned self-abuse into an art form. In between orgasms I enjoyed flexing my erection, a kind of calisthenic that I hoped would further develop my newly developed penile strength. It was difficult for anyone near me to ignore my crotch while the bulge under my jeans pumped rhythmically, a second heart, true to the core of my being.

I was waiting for Ted in the 'Tute's lobby, surrounded by two suitcases, bundles of books, and a cigar box with various souvenirs, when I unleashed my final splooge as a ceremonial farewell. Rosemary the receptionist shot me a look as if she could hear my fingers kneading my penis through my jeans pocket. I had managed to liberate my tool from its confines yet keep it out of sight within the ample folds of my violet JCPenney coat. I wavered among several arousing triggers— Rosemary's curious look, her voice, her cleavage as she leaned into her computer. In any case I felt lightened by my release, even if I had to sneak. "Pop Goes the Weasel!" had become my theme song.

Rosemary must have sensed something, a quickening of my breath or a small whimper in my throat. In any case she looked at me with what I thought was a knowing smile while I blandly stared back at her until, finally surrendering to our locked stares, we both let out a burst of laughter.

"I bet you're glad to be going home, Adam," she said. "We're going to miss you."

"I'll miss you, too," I said, my voice choked with emotion. "Well, not everyone. But certainly you, Rosemary."

I had tucked my pud back into its home inside my jeans and was wiping my hand on the lining of the coat when Ted marched into the lobby, ready to take charge of my packed belongings. We shook hands. I couldn't help feeling a small sense of triumph that the hand that had performed such a fine stunt was now engaged in this first touch of reconciliation with my brother. He was tender with a kind of macho horseplay, starting to give me a hug but opting instead for a friendly knuckle noogie. I let out a mock "Ouch!" I was, in fact, moved by this act of rough affection.

He noticed my eyes welling up. "What's the matter, small sibling?"

"Nothing," I said, my voice cracking. "I'm happy to be going home."

I watched how gracefully he moved, using his ropy arms to lift my bags as I held against my chest the cigar box with the assortment of more than a hundred meds accumulated through clever trading and bold thieving during the past three years. Ted handled himself with muscular solidity, his face calm and his gaze steady. His skin had cleared, and his cheeks glowed from the crisp fall air, a luminous russet sheen, as smooth as a Red Delicious.

"Man, it's been years," he exclaimed as he slammed the trunk and ran to open the door for me.

"Thanks," I mumbled, not quite recovering from his calling me "man," in a kind of brotherly solidarity that celebrated our shared masculinity, a switch from when he considered me an embarrassment to our common DNA.

"Mom's been preparing all day," he said. "We're having tofurkey in your honor. It looks more like a duck, but it's guaranteed to provide all the holiday cheer of the real thing."

"Great," I chirped happily. "I looooove tofu." This last statement was not entirely true. It's hard to like tofu for its own sake, but it does make a nice sponge for sauces. Still, I was not going to turn this feast into the horror of the Thanksgiving three years ago. And it's not like I had the same options. Auntie and the 'Tute had done all they could. My next step might be a serious institution. No, thanks!

"There will be lots of other goodies, too," Ted said happily.

"Great!" I nodded rhythmically as if the thought was delightful beyond words. It was at that point that my bobbing head went on and on and I was powerless to stop it; Ted took his eyes off the road and gave me a hard look. No problem, I thought as I clapped my right hand on top of my head to bring its motion to a halt. I gave him my most disarming grin.

"So who else is going to be at dinner?" Mother and Father were known to invite the occasional holiday orphan from work, a nerdy office assistant or a sweet cashier from the grocery store who might have revealed her loneliness by staring enviously at Mother's cart loaded with Thanksgiving bounty.

"Who were you thinking of?" Ted frowned.

"Oh, nobody." I shrugged. "Thought maybe Iris had a boyfriend. Or you a girl."

This last point might have been inadvertently cruel; Ted had never, in all the years he'd been my brother, had a girl. First there was his general oafishness, then body odor, then pimples, then a nasty personality, all combined into one unattractive composite. It was only now that Ted was coming into his own. He could turn into a very attractive person, eventually.

"Iris has a married boyfriend, but everybody hates him. Including Iris."

"Just family, then."

"Just us on this special day." He gave my shoulder a light jab. "How about you?" he added. "There's that girl you ran away with years ago. What was her name?"

"Can't remember," I said, shooting him a puzzled look. He might have doubted my sincerity, but he let the subject drop. Pia remained an obsession that, if revealed in its full dimension, might spark doubt in my newly certified recovery.

"Sure, you do," he said. "It's kind of amazing how things turned out for her."

"What do you mean?"

"She lived in that big house in New Canaan."

"Okay," I said, finally giving up on any desire I might have had to protect that precious moment of my life. "Francine."

"Right," he said. "Something like that. Well, that was some prank she pulled on her folks."

The truth is, I didn't know what he was talking about. Dr. Clara and Dr. Auntie and the rest of the staff at the 'Tute had systematically avoided any hint of Pia's existence.

"What prank?" The substance of our conversation years ago was starting to replay itself.

"Oh, it might be easier to show you." Ted smirked. "We'll take a small detour." He turned off the freeway onto Snelling and headed past the mall, familiar as the site of my adventure with Miss Entropia, then off into the meandering roads of New Canaan, the large houses nestled within pockets of poplar or elm, occasionally fronted by circular drives and rolling lawns. My heart quickened. Even after three years the route was lively in my memory as we approached the cul-de-sac where I had met my first and only true love.

There was the faint smell of a dead fire, not mounds of autumn leaves smoldering on people's lawns or the scent of fragrant wood smoke from chimneys but a reek of lumber, plastic, curtains, upholstery, carpeting. The stink grew heavier, disturbing the suburban clarity of a crisp fall day. Something was rotten in New Canaan.

The house was well recessed in the circular drive and hidden from neighboring houses by a stand of elms. As I glimpsed the pillared portico of Pia's neocolonial, I recoiled at the sight of a burned skeleton, sections of the charred roof still supported by blackened columns and walls, surrounded by shards of glass from the blown-out windows.

"When did this happen?"

"Weeks ago," said Ted. "It's been a running story in the news. The insurance company is still investigating. They don't want to pay because they're sure it was arson."

"Really?" I tried for an expression of profound disbelief by raising my eyebrows and shaking my head.

"They think the owners of the house had it torched because the man was having business problems. Light a match, collect an easy million once you add the value of the antique furnishings, fancy knickknacks, fine art collection, the lady's jewelry."

"Was anyone hurt?"

"No. The parents have gone separate ways. The woman is in Texas, and the guy claims he's bankrupt and living in a motel. Your girlfriend could be anywhere." Ted smirked in that old way of his. "The cops would like to talk to her as well."

Of course she did it! I wanted to shout triumphantly. She had been mulling over the possibility for years. I could still hear her talking about it that night in our snowbound van. Ah, Miss Entropia, what an example you are to me. After three years at the 'Tute my id had been sedated into a smiling wait-and-see imp, less a little shit than a quirky witness, guaranteed to provide commentary, whisper hints of madness, but with its hands off the steering wheel. I envied Miss Entropia's progression into fierce spontaneity. Her vision of the family manor going up in flames could elicit only fear and awe. Kali lives!

Ted stopped the car on the driveway. Somebody had gone nuts with the crime-scene look. Yellow plastic streamers were draped all over the structure from the eaves to the front porch and around the front lawn, blocking the walkway, doors, and windows. Even from a distance I could see through a broken plate-glass window the formal distribution of a gutted living room outfitted with charred furniture and water-soaked carpeting.

"She did it, you know," I said.

"Your girlfriend?"

"Not quite my girl." I sighed.

"Her parents think it's her doing, too," he said. "According to news reports, they're scared of her. They think she's fucking homicidal, that she meant to incinerate them. Nobody knows where she is, and the insurance company can't deal with demolition and cleanup until they're done investigating."

"There doesn't seem to be anyone around," I said. "I'd like to go inside."

"Inside where?"

"The house. Her room. It would be important for me."

"You're nuts."

"I used to be. But I'm better now." I gave him a little punch on the shoulder to let him know I was sane enough not to take my sanity seriously.

While Ted complained, I was out of the car, running across the circle driveway and ducking under the yellow tape to the boards that had once been the front door and were now secured to the doorjamb with plastic twine. The stink of the fire carried a mix of molten plastic, upholstery stuffing, electrical wiring. The soaked carpet was mushy as mud under my feet. The staircase had been deemed unsafe, and a ladder provided a way to the second story. I climbed up and found myself standing at the head of a narrow hallway with collapsed doors along the blackened walls, leading to the one door that had not burned down and was instead neatly shut against the surrounding chaos. I opened it and found myself inside Pia's bedroom.

Through the gloom, I could see a pattern of roses blistered and peeling away from the wall, now stained and sooty and so appropriate to Pia's dark persona. The room looked much as she might have left it in her rush to school—bedcovers in a tumult, shoes and belts and clothes strewn about the floor. The surface of the writing table by the window was cluttered with books and notepads, a laptop, a mug full of pens and pencils, a letter-opener dagger topped by a cross, and a pair of goggle-sized sunglasses. I put on the sunglasses, with a D&G logo in rhinestones. From the center drawer I pulled out an orange prescription bottle. I happily shook out on my palm a dozen of the familiar pink triangles for those noonday demons, then poured them back in the bottle and pocketed the whole thing. I wasn't stealing; I intended to give them to Pia when we met again. Startled by Ted urgently blasting away on the horn, I rushed out of the house.

Ted, unsurprisingly, had no sense of adventure. I don't know what else I might have found inside. For now the big sunglasses served as a talisman to bring me closer to the goddess, to view the world from her point of view.

As Ted headed home, it was time to shift mental gears from the reemergence of Miss Entropia in my life toward the immediate future. "So how is everyone doing?" I asked tentatively

"Nervous," he said.

"About me?"

"About everything!" he said. "The war, the flu, the Vikings, the economy, the kids."

"But mostly about me."

"Yeah, you. And Cousin Iris's new boyfriend."

I felt a surge of gratitude to Iris. At least I was not alone in causing the family grief. I had an idea why her married beau might be a concern. But I was not up to joining the rest of the family in worrying about her. For now, as long as the boyfriend wasn't a serious sadist or a butcher, I felt the burden on me lift.

"Is he a criminal?"

"Yes, a religious one."

"What kind of religion?"

"The hypocritical kind." Ted shook his head. "He's Bob Gamaliel, the minister at the evangelical church in Spencer. He's married but says God means man to have many wives. Apparently he has not let his wife in on this."

"He's a Mormon."

"No, a moron."

"How did she meet him?"

"She conducts workshops for preachers. Ritual as Sacred Dance. He was one of her students, and they started hanging out after class."

Finally I was home and struck by how much everything looked the same. It was almost as if the Thanksgiving of my undoing had been going on uninterrupted. A festive wreath of dry twigs threaded with ribbons adorned the front door. On the table were the good silver and china and a centerpiece of maple leaves, pinecones, and sunflowers. Inside was one of those multisensory assaults that define the big-deal family gathering: Mother's Barry Manilow on the stereo, candles flickering, turkey smell wafting from the kitchen.

Albert and Marjorie had dressed up—the silk dress with the little purple flowers for her, the white shirt with the pumpkin-pattern tie for him. Iris looked strange in a blue suit and lace blouse. I was flattered, sensing that much of the effort had been for my benefit.

I had not put on anything special for the occasion. At seventeen, with spotty facial hair and a rangy build, I no longer looked so convincing in Mother's dresses. Instead I wore my flower-child look, bell bottoms, a paisley pirate shirt, authentic rudraksha beads from Varanasi guaranteed to shield me from impurity.

I thought it was going to be an evening free of surprises as we gathered around the table and proceeded to pass the beans, the yams, the tofurkey. Then Cousin Iris stood in front of the table and quieted us down with the tinkling of teaspoon on glass. There seemed to be a collective sigh as she raised her palms in a gesture of blessing. Mother looked on benignly, Father frowned, Ted rolled his eyes.

Iris started right in: "Oh, how our Lord must be rejoicing up there in angel-land over the return of our own little angel, Adam! We thank you, Jesus, for this happy day."

I could hardly believe what I was hearing. The beautiful Iris, once so ethereal and delicate, was pretty much intimidating us into piety. Ted started to clap, but Iris was not done yet.

"And we thank you on this day of Thanksgiving for the bountiful harvest on our table and the harmony in our family."

There, in one single holy maneuver, God had provided the Webbs with boiled beets and mashed potatoes, with white meat and dark meat and tofu meat, with stuffing in the turkey and me at the table. I found myself sinking into my chair, feeling like another sacrificial bird. The responsibility, once Jesus had gotten credit for my presence, my state of mind, my goodwill, was overwhelming. Would I be able to rise to the occasion? Only God knew.

Iris sat down, but she wasn't quite done. She reached for my right hand and Mother's left, then signaled that we should all clasp hands. I was thus connected to Ted and he to Father, who in turn held Mother's hand. Well, even on our best behavior our family gets uptight when pressed to the most elemental physical contact. We don't handle it very gracefully, and with Iris prolonging the act beyond a simple squeeze as she closed her eyes and waited for divine inspiration to quicken her tongue, I felt us stirring uncomfortably, our hands clammy and lifeless in each other's clasp.

"We are waiting, Jesus. If you choose to save us now, though we know not the hour, we pray you will lift us together, as a family, into your heavenly house."

She waited for almost a minute, head tilted upward and eyes rolled back so that only the whites showed. I think I was the one who broke the spell; the possibility of being lifted to God-knows-where struck me as unappealing. I had things to do. I'd just gotten out of one institution; I was not prepared to be whisked to another. I wanted to live a normal life: go to college, listen to rock and roll, travel to Oaxaca, take the mushrooms, write a novel, find Miss Entropia. "Okeydokey!" I let go of the hands on my right and left and rubbed my palms gleefully. "Pass the yams."

Iris shot me a look that told me I was being a boor again; clearly there was an etiquette to the Christian thing. "Amen!" I added, to be on the safe side.

"Amen," everyone mumbled as we set upon the victuals before us.

One good thing about this particular Thanksgiving was that I was no longer the kook-in-residence. That distinction had been snatched away by the once graceful and lovely Iris. She was still nice to look at, but she had hardened into a pious rigidity, her feet encased in clunky shoes, the vaporous skirts and blouses of the past replaced by boxy blue suits and gray tops. I suspected I would never see her naked again.

On the other hand, even as she looked like a nun in civvies, we knew she was communing with Pastor Bob outside the workshop. Iris seemed preoccupied as she nibbled on the slivers of white meat, the spoonful of mashed potatoes, and the dozen green beans on her plate. Her bland expression took on a blush when the phone rang and Father said it was for her. "Some gentleman with a deep voice," he said. "Maybe God."

Iris pushed back her chair and went into the kitchen, primly closing the door behind her. We could hear her rushed, almost breathless muttering, as if she had been waiting to pour out a stream of pent-up emotion.

"Hurry, dear," sang Mother, loudly enough to discreetly cover up Iris's rant. "You don't want your food getting cold." There were things Mother knew about the ways of the heart that made her a trusted confidant.

"Talk faster, Iris!" Father chortled.

"Faster Pastor!" spoke Ted, loudly enough, I think, to be heard on the other end of the line.

"Faster Pastor!" I laughed along, enjoying the rhyme as the cleverest thing Ted had uttered in his life. "Faster Pastor, Faster Pastor . . ." I was suddenly bent on a repetitive behavior syndrome, the verbal equivalent of the eye tic or the restless knee bounce, knowing what was happening but incapable of ordering my voice to stop. Ted finally, mercifully, walked around the table and stood behind me to gently clap his hand over my mouth, pressing on my lips until the slightest utterance was stilled.

"Thank you," I muttered.

Iris came back into the dining room, looking dazed.

"What on earth is happening, dear?" asked Mother.

Iris stood at the table as if frozen in uncertainty. "I think I've lost my appetite," she said, then turned around and headed up to her room.

Mother was not about to let the holiday spirit be disrupted. "Enjoy, everybody!" She believed food cured the malaise of the soul. The tryptophan in the turkey, the sugar in the tiny marshmallows, the allspice in the pie.

And there it was, sitting in front of me, a brilliant example of cultural adaptation, a lump of tofu shaped like a football, varnished to a golden brown with soy sauce, two celery stalks on either side as thighs, a baby carrot serving as a beak, and a glop of bread stuffing shoved up the rear. It was beautiful; I didn't know where to begin its demolition.

"Wait," Father said. "We've got to get a picture of this."

Out came the camera, and Albert went around the table taking pictures of the food, of the centerpiece, of the family, in pairs and threes and by ourselves. Only Iris was missing. That was the beginning of her project to fast her way to heaven.

Chapter Eleven

ris sure knew how to pick a boyfriend. And it took a special kind to pick her. This married guy, Pastor Bob, had fallen in love with her while she was teaching him modern dance moves. She concentrated on the use of the vestments and how to move about like a winged messenger of deliverance. *He is a living presence amongst us,* and all that.

She spread the word that she thought nondancing people, especially men, moved like clods. With her talent and good looks, she soon had a class of about twenty ministers and a couple of rabbis, all of them men. Bob Gamaliel, charismatic leader of the church in Spencer, was her most enthusiastic student.

She found him intriguing. Here was this big-deal preacher, a stalwart of the evangelical movement, leader of the newly reborn, getting all moony over his movement coach. Iris liked costumes. Pastor Bob was all of a piece, showing up for class in a Hugo Boss suit, with the perfect hair graying at the temples, combed in a pompadour that looked sculpted on top of his head, and the cologne that enveloped him in a syrupy aura of apples and vanilla. Outside church, he liked to project an aura of optimism. Ready to be saved? Show your joy.

The first time he invited her for coffee after class he wanted to talk to her about the state of her soul. She listened; she'd been acutely aware of her mortality ever since the unexpected death of her parents. Living with fear made her a ripe candidate for salvation, more urgently now, with the End Times practically upon us.

She started seeing Gamaliel on Thursday nights after class. Soon, because the class gave him good cover to be home late, it became a weekly dinner. They went to fine downtown restaurants where he was not likely to be spotted by his suburban parishioners. One night, after they'd been going out for a couple of months, Bob took her to the Meridien Hotel. Instead of having dinner in the restaurant, he whisked her twenty-six stories up to a room where a rolling table with crisp linens, heavy silver, Riedel glasses, and a grigio chilling in the ice bucket awaited. She was so flattered by his meticulous planning that she began the affair that would lead to the current troubled situation.

She could bolster her self-esteem by getting this big preacher down to his silk undershorts, moaning under her as she gave him oral thrills that in his marriage he had only fantasized about. He persuaded her that she was on a higher mission, relieving the man of God of tension so that he might do a better job in the spiritual department. It was, to be sure, a complicated arrangement.

Initially sex was interrupted by the singing door chime. Pastor Bob would duck into the bathroom, and Iris would let in the room-service waiter. She was partial to dishes not usually found at the Webb table—chanterelle mushrooms, roasted quail, oxtail soup, and for dessert a litany of soufflés and crèmes.

Eager to get on with his thrills, Pastor Bob gulped his food. Iris would savor every bite. Fine cuisine was new to her. He wanted sex. She felt better about herself when she avoided sex. Usually, if Iris was particularly absorbed in the feast at hand, there would be no time for a second tumble. The pastor was expected at home. Iris would peck him on the cheek, then stay at the Meridien, lolling in the fine cotton sheets and watching Letterman. She was on a diet six days a week; on the seventh she was a whore for food. It began to bother her that she was selling her soul for a bowl of vichyssoise.

Bob was a slow learner; he started bringing little presents—body lotions, pretty soaps, bath salts—to their TGI Thursdays, as she called their dates.

His eventual resentment was inevitable. Bob was feeling a gnawing hunger for more of a relationship than Iris was willing to feed him. He wanted her to be his second wife, he said, so that he could be a holy bigamist just like Moses and Abraham. Iris reminded him that he was already in more relationships than he could handle, with his wife and kids for starters. They're not the same thing, he whined.

ris had run to her room after hanging up on Pastor Bob, and she stayed there for most of the afternoon. Then, as Father, Ted, and I were lined up on the couch in front of the football game, snoring and farting and groaning (it was an easy way to establish solidarity with the males in the family), I overheard her and Mother having a talk.

"I've created a monster," Iris blurted out.

"Who? Your boyfriend?" Mother asked, going heavy on "boy."

"*Me*," she said. "I'm the truffle monster, caviar monster, brie-and-apple-soup monster. I've become a pig for food that I can't afford. I must've lived in famine in a previous life."

"You've got to kick cold turkey." A nice metaphor, I thought.

And that was what she did. No gradual sliding from feast to snacks to coffee and cookies. The following Thursday evening Iris called Bob in their usual room at the Meridien and caught him dripping wet from his presex shower.

"What brought all this about?" he asked when she told him she wouldn't be there that night.

"I intend to reclaim my dignity," she said. "I've become a puppy begging at the table."

"Come over anyway. You can have a salad and herbal tea."

"No," she said.

The following day a box addressed to Iris arrived by messenger service. The driver asked if I was Iris because I happened to be wearing Mother's old silk Chanel knockoff, dredged out of the Salvation Army bag. It was a test to see how tolerant the family might be of any possible relapse. I wasn't planning to slide down the slippery slope of my eccentricities again, but who knew what might happen once the 'Tute's support system was cut off. Besides, I liked that particular purple shift, belted in back and with a row of pearly plastic buttons from the collar to the hem, for a variety of visual teases from cleavage to thigh, from chaste to wanton.

"I'm not supposed to let anyone sign for this except Miss Iris Fallon."

"I'm Miss Iris," I said, ignoring the man's wide-eyed stare and reaching for his clipboard. The sender was listed as the Meridien Hotel, Minneapolis.

I signed with an illegible doodle. I was carrying the package inside, nearly breathless with excitement, when Iris appeared in response to her name being spoken.

"Hey, Iris," I mumbled. "I didn't know you were home."

"Someone asking for me?"

"Wow, a prezzie for you, Cousin!" I suspected a gift from Pastor Bob, given their history at the Meridien Hotel, so I handed her the box and hovered. It was too heavy for lingerie or shoes. There was some muffled rattling when she shook it. "Can I open it?" I pleaded.

"Take it into the kitchen." She handed me the box and pushed me ahead of her.

I tore the box flaps with a butcher knife and revealed the previous night's untasted meal neatly wrapped in foil: fennel-encrusted sea bass on a bed of green-pea risotto, orange-infused rutabaga soup, a bottle of White Stag cabernet, three flavors of crème caramel in individual pots, each one sealed in cling wrap. There was no note.

Iris rolled everything back in the foil and sealed the package with strapping tape. She had me drive her to the post office and sent the box back by parcel post to Pastor Bob's church. No note.

"Any insurance?" the postal clerk asked.

"No," Iris said. "Nothing valuable."

"Proof of delivery?" he asked. "Somebody will have to sign for it that way."

"Yes, that's great." Iris nodded enthusiastically. "I want the whole congregation to know what's in the box."

"It could take three days," the clerk volunteered. "We can get it there faster if it's urgent."

"No," Iris said. "Slow and sure is fine."

Chapter Twelve

The next week on a Monday evening Father rousted us all out of our rooms for a family meeting. He kept marching up and down the hall, knocking on doors, exclaiming that the time had come for a serious talk. He liked airing our respective transgressions publicly, in a kind of kangaroo court with a rigged verdict so that the concerted pressure of the family would straighten out the transgressor. I had been a stellar family citizen since returning from the 'Tute, so I imagined when we all gathered in the living room that the subject had to be Iris. She was the one involved with a married preacher, drifting into a rapture cult, and courting an eating disorder.

But no, it turned out that the subject of the intervention was little me. It took a quick glance at Mother to catch the drift of our family conclave: she had on the purple dress with the endless row of pearly plastic buttons that I had worn three days before. Man, I must've looked as dowdy as a Republican nun! Ted scrunched himself close beside me on the couch to prevent me from bolting, his massive arm around my knobby shoulders. I stirred to test his resolve and felt his hold tighten. "Relax, bro," he breathed moistly into my ear. "This is not a big deal if you don't let it." I didn't quite understand how the bigness of the deal before me was under my control.

Iris had ratted me out. I looked around the room. Dressed in white for the occasion, she was the picture of innocence, her face clear of makeup, her hair brushed back primly, her feet together at the ankles. She wore a heavy gold cross that these days hung from a chain, letting Jesus nestle between her breasts.

Father started right in on me. "Take a look at your mother, son," he said. "She loves you so very much. And you love her. Is that why you want to dress like her?"

I could tell he had been talking with Dr. Auntie. It was the kind of analytic babble prevalent at the 'Tute, and they were still throwing old Oedipus at me. The effort was laughable. So I laughed. I don't know how long I went on, maybe three minutes, with a *ha ha ha* that sounded mechanically out of control, until Ted tightened his hold on my shoulders and stilled the shaking of my body, which in turn slowed the hilarity to a soft snicker.

"If you're done," Father continued, "we can finish our conversation."

We didn't carry on with our talk because just then the doorbell rang, and I escaped Ted's embrace to see who was visiting us. It was a UPS guy delivering a package for Miss Iris Webb from R. Gamaliel, Grace Church, Spencer.

"Dinner is here," I announced. "Courtesy of Pastor Bob." Oh, how I wanted to laugh. The impulse to break into another fit of laugh-o-mania was nearly overpowering. But I held fast, signed for the package, and took it into the living room. Before I could deposit it at the center of the group, Iris pushed me back past the kitchen toward the back door.

"Oh, not again," she whined. "Take that stuff outside."

The fishy smell was so intense that UPS had affixed a sticker to the box: "Warning! Perishable Contents." Iris took the parcel to the picnic table in the backyard. She carefully unpacked the box and spooned the whole mushy mess, from fish to 'shrooms to crèmes, into a Tupperware box.

We drove the package to Bob's home address and left it at his front door. She enclosed a note: *Bon appétit, your reverence. I am no longer your food whore.*

Iris won the food fight.

Fortunately my trial on charges of flamboyance and perversity had been interrupted; Iris was again the center of attention. Pastor Bob was banished, but her expectation of being plucked aloft was growing more urgent. She kept studying the headlines for signs of the coming tribulation, evident in every disaster from terrorist mayhem and Catholic priests' sexploits to earthquakes, floods, and drought. Even sunspots, eclipses, comets, meteor showers, and new planets fueled her sense of the coming cataclysm. She followed the fluctuations of the Official Tribulations Index (OTI), adding or subtracting points according to the vagaries of the visible universe. Day by day the numbers rose or dropped from a baseline of 148, where the tribulation might happen or might not, to the nosebleed 160s.

One day, when the OTI had broken 170, she paid bills, cleaned her room, washed clothes; she explained that she had no right to expect the family to deal with her mess after she had sprung aloft. She said one couldn't know the time or the hour, but one had to make peace with one's soul and be ready. She considered herself good to go.

The next morning, when a predicted tsunami off California's southern coast didn't happen, the index was down to 142, and we all breathed easier. Iris's idea of heaven did not appeal to me.

Still, I couldn't get too caught up in the twists and turns of our family. Somewhere on the planet Miss Entropia awaited. During the last three years at the 'Tute I had thought of her often, at first with lust and then, as the memory of that first experience of touch and release softened, with a kind of romanticized idealization. I nightly conjured the image of her face, her voice, her scent, and fell asleep to the remembered whisper of her breath on my cheek. I wondered if I would recognize her if she crossed my path.

For a couple of years I had harbored the illusion that she might end up at the 'Tute. As my graduation approached, I gave up on that thought. I begged Auntie for information—her address, her phone number, her school. No dice. It was information that had become irrelevant, and the files had been shredded. Plus, they would be liable for God knows what legal heat if I turned out to be a stalker, or worse.

"I wouldn't bother Pia," I complained. "I love her."

Auntie winced at the sound of the words. "Do me a favor," he said. "Don't go around saying 'love.' Nobody strikes more fear into the minds of doctors, teachers, cops, and parents than the crazy guy who says he *loves* the girl. Wouldn't do a thing to hurt her, blah, blah, blah."

"Will I ever see her again?" I nearly whined.

"*Qué será será,*" said Auntie.

I decided he and the 'Tute had done all they would ever do for me. Even if my mind was still a brambly kind of garden, I had learned to blunt my thorns and put on the virtues of the well-adjusted kid. Gone, for the most part, were the rages, the babbling, the fits of sneezing and groaning, the knee jerks and head bobs that had marked me as a child to be reckoned with. I had a firm handshake and a steady gaze.

I swung around and was about to congratulate Auntie on his acknowledgment of the play of the fates in affairs of the heart when I spontaneously decided on the analytical approach: "That's Spanish, isn't it?" I tried to sound thoughtful. "The *qué será* business."

Auntie nodded and gave me a suspicious look. "It means 'what will be will be.' "

"*Sí, yo hablo español,*" I said.

"One of your many talents," Auntie said.

I can dish out passive aggression as well as anybody. "I imagine you used the Spanish because it makes that bit of wisdom sound more profound."

Auntie sighed. I was getting at him from an unsuspected angle, and the effect was fun to watch. "It's just a tune, Adam. From before your time."

"You don't think I know that song."

"You act as if you've never heard it before."

"No, what I'm wondering is why you would choose a simple refrain to reveal this stuff about fate and destiny and the play of the planets."

"No reason, Adam. The song came to mind."

"Because it's more poetic that way?"

"Time's up, Adam. Go away."

I checked my watch and realized we still had twelve minutes to go. I started to protest when Auntie jumped right in on my thoughts. "And don't come back."

"Because I'm cured?"

"Yes, Adam. You're cured."

"Yippee!" I shouted. It was the second time I had been declared cured in as many years.

Chapter Thirteen

Once I was readmitted to the 'Tute for the long haul, my family breathed a collective sigh of relief. I had been, after all, the dangling participle, the loose cog, the sour note causing disharmony. Thousands of dollars and four years of harsh attitude adjustment had been spent on getting my head screwed down to a semblance of coherence and stability. Now, on my return home, I realized that the fabric of the family was fraying, that things had gotten worse without any help from me. Iris was a born-again, rapture-ready, anorexic adulterer. Ted had a secret hobby that was getting him beat up with some regularity.

More seriously, an unspoken tension was brewing between Albert and Marjorie. I could sense that something was wrong in the way they warily moved around each other. In the past they had been united by their concern over Iris, Ted, and especially me. Suddenly their focus had turned inward.

Their routines had not changed much. Albert still pulled his brown hat to his ears and settled down to watch the twenty-four-hour news for more evidence that the country was unraveling. Sometimes, after three hours in his La-Z-Boy, he would come out blinking into the brightly lit kitchen and discover that Marjorie had been gone all day. He would ask me if I knew where Mother was, and I would have to admit I did not.

When she showed up with no explanation to whip up a stir-fry for dinner, Father would barely acknowledge that she had been away. I tried to ask Ted and Iris what they thought, but they were too self-absorbed to notice anything beyond their noses. It was up to me, newly sane from the 'Tute, to figure out what was happening. I owed it to my parents to watch them for signs of stress since they had put up with my eccentricities for years. In a little spiral notebook I wrote down clues pointing toward a fraying of their relationship: Albert wolfs his food down without a word of appreciation. Marjorie returns home without announcing her arrival (*Honey, I'm home*). After Marjorie goes to bed Albert stays up for hours, flipping through the news channels, before deciding that Blitzer, Wallace, O'Reilly, and their ilk are idiots.

In the morning my parents circled each other in the kitchen, getting coffee, toast, milk in a kind of glum choreography. Small details, to be sure, but significant in light of their previous relationship. When Mother asked what I was writing, I said I was keeping a secret journal.

On the surface there was nothing major to record. Father would start the week systematically, sitting down to his breakfast of oatmeal with bananas and many cups of weak coffee. He dressed for comfort and agility in a soft corduroy suit, his brown fedora, and rubber-soled shoes suitable for climbing on rooftops. I could always tell when he had beaten me to the table because of the clouds of bay-rum after-shave that followed him down the hallway and stairs, through the living room, and into the kitchen. He checked his sample case, made sure he could demonstrate the virtues of Mightyplate Roof Coating: no tar, no stink, no cracks, no leaks. He would check his appointment book over breakfast, then set out. He was as resilient as the black, rubbery gunk he sold. He'd try to lock in six appointments a day, aiming for two firm orders. If he made four sales, the next day he would stay home and watch the news.

Unfortunately, he had little repeat business; once he treated a roof, it kept the rain out for seven years. He made cold calls, reaching further and further out of state, looking for strip malls, warehouses, schools, any structure with a huge expanse of flat roofing. Sometimes he hit an unsuspected jackpot. Often he would come home drained, his spirit numbed by the repeated door slamming and heel cooling, and it would take him a few hours of TV crisis watching and beer drinking to regain his sense of rightness in the world.

Mother, on the other hand, had always been hard to pin down. Through the years she had changed jobs on a whim: part-time librarian, school-bus driver, welcome-wagon lady, zoo docent, proofreader, department-store undercover security guard. She could afford to be flaky with a trust fund to her name. Her current adventure, however, remained a mystery. Every morning she would get break-fast ready, then leave the house even as we kids were taking our seats at the table.

"Where to, Mom?" Ted would call out.

"Just here and there," she would answer with a wan smile. Then she would bend down and kiss Father on the forehead, which I could see frustrated him. He probably thought it was out of place for him to have to ask what she was up to and even more so for her not to tell him. Therein lay the root of their dislocating relation-ship. Whatever Mother was doing, her comings and goings were un-predictable. She might take a weekday off and work on Sunday, sleep in, then stay out until midnight. It became rare for Marjorie and Albert to be in the house at the same time. And then they engaged each other politely, making fleeting contact for a comment on the weather, the world, the kids, perhaps a touch for hello or good-bye. It was an unsettling thing to witness. All my life my parents had been the anchor that tried to keep me from floating away in a sea of ambiguity.

Suddenly untethered by our parents' slip from their rock-solid stability, Iris was deepening her allegiance to the apocalyptic cult and Ted was skirting the edge of disaster with increasing mindlessness. I felt it was up to me to set the normalcy standard for the family; I would work on their shaky equilibrium. It was time to apply those hard lessons learned in the care of the 'Tute and Dr. Auntie; I would be the light in the prevailing murk.

I made myself useful. A soon as everyone went to their jobs, I performed significant acts of organization. I vacuumed, dusted, polished, mopped, washed, mowed. I saw myself as the coherence fairy, intervening in small ways to make life orderly.

A part of my day was dedicated to the books in the family room. There must've been about a thousand of them, arranged alphabetically by author. I entered the world of our family literature with a restless vision. There had to be a better way to organize books. I started arranging them alphabetically by title. It made sense because one looked for *Leaves of Grass* specifically, not "something" by Whitman, W. This approach satisfied me for a day or two. Then I realized that there was something messy and undisciplined about titles, each standing lonely without obvious relationship to the books beside it, as if a book were an island sufficient unto itself, disconnected from the literary mainland. I switched from alphabetical by title to filing by literary genre: poetry, fiction, memoir, biography, pornography, and finally alphabetical by author. It was interesting how much porn had been lurking on the shelves, revealed once the different titles coalesced into their own category—De Sade, Masoch, Hewett, A. M. Homes, A. M. Le Deluge, A. N. Onymous.

After that I cut loose. For a while books were arranged by color, then by age, typeface, or author's first name. I reached my zenith as a book classifier with the filing of the books by size, visually intriguing, I thought, from the smallest to the largest. If one were searching for a long book versus a short book, then one could see what was available. To keep things from looking too tilted to one side, I had big books at the ends, then scaled down by height and width and number of pages toward the middle, with the thumb-sized *Hail Mary from Lourdes* dead center. The shelf above would reverse the progression, and so on. The effect was so pleasing I let it stand to give the family a chance to admire my handiwork, a literary pipe organ to be played from thunder to chirp and back again, arpeggios of love and adventure and transcendence all at our fingertips, the library as symphony. Not a word through the whole weekend.

Then on Sunday night Mother wailed that she couldn't find her copy of *Teresa of Calcutta: Deva or Diva* by Mark Lockwood, the hack biographer. It was the first hint of what Mother had been up to in her mysterious wanderings. Why wasn't it under the Ls, and where were the Ls, anyway? Or the Ts? How about S for saint, N for nun, C for Catholic, I for India?

I watched her run her fingers along the book spines like a pianist playing scales. I waited for the reaction to the tingle on her fingertips that would signal the presence of the desired title. I believed in the tingle; Mother didn't.

She turned to me, having intuited that the new arrangement was my doing. "Adam!" she called. "How does one find the biography of Saint Teresa in these shelves? It's enough to drive us all crazy."

"It takes more than that, believe me," I said calmly as I sauntered over to the exact spot where *Teresa of Calcutta* was wedged, right between *Gravity's Rainbow* and *Lolita*. I took it from the shelf and handed it to her with a small bow. "It's a workable system once you understand it. You find what you're looking for and maybe something unexpected, wonderfully serendipitous."

"You are all the serendipity I've ever needed."

I decided I felt flattered, though I didn't fully understand the implications of her statement. Had she wanted a girl and gotten a boy? Expected a normal kid and wound up with a nutcase? Wanted a simple roll in the hay and ended up complicatedly pregnant?

The other question left dangling: Why was my mother so eager to read a sappy biography of Mother Teresa? In any case, she curled up with all five hundred sixty pages and spent the weekend absorbed in the comings and goings of the withered old Croatian with a loving heart and the will of an inquisitor.

One day my father decided to come to me for help, maybe because he felt that my affinity with Mother might shed light on her latest quirks.

"The family needs you, Adam," he began calmly as we sat down to watch a discussion on a congressional race in South Dakota. "I think we are losing her to some secret adventure."

"So ask her what's going on."

Poor Dad, he was barely disguising his anxiety. "I have asked."

"And she says?" I was feeling quite adult in this exchange, my father and I consulting as peers on a potentially disruptive situation. And for the first time I was able to see my own behavior through others' eyes. In a sense he was the hub, and the rest of us were at different times the loose cogs that made the wheel of our family wobble.

"She says not to worry." Father scowled.

"So don't worry." Having had a hidden life of my own, I was tolerant of anybody else's flights into unknown regions.

"It's the secrecy," he said sadly. "When she spends the better part of the week on the dark side of the moon, I feel left out."

"I get it, Dad." Suddenly he appeared to have aged half a lifetime.

"See what she's up to," he said.

"Sure." Then I added, "But I don't have to tell you. Do I? She'll have her secret to keep if she wants to."

With that vague agreement I set out to snoop. During the first month her excursions had been irregular—some days early morning, others after lunch and into evening. She didn't seem to be dressing to impress: jeans and a sweater or a plain tan skirt with a blouse and good walking shoes. When the weather turned warm she opted for shorts and a pocket t-shirt. I didn't picture Mother doing anything exciting in those boring duds. I looked far more stylish in one of her charitybound dresses.

The truth was that investigating my own mother's hidden life had the potential to unleash a raft of uncomfortable revelations. I waited for the right time to ask her what she was up to. Meanwhile, I watched. Even as Father seemed possessed by a kind of jittery distraction, Mother was newly focused on the small details of family life, confronting our every odd turn with a kind of equanimity and a serious regard for whatever our small crisis meant for us.

One morning, when the rest of the family had gone off for the day, she had brewed a pot of Earl Grey and we were sitting at the kitchen table with a plate of shortbread cookies between us. It was like old times, Mother and me and the gentle communion of tea. I tried to ease into a tentative interrogation. She was having none of it.

"Dear, dear boy," she cooed. "Are you worried about your mother?"

"Not really," I said with a self-effacing grin. "We are all wondering what you're up to."

"Am I the only one that has to be an open book?" She poured

more tea. "Everyone in this family has a private life. A room of one's own, some nook where you are unseen and untouched and undefiled."

She fixed me with a steady gaze. "You know what I'm talking about, Adam."

She was right. I had a whole castle inside me, with twisting hallways leading to a hundred rooms and dungeons. Pia was in one of those rooms. I didn't know how it would happen, but I was sure she would pop out eventually.

"You can't blame us for being curious."

"Who's curious?" She frowned. "I can't believe any self-absorbed member of this family wants to know what I'm up to."

"Father is curious."

"So he set you off to investigate me."

"He said he asked you," I defended him, "but that you told him he would know when the timing was right."

"Yes," she smiled. "I said I would tell him all about my adventures when I felt like it."

"You know Father," I said. "He doesn't like to be in the dark."

Finally she said, "Tomorrow you can come with me."

Chapter Fourteen

Time passed slowly the following morning as Mother got breakfast for Father before he went on his sales route, Ted rushed to
his job, Iris went out for her rapture meetings. By 10 or so the house
was silent, and I waited by the front door, ready to follow Mother to
her car. I sat on the stairs, dressed for mobility in jeans, sneakers,
t-shirt, and a rolled-up windbreaker tied around my waist. For once,
I thought, I did not seem likely to embarrass my mom.

Our first stop was Target, the men's-socks racks. Mother knew
exactly where she was going; she strode down the aisle while I hurried to keep up with her vigorous pace. She took a dozen pairs of
heavy white socks, the kind with extra thickness on the heel, rising
to midcalf. I wondered whom they were for; not even Ted wore
white tube socks.

"No questions, sonny boy," Mother said when she anticipated I was about to ask one. "You can tag along and watch and learn." Then she handed me the bag of socks, and I followed her across the parking lot. Whatever she had in mind, there was a sense of purpose to her stride, and I anticipated being part of something important.

Our next stop was Loring Park, a jewel between downtown and a tangle of freeways. On that brilliant autumn day, carpeted with the red and gold of fallen leaves, a cloudless blue sky already promising the radiance of the coming winter, Mother parked by the dandelion fountain. The Parks Board, a gang of anal-retentive vigilantes, had not yet decided it was time to shut off the water for winter, so the fountain was casting its starlike spray for perhaps the last time that year. Mother cut across the lawn while I followed, shuffling my feet against the crackling leaves, kicking up flurries of color. We must've gone two-thirds of the way around the pond when, after crossing the Japanese footbridge, Mother suddenly strode toward a solitary woman with a duffel bag taking up most of the bench beside her, heavy coat unbuttoned and face angled up to catch the sun's warmth.

I had over the years caught glimpses of urban wanderers, standing with a sign at an intersection or pushing a shopping cart down the sidewalk. I had never been close enough to any members of this club to absorb the impact of their individuality. In this instance the wide-open greatcoat in a military style, dark green with epaulets and brass buttons, revealed a solid, barrel-shaped woman wrapped in a maroon cardigan over a green v-neck over a lumberjack shirt, the tails coming below the waist of a brown corduroy skirt. On her head she wore a red elf hat with a white pom-pom, and on her feet high-top sneakers.

We stood silently for several moments a couple of steps in front of the woman until she finally opened her eyes.

"Why on earth would you be wanting to block my sunshine?" she asked. "If it's to get my attention, you have succeeded."

Mother quickly stepped to one side so the woman's face was again bathed in light.

"Thank you." I expected to hear a note of sarcasm in her words, but her voice had an even, mellow tone so that she did in fact sound grateful. She closed her eyes, as if declaring that our brief exchange was concluded.

Mother would not, however, let it rest. "My name is Marjorie Webb," she said. "And this is Adam, my son."

"Delighted to make your acquaintance," the woman said without opening her eyes.

"And your name might be . . ."

"Might be none of your business." She chuckled, pleased with her retort.

"No business of mine whatsoever," Mother was eager to reassure her. "Only in the sense that it is customary for people to exchange names when there's an introduction. We have introduced ourselves to you."

"More like intruded yourselves."

"I don't mean to bother you," Mother said. "And if you like, we can just go away without further conversation."

"I didn't realize we were to have a conversation."

"Like I said, we don't have to."

"But it is your intention, madam, to engage me in some kind of chat?"

"It is."

I liked watching Mother in her quietly relentless pursuit of whatever social congress she was after. It was the way she managed relationships in our family, and I knew she was pretty damn hard to resist.

"Fine." The woman sighed. "I'm Marlene Dietrich." Her soft laugh from deep in her chest turned into a cough.

"Pleased to meet you, Marlene." Mother stuck out her hand, which the woman clasped as her coughing subsided.

She then reached out to me as well. "And happy to make your acquaintance, young Adam." I will never forget the feel of that hand, a hard, fibrous thing, nearly skeletal in its sparsity of flesh. "Would you two care to join me in a little sun worshipping?" She dragged the duffel off the bench and edged to one side to make room for us. Mother sat on the end and pulled me by the hand to sit between them. For the first time I was assaulted by the sharp smell of the woman—tobacco, leather, burnt rubber, hot asphalt, and peppermint schnapps. Not an unpleasant blend. "Ah, this is nice," she said, tilting her face to the sun again.

"It is a lovely morning," Mother agreed. "Nice that it's starting to warm up."

"And what is it that brings you to my part of the world?" Marlene coaxed. "I should warn you that if you are in any way associated with a religious group, a rehab clinic, a political party, or a journalistic expedition, then our conversation will be zipped before it's begun."

Mother reassured her, "We are here out of simple human interest."

"Because you nice people from the burbs find the likes of my person interesting?"

"More an interest in your well-being."

"So there is something about me that gives you reason to suppose I'm not as fine as I could be?" She sat up to the full level of her dignity. "You saw a woman warming her old bones on a park bench and decided she deserved your concern. I'll have you know that I don't welcome spontaneous pity. I don't solicit alms like some panhandler. You can't come into my life uninvited and expect to buy yourself some warm fuzzies."

"I'm not here to give you money," Mother said.

"Or sympathy," the woman snapped.

"How about new socks?" Mother smiled.

The woman looked down at her feet, as if wondering for the first time what might lie inside her sneakers. By now I was feeling embarrassed to be caught between Mother and Marlene Dietrich; I didn't see why Mother couldn't leave the socks on the bench for the lady and say good-bye. It was like Mother to turn the simplest human interaction into an exploration of truth and intimacy. Mother had been edging closer to the woman and in the process pressing me against her. I felt an urgent need for air.

"I get it," Mrs. Dietrich said with a sudden laugh. "You're teaching your boy compassion, empathy, respect."

I practically jumped off the bench and stood on the walk shuffling my feet and edging gradually away from the two women.

Mother ignored me and slid a couple of inches closer to Mrs. Dietrich.

"Actually," Mother said, "I just want to give you some socks."

"You've decided I need socks?" The woman laughed. "My socks are fine."

"I bet they're not," Mother said.

"Just leave me the socks. I'll put them on later."

"Actually," Mother said, quietly stubborn now, "I want to make sure you put the new ones on."

Mother had managed to gently defeat Mrs. Dietrich. The woman blushed, untied the laces of her high-tops, and pulled them off slowly, one after the other, without a word, her gaze on her feet as if the operation required great concentration. By now I had drifted away and pretended to be absorbed in the art of sending flat stones skimming the surface of the pond.

"There." The woman looked up. "Happy now?" She had on a pair of socks that might at one time have been blue but now were rubbed to a shiny gray patina, with gaping holes at both heels; on one the unraveling allowed a toe with a black, bruised nail to peek out like an angry gnome.

"You can throw those away," Mother suggested kindly. Then, as the woman pulled off the socks, Mother suggested she wash her feet at the edge of the pond. "We don't want to put clean new socks on dirty feet, do we?" Mother handed her soap and a scrub brush she had packed in the bag with the socks.

When the woman came back to the bench her feet were bright pink with the cold. Mother handed her some paper towels. After her feet were blotted dry, the woman pulled on the socks, smiling for the first time at the luxury of the clean white knit warming her feet halfway to the knee. Once she had both socks on, she stretched her legs out to admire them. By this time I had gradually shuffled back to the bench, realizing that something significant had taken place between Mother and Mrs. Dietrich. Mrs. Dietrich put the high-tops back on and stood to shake Mother's hand. Instead of taking her hand, Mother opened her arms wide, and the woman stepped into her embrace. "This is the finest thing anyone has done for me in the longest time. Thank you."

"You are so welcome," Mother whispered close to the woman's face.

"You're a fucking saint, lady." She pulled away from Mother's arms. "I want to get a good look at you."

After that we walked around the edges of town for several blocks. I was now in charge of carrying the backpack with the socks, soap, and paper towels. Throughout the day Mother encountered two more candidates for new socks, both men. One, terribly drunk for so early in the day, was sleeping under one of the freeway bridges. The other was waiting in line for lunch at Loaves and Fishes, a Catholic shelter. The routine was similar. At first they refused to speak with her; more emphatically, they both told her to fuck off.

Mother was undaunted by the rejection. Eventually she wore her subject down and got him to pull off his shoes, dump his rotting socks, wash his feet. And always there was this transformation from grouchy monosyllables to profuse gratitude. I was not sure what was being worked out between Mother and her new friends, but I was proud to be her assistant.

On the way back to our car, by then a walk of three miles or so that would take over an hour, Mother quizzed me on my understanding of the day's events. The truth was that I had little sense of what had taken place. It seemed to me that if Mother wanted to give socks to the poor, she could give a box of them to Goodwill or the Salvation Army. A hundred people would get socks at once instead of the handful we might run into in a day.

"It's not about socks, silly," Mother said when I voiced my thoughts. "It's about touching someone's soul. Expose their sole and they bare their soul."

The truth was, I was dumber at seventeen than I had been at fourteen. It was all word games to me. I had seen what she meant, I just hadn't yet understood the significance of Mother's act. But when she asked me if I would go back out with her the next day, I eagerly said yes. And when Father asked me a couple of days later what was going on, I said Mother was helping the homeless.

"I carry stuff," I said with a shrug.

"Good," he said. "Keep busy while you decide about your future."

Fine with me because, after three years at the 'Tute, making decisions was not my strongest suit. I'd liked having my day broken up into discrete parts at the ring of a bell: awaken, exercise, eat, learn, eat, learn, analyze-therapize-socialize, eat, recreate, study, sleep.

Now, after a few months hanging around our house, my sense of place in the world had become disjointed. I slept late, grew soft, forgot to eat or forgot to stop eating, fell asleep reading, then walked around naked half the night, through the house and into the back-yard until the chill in the air drove me back under the covers. Mother's excursions into the world of the sockless gave my life order.

Fall drifted into winter, and rag wool replaced cotton. It became harder to maintain a cheerful facade as I tried to keep up with Mother on her rounds of shelters, bridges, and the occasional parked van. It was harder to find a source of water for the requisite foot washing, so I was in charge of carrying a gallon jug in my backpack, which we would use and then refill at various drinking fountains. We trudged through snow, fairly skated on ice, clomped in the slush and mud. The walking and hefting were toughening me up. Whenever I did try to hang on to my warm bed, Mother shamed me into rising to join her.

"It's trench-foot season," she would scold. "Somebody's toes could rot off because you're a slugabed."

I had seen enough feet wracked with blisters and scrapes, toes hammered and stubbed, to know that the ravages of the street would not be an easy burden on my conscience. I pushed myself off the bed and into the bathroom for quick work on face and teeth and hair. After coffee I would lace up my boots and zip up the violet coat I'd acquired three winters ago under the tutelage of Miss Entropia, pull a wool watch cap to below my ears, and follow Mother into the car.

"That's a weird coat," she said.

"It has sentimental value," I said, "and it's warm." Also, it made me a walking beacon for Miss Entropia. While I wasn't actively look-ing for her, the thought that she might recognize me and come to me was never far from my imaginings.

By winter Mother had been passing out free socks for three months and had built a bit of a network. One happy recipient would steer her to where more of the city's indigent hung out. We navigated a secret movable suburb, beneath the urb in the literal sense, nooks and pockets of tents and bedrolls and squats right under the twitchy noses of the safely respectable.

Winter made the luckless cases harder to find and more needy. We often wished we could provide a safe haven, a warm meal, a bus ticket. Ours was a low-budget mission. Mother had a single message: feet need to be kept clean, toenails trimmed, shoes dry. Occasionally we helped someone with directory assistance or a couple of minutes on our cell phone.

Our mission ranged farther afield. With the public parks turning into tundras and their restrooms closed for the season, we found the malls to be fertile ground. People in dire straits might lose job, home, credit, but they will hang on to a car. Usually the soccer-mom van or the daddy's SUV, something with reclining seats, a loud sound system, space for storage. There are social and educational advantages to living in a car, even if the family is cramped. The kids don't have to change schools or make new friends. The car can move around from mall lot to lake to river road to park and still stay in the neighborhood.

Mother got to be quite good at spotting clients for her socks. Dirty cars visibly packed to the roof on the edges of a mall parking lot, motors idling to keep the heater going, the twanging and thumping of contemporary country or classic rock providing audible evidence of domesticity; you can't beat Shaina or Bruce for comfort.

In the morning we cruised the parking lots for cars-turned-homes. During the day the kids were apt to be at school and the parent, usually one, as it was rare to find a whole nuclear family adrift, would find some comfort walking around the mall, nursing a jumbo pop with fries at the food court or sitting at a Starbucks with a clutch of keys and some bill envelopes and a checkbook on the table to provide the semblance of a role in the real world.

Mother spotted a client at a food court at Ridgedale Mall. He was about fifty and newly pudgy, as evidenced by the rolls protruding over his belt and between his shirt buttons. He read a newspaper, methodically working his way from front page to classifieds. He refused to look up and acknowledge Mother's gaze, maintaining his eyes on the page with the intensity of a proofreader. Here was a man in no particular hurry. Or no particular place to go, which was why, when Mother took the table adjacent to his and asked if he knew where the nearest Laundromat was, he looked up at her with sad, tired eyes and simply shook his head.

"There's a reason I'm asking," she insisted quietly. Then she gestured, and, right on cue, I produced a pen and a notepad.

She wrote in her neat hand, *I'm sorry to inform you that your feet smell as if they're rotting.*

He crumpled the paper and tossed it toward a trash can. "I like sitting here," he said. "And was enjoying myself until you and the weird kid showed up." He said this loudly, as if he were trying to make himself the annoyed party, hoping security might ask us to move on. After all, we were the true loiterers since our family refused to eat junk food.

Mother saw her opening. "Maybe," she said, "if you invited me to sit at your table we could chat."

"What do you want?"

"Five minutes," she said.

He pushed his keys, bill envelopes, checkbook, and newspaper to a corner of the table. I stayed at our original place, as Mother thought that my presence cut into the frankness of the discussion with some clients. This guy was particularly shy. I grabbed the comics from his newspaper and pretended to study them, from *Peanuts* to the *Flying McCoys*, while Mother wove her gospel of new socks and clean feet.

"So what kind of Christian are you?" he asked.

"The kind that saves soles," she said happily.

I got the joke because I'd heard it dozens of times, but the guy just stared, trying to hide his bewilderment. Mother went on to explain, "It's not enough to duck into a men's room and splash around. You can't wash your feet at a sink and then pull dirty socks back on."

"How do you know my socks are dirty?" He stared down at his boots.

"Sir," she began, "you know that squishy feeling you get as you walk around? The way your foot slides around inside the boot? How your socks start out stiff in the morning, then miraculously soften up?"

He stared at her as if she had been reading his fortune.

"Your socks smell. Like cheese, like road kill, like gas."

Like turkey, I wanted to add, but didn't because I knew my role in the small drama. My role was to pull a brand-new pair of rag-wool socks out of the bag then and there. They were natural beige, soft and thick and scratchy at the same time, and Mother took them from me and held them close to the man's face. "Smell," she coaxed. "Breathe in the pure fragrance of a brand-new wool sock."

Around us trays clattered and potatoes sizzled, cell phones chimed, double cheeseburgers and chicken nuggets were announced from the counter. But Mother and the client seemed to exist in their own universe; the exchange about to take place was a momentous one.

"First go wash your feet," Mother directed gently.

There was a moment when Mother's clients would show in their expressions a deep humiliation at being so exposed. The man pushed himself away from the table and gradually stood up, as if any sudden movement would attract attention. Then he walked purposefully to the restrooms at the end of the store, first grabbing the key from the counter, not some vagrant weaseling his way into a privileged men's room but a man who had every right to piss away the coffee he was paying for.

"Let's see your feet," Mother said when he came back to the table. His sockless ankles showed white above the tops of his boots. He pulled off first one boot, then the other. She nodded and handed the man his socks. "You're fortunate to have a car to move around in," she said. "I've seen feet so mangled, it's a wonder they don't fall apart."

She waited while he pulled the socks on and slipped on the boots. He smiled for the first time, and I imagined him wiggling his toes in the new pillowy softness. "Now," she said, "tell us your story."

By then Mother had figured out that her clients needed to talk as much as they needed the comfort of dry, clean feet. She nodded at me, and I pulled my chair to their table.

"My name is Harold. I used to live with my wife and daughter in a fabulous house in New Canaan. The house burned to the ground, and the cops and insurance investigators think it was no accident. For the insurance. My teenaged daughter and wife have gone off in different directions. The wife ran off with some guy to Texas. My daughter disappeared after the fire. She's been hanging out with friends. She uses an ATM card to get the money I put in her account once in a while."

"It's good of you to look after your daughter," Mother said. "The streets are no place for children."

He nodded. "Last I heard she was sleeping in one of those warehouses from the old milling days."

"I wouldn't let a child of mine live like that."

"I'm not sure I can do right by anyone again, lady. I lost my job, spent my money. The insurance company does not pay off arsonists, which is what they think I am. I did not burn my house down, but I have to wait until the investigations are concluded before I get the money, most of which will go to the bank, so I don't have a real sense of urgency. Meanwhile, I live in my last earthly possession, that nice Land Rover at the end of the lot. Now that I know I can't sink much lower, I'm pretty happy. Especially with these socks."

"You don't seem happy, actually," Mother pointed out gently.

"Ah!" The man smiled. "One key to staying joyous is not to flaunt it. Look happy and somebody will find a way to fuck it up for you."

He leaned back, put the cup to his lips, and drained it with a sigh. "Maybe it was an accident," Mother ventured gently. "There are many ways a house can go up in flames on its own. Oily rags. Frayed wiring. Gas leaks. It's a wonder more houses don't burn to the ground every day."

Harold gave her a knowing smile. "Oh, we had a serious torching incident here. The arsonist seemed to have gone on a rampage with birthday-cake candles. There were remnants of the stubs throughout the house, inside closets and behind curtains."

"Do you know who did it?" Mother asked, and at the sound of her question I very nearly let out a snort.

Harold shrugged. "I'm not admitting it was me. Or that I know who might have lit up the place."

Mother volunteered me to get a refill. I couldn't believe my luck; here I was sitting across the table from Miss Entropia's dad, and he didn't have a clue who I was. I felt the tiny shiver of delight I got when I sensed I had the inside track to a mystery of life.

Oh, ask me, ask me! The thought clanged around very loudly inside my head. Not that I was about to tell what I knew. I had the image of Miss Entropia dancing wildly through the house, tossing candles around with every twirl. I could hear her laughter, sense the breath of air as she flitted past me, smell the smoldering trail she left in her wake. It must've been a lovely thing to watch, that proud mansion starting to burn, curtains and carpets and clothes in closets first, then the fake wood paneling in the den and the plywood doors and the cabinets in the kitchen, the sharp chemical reactions of varnishes and glues interacting in one sweet, gigantic whoosh. I have often noticed in certain quirky personalities that the love of fire is more aesthetic than destructive. The loss of life and property is not the primary objective. *Burn, baby, burn,* that inflammatory slogan from the '60s riots, had more to do with the theater of arson than the redress of injustice.

Harold took a deep breath and, energized by the fresh brew, continued his story. "At one time our family was a perfect threesome. My wife, my daughter, and I seemed mentally intertwined to the point that thoughts of each other bubbled up unexpectedly. I'd pick up the phone for no reason, leave work early, stop for ice cream. Evenings were spent on a cushy sofa watching videos with our baby girl nestled between her mother and father. She would grow up feeling loved and secure."

Mother smiled. "Then you had to go and screw things up."

"I became an addict." He added quickly. "Oh, it doesn't matter to what. It's all the same—drugs, sex, work, food. It's not the stuff that kills you. It's the isolation that comes with the obsession. The whole of your life starts to revolve around finding the pleasure and then losing the pleasure. You're either anticipating, getting, or chasing It. Food tastes flat. Family gets in the way. God is a tease."

Mother was silent while Harold paused as if to organize his thoughts. Clearly nothing was getting in the way of his confession. He seemed to be growing lighter before our eyes.

"I was a money-making machine. I couldn't stop trading, hours upon hours of it, swinging in and out of investments that were like horse races. I made money in minutes, lost it in seconds. But when my house burned, I was all of a sudden free. My computer melted down to putty and exploded into gas. It was the only way to quit. By then I had so neglected work that, with my numbers way down, I had been reduced to marginal consulting. I didn't care. My occupation was to be trading, all the time, except when I was asleep. Sometimes the dealing was so hot I forgot who I was. My wife would call me to dinner and I would push away from the music of clicks to sit at the table, head down over the food, chewing without tasting, my mind humming with numbers. TMX up 3 1/8, SCV down 2 7/8, FVC up 4/5. I reeled with the possibilities. Wildcatting in the arctic. Online pharmacy. Linseed futures. I had my finger in a thousand pies." He paused to sip his coffee, and his eyes got a faraway look.

"So what now?" Mother finally broke in. "There are computers all over the city."

"I tried trading for an hour at the library, but I've lost the mojo. My clicking finger's gone stupid. It clicked on losers so often that I had to stop before the last of my capital went up in smoke. Like I said, I'm happy for the first time in years. I'm becoming myself. I've lost my home, my family, my job. It's as if all that frenzy were a big blanket smothering the life out of my real self. I'm not there yet, but the closer I get, the happier I feel. It's like smelling the ocean before you get there. You know what I mean?"

"Take care of your feet," Mother said to him as we picked up our stuff and left Harold to sort himself out.

Chapter Fifteen

By then Mother had identified a couple of unofficial shelters at the northern edge of downtown Minneapolis. As the warehouse district was being reclaimed for lofts providing a *La Bohème* kind of chic, a shuffling, foot-weary class was pushing its way farther north. There was nothing classy about the former light-industrial plants and storage facilities left vacant in the erratic swings of capitalism and now being occupied by a shifting underclass. A fixed address was irrelevant when you had a cell-phone number or a voice-mail box. A person could be anywhere, his embodied substance determined by the context enveloping the voice. Leave a message at the tone. I'm in a meeting. I'm in class. I'm in surgery. I'm not where you think I am. The weather is just fine here in California, Florida, Puerto Rico. Listen to the surf!

The building was called the Stitchery, dating back to the nineteenth century, when immigrant Germans had sewn the sacks that would be filled with flour from the mills. I could picture the vacant naves filled with long tables and an army of cutters and sewers making bags in fifty- and one-hundred-pound capacities, then sending them to a hand press where they would be stamped with Grain Belt, Gold Medal, General Mills. The real estate agent with the listing had opened it up as a shelter, and for a few dollars a head he kept the door open, the heat minimally on, and the water running.

It must've been a gloomy place to work. A dusty light streaming through the narrow barred windows barely revealed a dozen bedrolls scattered about, pushed into corners or surrounded by piles of stuff and cardboard partitions to provide a sense of privacy. An outside electric line had been pirated to fuel a couple of space heaters, humming, glowing, breaking through the chill, enlivening a pungent blend of fast-food grease, musky skin, oily hair, and dog fur. Mother and I stood for several moments letting our eyes adjust to the shadows. Most of the residents were bundled by themselves, with only an occasional couple evidenced by a large mound inside a two-person sleeping bag. I sensed we were far more visible to the established residents than they were to us.

There were dogs around, a couple of them in dog sweaters and bandanas or spiky collars, as if the lost children needed some creature to take care of. Even before anyone in the room spoke a word to us, a mutt came over to smell my hands and rub itself against me. I reached down to pat it, and the feel of tangled, sticky fur was shocking. I'm used to dogs whose coats are shiny and silky enough to take to bed. The dogs ignored Mother and clung to me, probably associating care and companionship with kids rather than adults.

I searched for the source of a tinny, rhythmical sound, perhaps insects or rodents chewing, mating, or whirring away within the crannies of the Stitchery. It took a minute or two for me to realize that the sound came from several earbuds hooked to a variety of music players. Salsa met hip-hop met funk met metal in a single buzz.

A voice sang merrily from a corner, "It's the sock lady."

"Hello, kids," Mother announced cheerfully. "Clean feet are the next best thing to a full tummy." She gestured for me to pull a stool next to her in the middle of the room. "Okay, I've got socks for everyone. Who's first?"

A gangly stick of a guy wrapped in an army coat emerged from the shadows holding a boot in either hand. He started to sit on the stool, but Mother pointed him to the rear of the hall. As gentle as she was, nobody used an imperial index finger as sternly as she. "You know the drill," she said. "Wash those feet."

"That water's fucking cold," he whined.

"Sorry," Mother huffed. "I'm not putting clean socks on dirty feet. Who wants to go first?"

I could hear water humming through the pipes, followed by loud splashing. At about 60 degrees even with the feeble heaters going full blast, the water must've been close to numbing. The skinny guy retreated, and a line formed. Most got socks; a few were sent to wash again. There were yelps and shouts from the utility sink in a corner of the nave. Still, we must've given a dozen pairs to kids my age and younger. I wonder if Mother intended that I receive a reminder of my blessings. The truth was, I felt guilty and vaguely irritated by the glum demeanor and silent hostility of these scruffy kids.

I imagined they felt superior to me, a certified mama's boy, as if the street life gave them an aura of the heroic and the romantic.

Finally a tall figure of a girl in a hooded black coat took her place at the stool. She was already barefoot, her feet rubbed red from the cold and the scrubbing. I remember marveling that she had taken the time to give herself a pedicure, her toenails glinting with black polish.

"My son has some fine socks in his backpack," Mother announced. That was my cue to pull out a pair and hand them to Mother, who in turn gave them to the client. The girl sat on a box and neatly rolled the socks onto her feet.

"Does that feel better, honey?" Mother asked. She held the girl's feet and squeezed them affectionately.

"Yes, yes. They feel wonderful," she answered softly. "Thank you so much." I don't know why I didn't recognize the voice right away. I expected a darker tone from the tall girl in black. But then she stood up and took a step toward me so that she could whisper close to my ear, "I like your coat."

I was about to speak her name. Ask her if she knew who I was. I should have expected her to be here since her father had said something about her living in a warehouse. She had already turned away from me, but even as she walked away, with a soft final thank-you for Mother, I wondered if my galloping heart could be heard by everyone in the building. My God, I kept thinking, afraid she might disappear if I didn't reassure myself of the reality of her sudden reemergence, *I have found you.*

It was dusk by the time we left the Stitchery, and I never did get another look at the girl I wanted to be Pia. She could've remained silent with her hood over her face and I wouldn't have known it was her. She had reached out to me.

As usual Mother and I made our way back to the car through peripheral streets on the edge of downtown. This part of the city always felt foreign to me, with the sidewalks cracked and buildings abandoned, their doors boarded up and windows broken, street lights burned out.

"Was that the girl?" she said in a tone that was more an accusation than a question. We had reached a dark stretch, which made our voices more intimate, more conducive to truth.

"I don't know," I said. "I couldn't make out her face under the hood."

"Typical," Mother said. "Hardly anyone on the streets wants to be found. Some have left behind a trail that they hope has gone cold. It's not our job to poke."

"I need to find her," I confessed, my desire suddenly quickened by the bare possibility of Pia.

"I expect you will," she said. "If she lets you."

Chapter Sixteen

In mid-December Mother slowed her ministry. Minnesota is not suited to winter vagrancy, and with the advent of the first frost many potential clients hotfooted it to milder climes. Our loss was Texas's, Arizona's, California's gain. I missed our excursions and was suddenly left to find a meaningful way to spend the time. I read, of course; *Don Quixote*, parts 1 and 2, absorbed me for the better part of January and February. I sent for college catalogs and found great amusement in picturing myself at Harvard, Yale, Stanford.

My college choices were based on the photos in the brochures. I particularly liked groups of students combining in one shot every possible ethnic permutation. All together now: smile for the camera with identical white teeth shining from brown and black and pink faces.

I thought of Pia much of my waking time. I had no life outside the house, and daydreams involving her brimmed with potential.

The night we'd jacked the 'Tute van had grown in my mind as the height of intimacy and adventure, my finest hour. I nurtured the fantasy that our destinies were interwoven and that encountering her at the Stitchery was proof of this. Sometimes during sleep, dreams came with restless, unsettling imagery. Pia running naked with a pack of wild dogs. Pia bleeding from a dozen bullet holes. Pia in flames. Synchronicity ran rampant, and I would be there for her when she most needed me.

I grew impatient waiting for Mother to visit the Stitchery again and decided to go alone. It took three bus connections to get within walking distance of the industrial ghetto where the old flour-sack workshop was located. Along the walk down Bledsoe Avenue I passed some wondrous urban destinations. There was the Skunkworks Gallery, which that month was featuring a show of artistic taxidermy—a chimp dancing, a dog rolling over, a mouse stalking a cat. On the next block Sally's Salvage, a cavernous warehouse crammed with the flotsam and jetsam of urban demolition, including vintage bath fixtures, elevator cages, leaded glass, columns, lintels, and tin ceiling squares.

Then a neon beacon that made my pud twitch: "Nudes! Nudes! Nudes!" But even as I was tempted to take this detour, a big man standing outside the door told me to keep walking unless I could prove I was twenty-one. Oh, how I yearned to look at a naked woman once again. It had been years since I had stolen a glance at Cousin Iris, and the photos and web images that I had since perused were only a pale shadow of live flesh.

"Are they totally naked?" I asked.

"Down to their shaved pussies," he said.

"You could let me in for like a minute," I said. "I took three buses to get here."

"You want me to lose my job?"

"No," I said sincerely.

"Good," he said. I could tell he liked me. "On your twenty-first birthday you get in for free. It's a tradition."

"I'll plan on that." I was not quite mollified.

The guy did give me a postcard with a drawing of a buxom blond promoting *Nudes! Nudes! Nudes! Happy Hour, with* FREE *Appetizers.* The idea of eating nachos, baby hot dogs, and fried curds while a naked woman hovered above them added to the appeal.

Finally, with a quickening heart, I found myself within sight of the squat brick building of the Stitchery. I was both eager to find Pia and afraid of finding her. I could tell her I had met her dad, or tell her that I knew her mother was in Texas, or that I knew people thought she had set fire to her house. But none of that was any of my business. I could ask her if those hours in the 'Tute's van, parked in the middle of the Alligator lot, had made as much of an impression on her as they had on me.

I pounded on the door until my fists reddened and some skinny guy in a recovering Mohawk opened it a crack.

"We're full," he said.

"I'm not looking to stay," I said. "I'm looking for someone."

"Most someones here don't want to be looked for."

"She's a friend," I said. I was stretching a little, but I didn't think Pia would deny me.

"What's her name?"

"She was Pia when I knew her a few years back."

"No Pias here today."

"Well, it wasn't her real name."

"No surprise there."

"Maybe Francine," I took another stab. "Or Miss Entropia."

"Nope. And you're out of free guesses."

"Can I come in and look around? Maybe I'll see her." I inched forward, hoping to catch a glimpse of the warehouse through the cracked door.

"Don't mind if I don't trust you right off," he said. "We are periodically visited by the building guy sending spies to make sure we're not breaking any codes."

"I'm just a guy in love." Yes, I thought, that was what I was. Even though he smirked, I knew I was harkening back to a finer time when men and women were maddened by love, turned into fools and saints by the free flow of pheromones.

"I have to ask. Tell me your name, and then if nobody objects to your coming in, I'll open the door."

"My name's Adam."

He closed the door, but I could hear him shouting, "Anyone mind if Adam comes in?"

"I was here with my mother a month ago, passing around socks." I said loudly so he'd hear me through the door.

"He's the guy that came with the feet lady," the guy repeated.

I wondered if the conversation was over, if closing the door with a definitive snap was his way of telling me to go away. And yet I stayed.

After about an hour I wanted to think that I was meant to wait. That the gatekeeper knew I was still out here, with the cold seeping inside my shoes, my gloves, my cap.

I tried sitting on the stoop and leaning against the door. As the cold numbed my butt, I wondered if I wasn't in fact being put to some test. My character was being gauged—my resolve, my sincerity, or my docility. I had heard of aspiring Zen monks being made to wait for days, getting baked by summer heat or blanketed by winter snow, before being admitted to the zendo. For me the test lay in the uncertainty of whether I was being put to a trial or had simply been forgotten, so nobody would be the wiser whether I stayed or left.

I felt in succession angry, stupid, humiliated, and thirsty, which soon overpowered every other reaction. My mouth was sticky and tasted of bad cheese. And still I resisted the impulse to pound on the door or to walk away. At different times I was sure I was being observed from an upper-story window. During those moments I sat more erect, cross-legged in front of the door, my face tilted to the waning sun as I tried to clear my expression, the scrunched brow, the tight lips, the squint, of any signs of stress. I waited for the secrets inside that building to be revealed. I hardly dared hope for a sign of Miss Entropia, since I didn't really know what I would do or say once I found her. I saw myself offering to be her friend if she needed one, even if that meant participating in her flight from justice.

I marveled at how readily Mother had been welcomed at various squats. Just weeks ago she had walked into the Stitchery as if she belonged there. Even before people knew her, they had heard of her mission to clothe the world's wounded, battered feet. Without her I was just another stranger at a loss as to how to communicate my utter harmlessness.

Near dusk there were signs of activity. At first when the door opened, I thought I was finally being allowed inside, but it was only to let a nocturnal resident of the Stitchery slip out and, with hardly a glance in my direction, head toward downtown. I called him in a belated effort to get a sense of what was going on. "Hey, man!"

He turned and looked at me with surprise. "Hey, man," he repeated after me. "You were talking to me?"

"Well, yes." I hesitated. "I just wonder if the people there know I'm sitting here, waiting to go inside for a visit."

"Yeah, we know you're out here."

"Great!"

"Yeah, great," he echoed, his voice flat.

"So what can you tell me, man?"

"What can I tell you?" he repeated. "Tell you about what?"

"About why I'm sitting here."

"Ah!" he exclaimed as if finally getting the drift of our conversation. "Now, that is a question you can answer."

I could only shake my head in wonder. "You guys are nuts."

"Well, we're not sitting out in the cold waiting for a door to magically open."

"Can you give me some advice?"

"Bring doughnuts."

returned to the Stitchery early the next morning with two bags of goodies. The allowances I had saved while at the 'Tute were vanishing, but I was glad to splurge for the sake of Miss Entropia. It was around 8:00, and I was hoping it was early enough that the restless denizens of the Stitchery wouldn't have gone out yet. I had a dozen doughnuts, and I also included food that might better feed kids on an erratic diet—peanut butter, multigrain bread, instant breakfast, soy chips, Reddi-wip. I felt like Santa Claus, down to my red Christmas hat with the white pom-pom. Instead of knocking I shook a set of chimes.

Somebody yelled, "Come in!" and I pushed the unlocked door open with my foot and slipped inside with a bag in either arm. The yawning nave that had once been the sweatshop was sunk in gloomy light, a contrast to the bright winter sky.

It took a couple of minutes before I was surrounded by the softly breathing ghosts of the Stitchery, crowding me, reaching into the bags, picking out a package or a doughnut and finally tipping the bags over, scattering their contents. I sat down on the wooden floor as about a dozen figures gathered cross-legged around the groceries.

"Ooooh, whip it up!" a voice exclaimed, and the silence was broken by a rising hubbub as the cans of Reddi-wip were passed around, squirting into mouths, onto fingertips, over noses. I was pretty much ignored until one boy handed me one of the cans. "Shake it up and mainline it into your mouth," he recommended.

I was brought into a circular feeding frenzy, hands reaching to grab the cans out of other hands, the squirts blending in with giggles and sighs of contentment. I felt a sense of communion. The sweet foam invading my mouth seemed to crowd out the numbing cold, the darkness, the dense smell of smoke and skin and clothes gone biologically sour. The surrounding figures took on personalities, a head crowned with a Mohawk, lips and ears and noses dangling rings, a couple of large dogs with studded collars. I looked about for Pia.

After less than an hour the circle broke up as kids retreated to their spots along the wall, to the bedrolls and backpacks that made for personal space. They had picked through the goodies like crows. Before us lay a scattering of empty cans, wrappers, crumpled bags. Finally it was just me and the guy from the previous day who had suggested I come back with food.

"You've been helpful," I said. "What's your name?"

"I wouldn't give you my real name. Make up something and call me that. For conversational purposes, anyway."

"Doorman?"

"Yeah, I like Doorman."

"Okay, Doorman. I'm looking for someone. I saw her the last time I came with my mother."

"We come and go."

"I knew her a few years back as Miss Entropia," I added quickly. "Maybe more people know her as Pia. I think she was actually here when we brought socks."

Doorman pondered the question, shutting his eyes and breathing deeply as if entering a trance.

"Seriously," he said, opening his eyes, "most of us don't want to be found."

"I don't mean Pia any harm," I said. "I'm just in love with her."

"Most women don't want to be found by guys who claim to be in love with them," he laughed. "You might get oral from someone, but not her name."

"I'm not looking for sex," I said.

"That just makes you more complicated." He laughed again. "You're a wacko, aren't you?"

"What do you mean?"

"You've done inpatient time, you're on meds, you imagine stuff and think it's real, you fall in love with women who don't exist."

"Ms Entropia exists."

He sighed. My heart started pounding because I sensed he had come to trust me. "Okay, I know who you mean. She liked to make fires to roast marshmallows."

"Yes!"

"She doesn't stay here. She stays with a friend."

"Where can I find her?"

Doorman shrugged. "Should be easy. She's always online. She borrows people's laptops, hangs out in libraries and cafés. We miss her checking our e-mails."

"Will she be back?"

"I imagine." He shrugged.

Chapter Seventeen

I had a strategy. If Pia would not be found in the parks and communal houses of the city, I would find her in the shifting ether of the internet. Her disembodied roaming would leave clues; her personality would shine through any number of aliases and user names. I would send out hooks, and eventually her true identity would rise out of the electronic murk.

I became a hermit, coming out of my room into family life only to eat. I declared that my new mission in life was to bone up on serious academics and apply to college for the coming fall. In reality I became a chameleon. Or, as the 'Tute mavens might've put it, I adopted a multiple personality disorder that kept me swinging among a dozen identities 24-7. I spent my waking hours online, alternating one persona with another. Giving advice, sympathy, love of the distantly cerebral kind but also attempting seduction, threatening racial war, planning mayhem. At times I felt my head had swollen to the size of a small planet because of the stuff I learned. School problems, child abuse, romance, lust, authority issues, hormonal crises, parental stifling. Most of the chitchat was the stuff of life—family vacations to the North Shore, birthdays, dating, college apps, and deaths. I spent much of my time sending best wishes, condolences, congratulations. I had an extended network, and I was boy or girl, black or white, geek or stud. The richness of my online existence made the everyday minutiae of my family's ongoing life seem trivial. I was living in shades of gray. I waited for like-minded combustiphiles to make themselves known.

In the quiet of the night, in the glow of the screen, in the privacy of my room, I cast the first lures in a dozen chat rooms:

> PyroToy:—hello. anyone here feel the need for True Beauty?

I also logged on as Mr. Flame, Sparky, El Fuego, Ignitius, Matchstick, 5Alarm, FuseBoy, Hottie. There were a couple more, but PyroToy seemed to attract the more interesting personalities.

I was peppered with replies.

> Annabelle:—got milk?
> MisterMan:—how old r u?
> Twi9nkle:—u boi or grrrl?
> BluGlo:—define true

Most replies I ignored. They were either trolling for victims or perverts. I answered BluGlo:

> PyroToy:—true like ice like fire.
> BluGlo:—yeah . . .
> PyroToy:—u know?
> BluGlo:—know what
> PyroToy:—true beauty
> BluGlo:—define beauty
> PyroToy:—u e-mail?
> BluGlo:—slow down, toy
> PyroToy:—i'm in luv
> BluGlo:—bonehead, going now
> PyroToy:—noooooo!!!
> BluGlo:—later

Then BluGlo disappeared into the ether. I spent the next few days trading simple-minded utterances with various chatty chatters. Wasted hours staring at the flickering voices, indistinguishable one from the other, seemingly devoid of personality and intelligence. I would entertain simple little exchanges with my hooks designed to smoke out the true pyromaniac.

> PyroToy:—fun stuff to do:
> roast marshmallows
> set bugs on fire w. magnifying glass
> write your name on the pavement with lighter fluid
> glass blowing
> watch paper, curtains, straw, leather, hair, etc., all burn
> with their own particular beauty

The one thing that kept me focused on the screen was the hope that BluGlo would resurface. I started moping around the house, confident that BluGlo was Miss Entropia.

And then she reappeared.

> PyroToy:—set a fire, celebrate the cycle of life and death. born as a spark, it feeds and grows and lives off oxygen, finally goes cold and dies. burn baby burn something today!!!!!
>
> BluGlo:—yeah, but the downside is stinking of smoke. hair, clothes, skin. after the light comes the darkness. some days I get the feeling the whole world can smell me. even showering doesn't get rid of that smoky aura.
>
> PyroToy:—try dr. bronner eucalyptus.
>
> BluGlo:—you an old hippie?
>
> PyroToy:—born too late. but i identify.
>
> BluGlo:—me too. golden age of pyromania.
>
> PyroToy:—LED ZEP!
>
> BluGlo:—i meant the kind with matches.
>
> PyroToy:—burn baby burn.
>
> BluGlo:—whole neighborhood up in flames
>
> PyroToy:—what a sight
>
> BluGlo:—ever burn down a house?
>
> PyroToy:—no . . . you?
>
> BluGlo:—no
>
> PyroToy:—really?
>
> BluGlo:—yes. but i've wanted to
>
> PyroToy:—u boi or grrrl?
>
> BluGlo:—i'm gone gone gone
>
> PyroToy:—no wait . . .
>
> —BluGlo has left the room.

Mostly my leading hooks were ignored. Pyromania is not a prevailing obsession among chatters. The stream of conversation, if you can call it that, is banal to the point of numbing. I realized that I had little in common with my contemporaries beyond our shared interest in each other's body parts.

One recent exchange:

> PyroToy:—anyone hot out there?
> Snake:—hot how?
> PyroToy:—hot like fire?
> Snake:—hot like ass
> PyroToy:—yours?
> Snake:—u boi or grrrrl?
> PyroToy:—boi
> Snake:—fk off

Then, when I least expected it, BluGlo spoke from the screen with such truth and power that I couldn't tap out anything coherent for several minutes:

> BluGlo:—hey, pt, how goes the heat?
> PyroToy:—I know you
> BluGlo:—maybe
> PyroToy:—tell me about u
> BluGlo:—i am totally hot, especially when the lovely flames
> of a fire let their shadows dance across my face and the fire
> puts a light, lovely, and heavenly beautiful glow around and on
> my body like a goddess of the fire. all in the dark of the night
> but light of the fire and the moon

PyroToy:—please don't leave this time
BluGlo:—was there another time for u and me?
PyroToy:—yes yes yes
BluGlo:—when
PyroToy:—u know when
BluGlo:—u 1st

And then, my breath running short with the excitement of finally having made contact with Miss Entropia, I pulled back from the keyboard and considered the proper response, the one that wouldn't get me blown off again. The chat room is an unforgiving medium. People cut you off without a word, never speak to you again, block your every utterance. It's easy to lose contact in the fog of anonymity.

PyroToy:—u keep running off
BluGlo:—you have something to say to me, spit it
PyroToy:—years ago we jacked a van and ran away to
the mall, talked through the night, had an adventure

A long time passed before her name appeared on the screen again. I was sure she had disappeared; a dogged kind of faith kept me staring at the chatter scrolling in a hundred interweaving flickers. I had been in my room for hours so that in the dark the pale radiance from the computer screen cast a milky light on my desk and hands. Through the open window the starry night sky shimmered as if in reaction to my barely contained excitement.

BluGlo:—do u know my name?

She was giving me the first real opening.

PyroToy:—Miss Entropia
BluGlo:—what????? never heard of her

I had been kicked in the heart. The searching of the past weeks was slamming to an end, with nothing to show but red eyes and black dreams. I wanted to tell her that I knew who she was, that she would evade me no longer. And, then, like a sudden ray of light, her voice appeared again.

BluGlo:—LOL!!!!! hello Pyro
PyroToy:—c u?
BluGlo:—why?
PyroToy:—cause I love you
BluGlo:—bonehead
PyroToy:—yes yes yes it's u!!!!!!!!
BluGlo:—i'll be at sistersludge tonite
PyroToy:—what time???
—BluGlo has left the room.

Chapter Eighteen

There was no running after her once the virtual door had slammed shut, but the thought that our next conversation would be in person filled me with giddy anticipation. I would be at Sister Sludge coffee shop by 6:00 prepared to caffeinate myself into a jangle of jitters until Pia showed.

Meanwhile, I wandered through the house in a restless drift from nervous munching in the kitchen to unfocused TV watching to a long shower in a kind of ritual cleansing for my seeing Pia. I borrowed Cousin Iris's fragrant confections, lavender for the hair, ylang-ylang for the body, tangerine-mango for the teeth. I had hoped to streak the few steps to my room unseen when I crossed paths with her in the hallway, not unlike the nude night wanderings of yore except this time she was the one dressed. She congratulated me on smelling good for the first time since I'd arrived from the 'Tute.

"Thank you," I said. "I have a date." I made this announcement barely able to contain the note of triumph in my voice. Not only was I going to see Pia after all these years, but it was my first real date ever.

She frowned. "I thought you might have cleaned up for a higher purpose than romance. First the body, then the spirit. A shower is good preparation for the rapture."

I could think of no higher purpose in my life than my long-fated reunion with Miss Entropia. "Well, I'm in love," I said, enjoying the flush that just saying the words brought to my skin.

Iris was not sharing my excitement. "What's the point of cleaning up for sex when you will be soiled again?"

I was suddenly anxious about being naked, and while I might at one time have found nudity with Iris exciting, her fervor for the second coming was downright stultifying. "I should put some clothes on," I said, hoping to edge past her without brushing her white dress.

"Not on my account," she said. "I have trained myself not to see people's bodies anymore. Just their souls as reflected by the light in their eyes."

It was true that her gaze had not wavered from my face, her eyes locked with mine.

"That's nice, Iris," I said.

"What I do see," she went on, "is a veil of darkness where the light ought to be."

It was almost 5:00. I smelled sweetly of Iris's flowery concoctions. I had borrowed Ted's red flannel shirt and chosen my least dirty jeans, which happened to be black for a properly anarchist look. That Saturday everyone was home, and I had a hard time avoiding the family while rattling around the house. By then they had, through my virginal fidgeting or Iris's babbling, figured out that I was going to see a girl. Mother acted all cheery and bubbly, and Dad exercised a kind of affable bonhomie. Meanwhile, I was starting to feel like a fraud because Miss Entropia had guaranteed only a shared coffee at some unspecified time.

"Nice shirt, little bro," Ted sang as he stood at the kitchen door blocking my way. I was in the grip of the munchies and had scrounged inside the refrigerator for sustenance—mayonnaise and capers for a superb sandwich. I nearly dropped the plate as I turned to leave the kitchen and found myself facing Ted's broad grin.

"Going somewhere?" he asked.

"Yeah, to my room to eat my sandwich."

"If you get mayo on my shirt, you're in deep feces." Then he added as an afterthought, "Especially since you grabbed it without asking."

"Want half a sandwich?" I retreated to the kitchen table, giving up any hope for privacy.

"Thanks, kiddo, but you'll need your strength." He sat opposite me, held his head between his hands, and looked skeptically at the sandwich. "A guy your age is expected to go all night. I'm sure you got a lot of practice boning the nutcases at that place where you were sent."

I realized that he imagined our little group-therapy sessions at the 'Tute turning into free-for-all gropes, leading to late-night dormitory wanderings and happy sleepovers. Actually it was common knowledge that chemicals were added to the water to reduce our libido. In the few cases when two of us managed to hook up in any significant way, the emotional side effects often led to increased medication, separation, isolation. The parents did not want pregnancy and heartache further complicating their children's lives. Dr. Clara would nip blossoming love in the bud.

"Oh, yeah," I said. "You haven't lived until you've fucked a schizo. Man, when all those personalities kick in, it's like being with half-a-dozen girls at the same time."

Ted gave me a long look. "So who's the lucky woman?"

"Somebody I met online."

"Really?"

I had his attention. "Yeah, her name is BluGlo."

"You don't know her real name?"

"Not exactly."

"Or what she looks like?"

"I have a vague idea."

"She could be a he."

"I don't think so."

"Or a hooker after your money."

"Cool. I have no money, but I could use a hooker."

I munched happily on my sandwich and wondered how much to tell Ted about my reunion with the elusive Miss Entropia.

"So what's the plan with this mystery girl?" Ted asked.

"We're meeting at a coffee shop."

"That's good. A public place in case she turns out to be weird." He leaned across the table and lowered his voice. I was to get some advice after all. "Listen. Here's what you do in case you don't want to be with her for even one minute more than you have to. If she turns out to be weird or butt-ugly, you ask her for a quarter because you have to feed the meter. Asking for one makes your escape plausible. You have to hurry because you don't want a ticket, but say you'll be right back as you sprint out the door, and keep on sprinting until you're a hundred blocks away from her."

"I keep her quarter?"

"Win–win."

I was appalled. "Christ, Ted. That's harsh."

"Not as harsh as staying out of kindness. Then seeing her again and again, all the time wishing you had the guts to break up. Finally getting engaged and married and finding out after thirty years that you should've run when the running was good. Now, that's a harsh life for you."

"What if I love her in spite of the fact that she may be weird?"

"That's worse. Do not fall in love. Ever. All miserable couples were once in love. The best marriages are out of convenience. You know, fat rich guys with trophies. Fuck buddies. Homo-lesbian breeding contracts. Arranged marriages in India, Dubai, Arkansas."

Whatever he thought, none of it could apply to Miss Entropia and me. Some things were meant to happen. And whether tonight's date would lead to misery or bliss, it was beyond my ability to change the direction of the fates. Ted's spiel had given me an idea, though.

"Can I borrow your car tonight, Ted?"

"For a quicker getaway? Sure."

I was in luck. Ted's 1988 Corolla would make a fine sequel to my first carnal experience with Miss Entropia in the 'Tute van. It had an ample backseat, a box of old CDs for the six-speaker player, and a cooler in the trunk usually stocked with Dos Equis beer. I could picture us, watching the glittering skyline beyond Lake Calhoun while sipping brew and grooving to the Zep. We'd sit close, our feet on the front backrests, maybe our fingers brushing, our shoulders rising and falling with our breath in sync. I dared not imagine more. Every day I was growing closer to the previously tedious Ted.

Mother got all weepy when she came into the kitchen and found Ted and me deep into our conversation on the vagaries of romantic love.

"Our boy here has a social life," he bragged. "I'm lending him my car in case he gets lucky." He snorted.

"I hope you're not giving him any bad advice." She took a disapproving look at my unfinished caper sandwich and sat down with a mug of tea. "Adam will know how to behave himself."

"This is what a big brother does," Ted added with the same snort. "Give the kid the benefit of my experience."

I couldn't help feeling that Ted was playing a part, that the role of the wiseass hell-raiser no longer came naturally to him. Still, he seemed compelled to go on. "I couldn't get a clue as to who this mystery woman is. Somebody he met online. Can you imagine that? A chat-room romance going real-time."

Mother was not rising to the bait. "I'm sure Adam will tell us about the girl when he's ready." As always, she knew more than she was letting on.

Father would have been surprised if he'd known I was about to reconnect with the girl who, in his mind, had lured me into hijacking the 'Tute's van. In any case he slipped me a folded bill as I headed out the door, happily clutching Ted's keys. Interesting how intensely my family was vested in my acting like a regular teenager.

I counted my money as soon as I was in the car. Ten dollars from Father, six and change in my pocket—enough for a proper evening, assuming I didn't have to gas up. I turned the key in the ignition and felt a surge of satisfaction at the rumble from the Toyota's rusted muffler. I rolled down the window and stuck my arm out, steering with a light pressure from my fingers. It was a triumphant ride in Ted's car through the quiet Highland Park streets, then onto Snelling Avenue and finally 94 toward downtown Minneapolis. I was wearing clean clothes, smelling like a prince, driving a car, with money in my pocket on my way to meet a girl! What could be finer than that on a starry winter night?

Chapter Nineteen

Sister Sludge was the anti-Starfucks, fragrant with the mingled scents of coffee and musty upholstery, a scattering of tables, rickety chairs, armchairs, and couches on ratty Persian rugs, dimly lit by teetering floorlamps with feeble bulbs under brown paper shades. It took me only a moment to recognize Pia sitting by herself on a loveseat.

She must've spotted me as soon as I walked through the door but waited for me to sift through the faces in the crowded room, my anxiety growing at the thought that she wouldn't be there. I soon found myself gazing into her large almond eyes. In any case she would have been hard to miss in an iridescent turquoise prom dress with a flared skirt topped by a sequined bodice, which appeared to have been plucked from the Goodwill racks. Her black hair was twisted into a bun resting on top of her head. On the sofa arm was draped a furry stole, perhaps rabbit. One leg crossed over the other displayed a black steel-toed boot.

"I know you," she sang as I approached her. "The Adam Bomb!"

"Miss Entropia." I tried a little bow as I felt a sudden choking in my throat so that the simplest greeting came out as a croak.

"Oh, so formal." She waved me off with a flick of her fingers. "Pia to you." She patted a spot on the sofa.

She asked for an espresso, and I was glad for the chance to escape the disturbing effect her presence had on me. I waited while the machine dripped out two doubles, a new experience for me, but I thought if there was ever going to be a time for new pleasures, this was it.

I set the two ceramic cups on a low table. Then Pia made me go back to get lemon peel.

"It supercharges the sensory dynamic," she said.

"I agree," I mumbled as I followed her example and twisted the peel before I dropped it into the cup.

The first few minutes went by in a strained sequence of social niceties. She was doing okay, she said, sometimes hanging at the Stitchery, sometimes sleeping at her former English teacher's apartment in the burbs, where Mrs. Ferguson, a spinster of the old school, offered a motherly blend of talk and tea but provided only a blanket and a lumpy futon because, Pia suspected, she didn't want her guest to get too comfortable. Pia was at a crossroads, having to decide whether to go south to her mother's new home in Texas or try to stay as long as she could in her friend's apartment, get a job, and help with the rent. For now she wanted to be a moving target.

"People I don't want to talk to keep wanting to talk to me."

"About your house burning down?"

"About Dad. They say he did it for the insurance."

"They don't think you had anything to do with it?"

"Yeah, they're curious about me, too," she said. "But I was in school at the time."

"Is that what they call an alibi?"

"Don't be a wiseass." She took a sip of coffee, noisily drawing it through her lips to cool it. I took it as a signal to move on from that particular topic.

"I've been so broke, I haven't had an espresso in ages. Such a huge miracle in such a small cup!" She closed her eyes and sipped again.

I felt wealthy. The first round of espressos had set me back four bucks. I still had twelve in my pocket. I would spend it all on Pia to make her happy. "Can I get you another coffee? A cookie?"

"Don't be a bonehead." She gave me a small punch on the shoulder that made me shiver with pleasure. "You can't let a girl suck up all your money."

"You're not just any girl."

"Okay, let's split a peanut butter–chocolate chip. It packs the most nutrition for the buck."

I let her eat most of it. She broke it into small pieces, chewing slowly, making it last. She finally picked up the last remaining crumbs between her fingers. I went back for another one. At a dollar each, they were a bargain. Whatever was going on with her life, I felt protective, eager to take responsibility for her well-being. I resolved right then that I would not let her go back to wherever she was camping. I had no idea how I would manage to ask her to come

171

home with me. Meanwhile, she evaded my questions, wanting instead to know everything about me.

"What do you do with yourself all day? You're not going to school and you don't have a job."

"I help Mother sometimes with her sock ministry. I read, I think, I wait."

"What do you wait for?"

"Love, money, friends."

"Sounds pretty self-serving."

"World peace, too. I wait for world peace."

"You expect those things to happen if you just sit around and wait?"

"I do meditate."

"Are you on any interesting meds?"

I made some stuff up to impress her. "I'm supposed to take two hundred of Ritalin and one hundred of Zafirr and two hundred of Lyminal, but I hoard them and get refills to trade or save for a rainy day."

"What's a rainy day like?"

"Wet and dark."

"No ex, no weed, no meth?"

"You have quality control in prescription meds. Pfizer, Warner-Lambert, Sandoz—they stand by their products." I added, "What are you swallowing these days?"

"Ferguson keeps me mellow with talk. When I was at home I could be delicately balanced in a space between normal and eccentric and nobody worried. If I let out a happy shout for no apparent reason or delivered a soliloquy, mostly effing this and effing that, the family thought, That's just old Francine being Pia. The Pia I know is different from the one they think they know. I'm like a cable twisted of many colors, each strand distinct from every other strand, yet intertwined to make a single blended rope. I know how to pull the right strand to keep from going overboard."

"What happens when you pull the wrong strand?"

"Be careful what you ask."

I was in love all over again.

I offered Pia a ride to her friend's apartment. As we drove through the quiet frozen night, I was planning to bring her home, stopping only to get her stuff and head back to my house. Still, I was biding my time to surprise her with the offer. So we stopped in the parking lot of a generic apartment complex, a bewildering city of identical boxes without any discernible focus. She told me where to park, and I switched off the ignition. We were silent for a couple of minutes while I searched for the right way to broach my idea. Finally she shivered in her green party dress and the furry stole.

"I can't ask you in," she said. "Old Fergie would not appreciate a guest."

"You don't have to go just yet," I pleaded.

"Yes, I do. It's freezing here."

"Two minutes," I insisted. "So I can say one thing to you and you can say one thing to me. Two things in two minutes."

"Okay," she said. And she moved toward me so that I could put my arm around her shoulder. At that moment I felt I would never be closer to Pia, the press of her body warming next to mine, the fragrance of her hair, somewhere between smoke and lavender, her breath gentle on my face; I wanted the moment to last forever.

"Come home with me," I blurted. "You won't have to sleep on the floor. There is a bed for you."

"You think I'm a stray puppy that's going to follow you home?" she said. "'Pleeeeze, Mommy and Daddy, let me keep her. I promise to take care of her.'"

"I will care for you," I said earnestly.

"Don't be a bonehead," she said.

We were quiet for what seemed a long time. The windows had fogged up with our breath, and the nearby light pole cast a faint glow inside. It occurred to me that Pia and I were inexplicably fated to have our most significant moments in parking lots. I switched on the radio to fill the gaps in our voices, but Pia reached out and turned it off.

"No noise," she said.

Neither of us spoke for a time, and with each passing minute the tension between us seemed to magnify our breath, making us aware of the stirring of our bodies in the nearly airless confines of the car.

After a while, as if to keep from drifting into a kind of waking slumber, I spoke again. "I will care for you," I repeated.

"I'd better go get my stuff," she said.

"I'll help you."

"No, she'll freak if I come in with someone. It won't take a minute."

We reached my house around 2:00 A.M., coasting down the street and into the driveway so as not to wake my family. I pulled off my shoes as we paused for a moment inside the mudroom. She held her boots, one in each hand, and followed me up the stairs, then down the hallway, sneaking past the closed bedroom doors. I was not ready to explain the girl in my room to Mother and Father, Ted, or Iris. I couldn't yet explain her to myself. I was relieved when I closed the door behind us. I turned a desk light on and indicated that she could have the bed. I would unroll the futon that I kept shoved against the wall as a couch. Pia stood uncertainly in the middle of the room while I fell onto the futon with a sigh. I patted a spot beside me, but she ignored me, choosing instead to look around intently, running her fingers across the book spines, picking up a beer mug I used to hold pencils, a scorpion encased in a paperweight. Then, still standing, she turned and asked me to unzip the back of her dress. Not daring to touch her body, I pinched the fabric in my fingers and slowly pulled the zipper down, feeling at that moment like an acolyte assisting in a holy ritual. I didn't say anything; I had already been called a bonehead three times that night. She shrugged her shoulders and the dress collapsed at her feet into a flower, her pale, thin body a pistil rising from its center. She slipped off her panties and turned to face me.

"Where's the shower?" she said as she stepped beyond the tulle circle and started toward the door.

"Like that?" I could hardly open my eyes wider.

"So lend me a shirt," she said, picking from my closet an obnoxious parrots-and-pineapples thing I had traded for at the 'Tute.

"Not right now, Pia," I fairly stuttered. "You'll wake everyone. Wait until later in the morning when the house will be empty."

"So am I going to be your little secret, stashed away like a criminal?"

I didn't want to point out to her that being an arson suspect did make her potentially criminal, and criminals are best kept out of sight. I would let her out eventually; but for now, making a naked appearance at 2:00 A.M. was not the best way to meet the family.

"You can have the bed. Go to sleep." I was not going to feel easy until Pia settled down.

"I can't go to bed without showering," she said, facing me as I stood in front of the door. "It's a ritual purity thing. And I won't sleep in your disgusting linens," she added, fixing me in a defiant look.

"Okay, I'll change the sheets," I said. I handed her a clean towel, and after checking the hallway for Father or Ted on a pissing excursion, I led her by the hand to the bathroom at the other end of the house. Nobody has ever looked more attractive in the dumb shirt, her skinny legs striding resolutely below the tails.

She admired Iris's collection of shampoos and rinses, the scratchy French sage soap, the natural loofah. "Okay, you can leave now," she said.

"The door doesn't lock," I said. "Somebody might be shocked. Father suffers from a heart condition. Ted is given to obscenities when startled."

"Fine," she said, shrugging off the shirt and allowing me to luxuriate in her nakedness for the second time that night. This time I stared at the sweet downy V below her rounded belly. She let me stare for several seconds, then snapped, "You can guard the door." I dutifully sat on the toilet while behind me the shower stall exploded in billows of fragrant steam.

Finally she emerged, all scrubbed to a rosy glow, and began to dry herself. Oh, to be the towel rubbing her hair, her breasts, her ass. She did that cute thing that I'd seen Iris do, wrapping the towel around her torso, tucking one end just above her breasts so that the lower hem barely covered her bottom. She wiped the steam off the mirror and combed out her wet hair in thick strands.

"You're drooling," she said to my reflection.

I closed my mouth, but I could hardly believe that at 3:00 A.M. it was no dream that this beautiful creature would be lying in my bed, all neatly made with clean sheets under a wildly geometric Mexican blanket. Even if she left the next day, the residual magic in those sheets would forever forestall laundering.

"Your turn," she said.

"To shower?" I asked dumbly.

"You don't expect to crawl in bed with me like this, do you?"

"I don't think I'm dirty," I said lamely.

"You're too dirty to lie with me, too dirty to dream, too dirty to die if that should happen to you during the night."

I was out of my clothes and into the shower in a flash, rushing to keep my now obvious tumescence out of sight. After a minute I declared myself clean and stepped out of the shower. I pulled my jeans back on without bothering to dry myself. It was my second shower in less than a day, a record for me.

All I had to do now was get Pia back to my bedroom without awakening anyone. The hallway was plunged in darkness, in contrast to the lights in the bathroom. The temptation to break into giggles was stifled by the door to Ted's bedroom opening a crack to reveal the glow from a reading lamp, then shutting suddenly with a crack that rang like a gunshot in the quiet house. A moment later we were safe inside my room, the door locked, the light off. I was relieved when she tossed the towel aside and slipped under the cover.

In the spirit of Pia's example, I took off my jeans and crawled into my sleeping bag. I waited nervously in the dark for some signal that would cue my next move. I was not at all familiar with the etiquette of sleepover guests. Once my eyes grew accustomed to the dark, I could tell that she was lying to one side, clearly leaving enough room for me. But now, with the moment of truth upon me, I was rendered indecisive. I couldn't believe I had come this far with Pia in just a matter of hours when earlier today she had been a made-up name in a chat room. I wanted to sleep and then find out the next morning that this was not a dream, that Pia was in my house, my room, my bed. It took about half an hour for me to get up the nerve to crawl from the futon to the bed, slithering along the floor and inside the covers like a belly-dragging alligator. The last thing I remember of that night, after joining Pia in bed, was the silken rhythm of her breathing, a sweet narcotic lulling me to sleep.

When I awoke a few hours later, around noon, the room was awash in light, the house beyond the door utterly silent. Pia was still asleep. I leaned up on my elbow and gazed boldly at her features, which had softened to a sweet vulnerability. I crept out of bed and looked out the window, noting with relief that none of the family cars was in the driveway. We were happily alone. Without bothering to dress, I stepped lightly down the stairs to the kitchen. Sticky notes in various colors signaled me from the breakfast table:

Where did you go last night, Bro? The tank was empty!!!!

Adam, it's your turn. Clean the bathrooms!!! Love, Mother.

Son, College apps are due!! Dad.

Cousin, The time is nigh! Have a blessed day!!!!!! Iris.

I felt assaulted by exclamation points, a reminder that my family would have to be faced eventually. The next few hours offered a respite from the awkward circumstances of my houseguest. I organized a fine breakfast—a pot of fresh Sumatra, a bowl of Cracker Jack, a banana, a bag of Cheetos. I arranged everything on a tray and climbed the stairs, careful not to spill the coffee from the large mugs. I could hardly wait to surprise Pia with breakfast in bed. Still, I found myself standing in front of the shut door, not daring to lift one hand from the tray with its contents threatening to slide toward the edge. I fidgeted indecisively before setting the tray on the floor, opening the door a crack, then picking up the tray and stepping inside. I kicked the door shut with my heel.

Pia was sitting cross-legged on the bed; she smoothed the blanket for the tray, then rewarded me with a luminous smile. I could hardly keep myself from staring at the tender brown tips of her breasts, which seemed to be winking at me in a greeting of their own.

"Oh, man," she said. "A naked angel bearing goodies."

Chapter Twenty

We eventually put on clothes—Pia wore my pineapples-and-parrots shirt, and I put on her turquoise prom dress. She zipped me up and made me turn and admitted that it fit me nicely. We'd been so close through the night that it was as if we wanted to get inside each other's skin. "I want to know what it's like to be you," I said. I could look in the mirror and see me as Pia, her face blending into mine if I half shut my eyes and gazed at the reflection. The reality was more complicated; the crisp folds of the dress were like a whisper down to the depths of my earliest life, the one I had before I became who I am, a time when possibilities coexisted, the undifferentiated zygote holding potential ovaries and testes. That must've been the happiest time. The next moment in my fetal history would have been one of harsh compromise.

I gave Pia a tour of the house. She peered into my parents' bedroom and marveled at the towers of newspapers and magazines against the walls, strewn on Father's side of the bed, arranged in a hidden system according to whether they had been read and were being saved for future reference or simply pushed out of the way until he got the energy to take them to the recycling bin.

"He reads them all?" Pia asked.

"Every word, it seems."

"He must know a lot of stuff."

"All bad," I said. "Don't get him started."

"And your mom?"

"She always has a new career. She's been undercover security at Macy's, an artist's model, a loan consultant, a hotel concierge, a tour-bus driver. She doesn't do any of it for the money."

Mother had been on her sock ministry when she was not at some job. She was naturally good-hearted, of course, but I think the main motivation was to overcome Father's despair with some small but tangible contribution to her fellows. She believed firmly that negativity spawned more of the same. Her wanderings among the homeless were a conjugal neutralizing of his nihilism.

"Mainly," I said, "she likes to do good works."

"Like giving away socks."

"Yes."

I opened the door to Ted's room just enough for her to look inside. The smell of menthol liniment hit us like a whoosh of cold air. Ted had turned his room into a weight-lifting gym ever since he'd realized that maybe he was not as attractive as he should be when a special someone came around to ease his loneliness. He wanted to be buffed and pumped in time for summer.

Pia caught sight of the bodybuilding pictures that Ted had pasted around the walls, a gallery of oiled, rippling, tanned muscles in fierce contraction.

"Is he gay?" she said.

"It would come as a surprise for everyone." I added, "The family has long placed their bets on me."

"And you're only slightly queer."

"Only Cousin Iris would care," I said. "She thinks we're all doomed, anyway. But especially queers of all stripes."

I had saved the best for last. I opened the door to Iris's room. Pia stifled a gasp. It was all cake frosting and meringue, from the wallpaper of pink-and-white roses to the fleecy carpeting to her bed under a gauzy canopy that tented down from a point in the ceiling, protecting a collection of stuffed creatures—a bear, a dove, a lion. And, sitting on a kid-sized rocking chair, a Jesus doll, about four feet tall, which could be Velcroed to a cross.

"She can't be for real." Pia shook her head in wonder.

"She believes in becoming like a child in order to enter the kingdom of heaven."

Pia pulled me into the room. "I love the shaggy white carpet. I bet it will feel good on your ass."

Her hand sneaked under the hem of the green taffeta skirt and ran up the back of my leg to land on my butt. I had always been fascinated by the vulnerability of dresses and skirts, every private thing so well concealed and so easily invaded. I could hardly breathe as she gave me small shoves, causing me to stumble and fall backward. Pushing the skirts up toward my belly, she climbed on top of me, and in the confusion of that moment I found myself holding her close as I tried to hump above the white shag carpeting. We were done in a few minutes, and Pia rolled off me, our fingers touching, our breath returning to normal, I felt a thrill at the happy desecration of Iris's space.

Later that afternoon we changed into jeans and t-shirts. As the erotic charge of earlier in the day dissipated, the elaborate folds and flounces of the prom dress felt clumsy and clownish. Pia used my Mac to check her e-mail. There were multiple messages from her father and mother, wanting to know where she was, if she was all right, if she had spoken to the detectives from the police, the insurance company, the fire department. Everybody wanted to talk to her.

"Nobody knows I'm here!"

"*I* know." I felt somewhat stupid for pointing out the obvious but at the same time proud to be the repository of a serious secret in Pia's life.

"I'll kill you if you tell anyone," she said. "And then nobody will know."

"You can stay here as long as you like," I said. "Actually, please stay with me. You will be safe, out of sight but better not online. They could find this computer, in this room, in this house, in a minute."

Chapter Twenty-One

Somehow, through the shaping of circumstances, it became clear by the next day, that, for the time being, I would keep Pia's presence in my room a secret from the family. My door would stay closed while I went on with my life, no one having a clue as to the excitement that thumped in my chest. Pia would remain hidden, as quiet as a ghost, sneaking off to the bathroom as needed but bathing only when the family was gone or asleep. Occasionally, during the day, she would be able to hang out in the yard or watch TV in the family room. On weekends she would have to keep to the room. I suggested she write a novel. But she laughed, saying only that she would meditate, sleep, read very long books—my *Don Quixote* was first on her list.

I thought that first night at dinner would be awkward, but I was a natural at dissembling and obfuscating. I was able to enjoy the family, the quizzing about my date (coffee and conversation with an online buddy), my plans (to get my college apps under way), my aspirations (Stanford! Harvard! Berkeley!), without so much as a moment's hesitation. Mother was taking a break from her sock mission, and I claimed to be attacking the college apps with great enthusiasm. I volunteered to do the dishes, which surprised everyone. It was easy enough to arrange some leftovers in an appetizing design on a plate (a clump of rice surrounded by broccoli, chickpeas, zucchini) and sneak supper to Pia.

Pia had made my room her home. She'd pushed some of my clothes out of the way to make room for hers in the closet. A space on the headboard bookshelf had been cleared for a small box containing a couple of pairs of earrings, a desk calendar with a selection of witches and druids for every month, a travel alarm clock, various pens and pencils. She was sitting cross-legged on the bed writing in a small spiral notebook labeled *Dreams*, which she closed and laid flat on the blanket as soon as I came in.

"You need to knock before entering," she said.

"It's my room," I argued weakly.

"Yes, well, I'm in it now, aren't I?" Then she added softly, "It's not like we're married. You should respect my privacy."

"I brought you something to eat." I set the plate on the desk.

"So you're not going to let me starve?" She rolled off the bed and sat in my chair.

She ate happily. Her mood lifted from the quick snap of a minute before, yet for the first time I realized I would have to be wary. The better I kept her invisible, the more she would depend on me.

It didn't take long to develop a routine. Not that Pia made it easy. I wanted her to take her showers during the day, while the family was out, but she insisted she could not sleep without a bath. I wouldn't let her out of the room until after midnight, once I figured everyone was asleep. And even then it was a dash down the hallway while I served as lookout. I would lock the door behind us and jump under the spray alongside her; if asked about the water running in the middle of the night, I could claim that a hot shower made me drowsy, better than getting back into the usual doses of Zonkers and Snoozers.

When Mother did comment a couple of days later about the shower going, everyone agreed that my bathing at night was a good idea, as the bathroom would not be jammed with everyone else trying to take off in the morning. I was the one unemployed, unschooled, unencumbered with obligations since dropping out of the sock ministry.

Mornings could be anxious. I had to cut off liquids after Pia's shower, but she often needed to pee just as the family was lining up for their ablutions. Hence the chamber pot. More precisely, a red plastic bucket. Pia was appalled at the idea. I kept having to remind her of the need to remain hidden, exaggerating the likelihood that she would be found and questioned under suspicion of arson (five to twenty years). I had to leave the room while Pia mastered the bucket. She insisted I empty the thing immediately.

During most of the day we led a normal life. She had a big breakfast around 10:00, which would tide her over until I brought up her dinner of what I could save from the family meal. When servings were small, I would keep some from my plate to add to her share. Weekends were tough; she had to stay in the room from Friday afternoon to Monday morning, with breaks to shower during the night. She was prone to prolonging these escapes. We would steal down the stairs and out the kitchen door to the backyard. She loved the sense of freedom she got from twirling naked in the moonlight. Her slender figure, her gleaming white skin, the flow of her strange dance made a lovely sight. But I anticipated discovery, exposure, arrest.

Fortunately, her escapes would last only a couple of minutes before the sharp cold drove her inside. I would wrap her in a blanket and rub her body back to a warm glow. Then it was back up the stairs, quietly, to our room. Her cell, she called it. She spent hours reading *Don Quixote*. She had decided she was going to use the solitude to improve herself. And then she wanted to discuss her reading. Being crazy myself, she said, did I think Don Q. was playacting or helplessly gripped by his delusions?

"What do you think?" I countered. "Being that you're somewhat warped yourself."

"He knew perfectly well," she stated flatly, "what was what in the realm of the real."

"Of course," I said, as if that point merited no discussion.

"And that didn't make him any less crazy," she added.

"Made him more crazy," I said. "What could be crazier than deliberately behaving as if you believe your fantasies are true?"

She laughed. "Most people don't really know how much in control we really are. I mean, you've had shrinks and parents and teachers fooled for years. You've even got me fooled."

I gave her my look—the raising of the eyebrows, the slight jerk of the head in surprise as if on the receiving end of a small blow, the deep shrug as if my head were trying to hide between my shoulders.

"You don't think I know why you're keeping me here?"

"Because I'm a bonehead?"

"Because you're a monster," she said. "A Jeffrey Dahmer type, getting ready to slice me up. And what's worse, you know it."

I feared Pia's boredom. It was starting to make her cranky. I brought her earphones so she could listen silently—classic rock, opera, big band, jazz, anything loud to cover her growing melancholy. She played music during most of her waking moments, ignoring me while I went through the motions of poking around the web looking at college sites and SAT cheating services. But my heart was not in it. I was loving my life, hunkered down with Pia, nothing much to do other than take care of her, flowing into the roles of lover, husband, servant, bodyguard, confidant, and warden. I was giddy with sex. I could only do the cat-that-ate-the-canary smile every time Mother or Ted remarked on my good humor.

I tried to make my errands as brief as possible because Pia, left alone, was unpredictable, as she was prone to ricochet though moods with unnerving randomness. I had to remind her to use the earphones whenever she played her favorite Rancid, Alice Cooper, Bartók, always at full volume, accompanying her loose, twirling dancing from one wall to the other in my room, sometimes crashing into furniture, knocking a chair over, falling exhausted to the floor. She had occasional bouts of conversation, more like argument, with herself. When

I asked her to please be quiet before the family overheard her shouts, she said I couldn't stop her from thinking. I was constantly having to reassure her that the heat from the investigations would cool down and she would be able to quietly slip back into the world of the living. I was not eager for this to happen.

"You are ranting again," I would point out.

"I'm thinking out loud."

"Well, keep it down, okay?"

"Not okay. If thoughts are screaming inside my head, they will come out as screams."

And then, as if on cue, she let out a piercing wail. I hurried to her side and coaxed her to sit down on the bed, putting my arm around her shoulders.

"What's the matter, Pia?" I said. "They'll hear you all over the house."

"Nobody's home, right?" she said, calming down. "I know how to be your evil little secret."

"Not evil, Pia," I said. "I'm looking out for you." And then, to prove my point, I opened the cigar box where I kept my collection of meds and handed her two little pink triangles from the bottle I'd found in her desk during my visit to her burned house.

"Thanks," she said, swallowing them without water. "You're a sweet bonehead."

Chapter Twenty-Two

By week two my waking life was dedicated to keeping Pia amused and out of sight, paying attention to her breath, her looks, her tone of voice for signs of unrest. Every day presented a potential crisis. She was increasingly demanding—hungry, bored, thirsty, restless. She wanted a phone, but I would let her use mine only if I was with her for fear that she would give herself away. She soon took over my computer. As a result she was online at all hours. I insisted on no e-mail in case her contacts were being monitored by the arson sleuths. Within days she was chatting around under a variety of aliases. She was "HotHead" in various chat rooms, with a photo of a redhead taken from the L'Oréal website. At last count she had collected forty-seven friends, including a few interested in pyromania. A couple, PyroSam and Torchy, were insistent that she call them to get together for a real date, maybe set up a little s'mores party. I was jealous; I had reconnected with Pia online, and I was wary of some jerk getting to her.

She broke into loud cackles, which I quickly stifled with my hand. I needn't worry, she reassured me when I let her speak again. Those two guys were bigger idiots than I was. They were, in fact, cops. And she was enjoying stringing them along. I warned her about having too much fun with them. There was no telling what a disappointed undercover cop might do to another fake persona.

I tried to keep her happy, providing her with books, music, sweet or savory treats on a whim. I often failed in spite of my best efforts. Like the night she wanted the balsamic fig gelato from Caruso's Gelatteria. I begged Ted for his car and drove to Uptown, where the Caruso shop was about to close, a near disaster, as I could've returned empty-handed. I inspected the selections behind glass, going from one tub of colorful confection to the next until I had to face that there was no balsamic fig. Caruso's had eliminated it from its repertoire because the only customer who asked for it was some strange girl who seemed to collect all her spare change for a small serving every couple of weeks. I tried to make up for the failure of my mission by buying pints of peanut-praline, mango-kiwi, passion fruit–rose petal. I went back to the house with the gelato softening in my backpack. I tossed the keys to Ted, who suddenly wanted to chat.

"Hey, bro! Mission accomplished?"

"Yeah, Ted. Thanks for the car." I paused on my way up the stairs to where Pia awaited my rapidly melting gift.

"Slow down, guy." He indicated a spot on the couch beside him. "We hardly see you anymore, you've turned into such a hermit."

"I've got to go to my room, Ted," I said, still trying to pull myself away from his bewildered expression.

"What do you do up there all day?" He laughed his familiar laugh, somewhere between a snort and a guffaw.

"Research," I mumbled.

"Is that what they call porn sniffing now?"

I wanted to laugh at him. *I* don't need porn. *I* have a girl! "College apps, transcripts, financial aid," I mumbled.

There was the snap of a door shutting.

"Somebody up there?"

"Iris."

"No. She's out with her End Times cohorts."

"Mother. Father. Who cares?"

"Nobody home but you and me, bro."

"The wind?"

He shot me a smirk that said he knew I was frantically equivocating. "I guess you'd better go see."

By then I was bounding up the stairs.

t was the Great Gelato Meltdown, a turning point in my life as host to my secret guest: Pia was in her underwear, sitting on the edge of the bed with her legs splayed, striking matches and tossing them all around her. The flames flitted in midair like angry fireflies, rising and then diving to the floor. I dropped the backpack and lunged to slap the matchbook from her hand. She laughed as I danced about the room putting out the tiny fires singeing the carpet and filling the room with a sharp stink. Pia kept laughing until she spotted the Caruso's containers I had set on the desk, which I feared were now turning into a syrupy mush.

"Which one is the balsamic fig?" She peered suspiciously into each container.

"They were out," I said. "They might have some next week. I didn't think you wanted to wait that long."

"It took you a while," she said, "considering you didn't even get the right flavor." She spooned out a dollop of the peanut-praline and frowned at the first taste. The mango-kiwi and the passion fruit–rose petal met with similar grimaces.

"You eat them," she said, pushing aside the dripping cups and letting herself fall back on the bed. "You were obviously getting flavors you like. Not thinking of me at all."

I tasted the praline while she sulked. I took another taste, from the mango this time, but the fruit seemed overripe and left a cloying film in my mouth. If Pia didn't like the gelato, I wouldn't like it, either.

She lay on the bed, a hand across her eyes as if to shield them from the light.

"I can get you something else," I said, although clearly I could no longer be trusted. I hoped she wouldn't ask for anything; I didn't need to arouse more curiosity from Ted or the rest of the family. And I didn't want to leave Pia alone if she was in a match-lighting mood. There were burn marks on the carpeting, on my notebook, in the wastebasket.

Pia had curled up in a silent funk on the far side of the bed, knees to her chest, her arms protectively around her head.

"Go away," she said, her voice muffled by the pillow.

"I can't leave you alone, Pia," I said as gently as I could. "You were setting my room on fire."

She suddenly sprang up and crossed her legs on the middle of the bed. "I was not."

"What do you call throwing matches around?"

"Oh, God!" she exclaimed in a deep-chested groan that I feared could be heard all over the house. "Oh, God, oh, God, oh, God."

"God lit the matches?"

"I was just bored. I would've snuffed out anything that looked serious."

"You set things on fire when you're bored?"

"No," she said.

"You just said you did."

"I mean, I don't just light up when I'm bored. There's more to it than that. A feeling comes. I start by imagining the dance of fire. I want to put my fingers close to a flame, have it lick my skin like a cat's tongue. I get the urge to smell something burning—wood, plastic, paint, hair. To hear the sirens blasting through the night. To warm myself with a real six-alarm fire."

"Like your house."

"I was in school when it happened."

"Why are you afraid to talk to the insurance company, then?"

"Generalized, unfocused, unearned guilt."

"Because you were glad to see your house go up in flames."

"I didn't see it burning." In her tone, mixed with adamant denial, there was something like regret. "Except in the news that night."

"Not the same as live, I imagine."

"So now you've decided to humor me?" she said finally, having given the accusation considerable thought.

She was right. Even now, as the night grew late and Pia had lain back on the bed, her breath relaxing into an even rhythm, I found myself wary of her next word.

"I want you to be safe," I said. "And happy."

I unlocked my desk drawer and pulled out the cigar box with its stash of about a hundred pills of different colors and shapes—Ritalin, Adderall, Zoloft, Xanax, Klonopin, Prozac—all the things I'd been on through the years and which, with great foresight, I had saved for a more pressing occasion. I picked out three different pills for their qualities of geometry and color—a pink triangle, a gray capsule, a blue heart.

"You're trying to dope me up?"

"A Zipper, a Zonker, and a Snoozer, for recreational purposes."

"What are you really giving me?"

"An antidepressant, a sedative, a reuptake inhibitor. All well tested on the troubled youth of today."

"But what will they do together?"

"Synergy is a wonderful thing."

"Could they make me weirder?"

"More normal, actually."

She held the pills in her hand and studied them as if they held the key to her future. I handed her a can of Dr. Pepper, and she delicately placed a tablet on her tongue, swallowing each in turn with blind faith.

Minutes later she was growing drowsy, and her expression had taken on a new innocence. I relaxed as well. For all her wound-up energy, when Pia finally slept she did so with rocklike solidity. I went over to the bed and pulled the Mexican blanket up to her shoulders. I unrolled the futon and set it on the floor beside her. It was the first night we hadn't touched. I felt I'd been banished to a cold steppe.

Chapter Twenty-Three

By the third week Pia had grown more anxious in her confinement. The brief nocturnal stretches in the backyard, her whirling moonlight dances, barely alleviated her restlessness. I feared she would simply walk away, making herself vulnerable to curious, blabby neighbors. I had in the past several days reveled in my newfound power. I liked Pia being dependent on me, like some rare creature I had trapped in a jar, even if she was a demanding, whining captive. I didn't question who had the power in our symbiotic arrangement; I was happy to be both her warden and her fetch dog.

I continued to dispense occasional meds from my cigar box that took the edge off her moods. She was sleeping a lot, for several hours at a time, her breath in deep slumber sometimes alarmingly growing soft and barely audible, and during those times I was able to relax my guard.

Keeping Pia quiet freed me to lead, to all outward appearances, a normal life in front of the family. As it was, they had grown curious about all the time I spent in my room, Ted accusing me of surfing porn and masturbating compulsively, Mother and Father questioning why it was taking me so long to decide on my education, Iris warning me that the consuming fires of Armageddon would spare no one but the saved. It was still possible for me to be among the chosen, natural for someone my age to become like a child and enter the kingdom.

I had dinner with the family in one happy circle around the table, resisting their attempts to feed me breasts, ribs, and rumps from various animals. I stuck to mashed potatoes and broccoli and beans of every color. As I ate and chatted and grinned at everyone's stories, an inner sense would signal when Pia was awake and starting to fester in her solitude. I'd excuse myself and sneak a plate upstairs.

She was usually chatting away on my Mac. She had developed a new identity: PRZNR. She spun out a narrative about being held captive by a wealthy pervert who at various times either tormented her or lavished her with pleasure: "Dispatches from a secret location in the Mexican Caribbean."

Some nights I stayed awake so I could check her postings:

PRZNR:—I am being fattened up by my keeper, Don Reynaldo, so he can eventually feed me to his pet shark. I'm fed six times a day. Fudge sundaes, avocado smoothies, tortellini alfredo, battered onion rings, Nutella sandwiches. He hasn't told me he plans to feed me to Fisho, but I can tell by the way the shark stares at me from behind the glass walls of his tank that my fate is sealed. Fisho is a rare blue shark with his fin the color of silver. Don Reynaldo, Rey for short, swears he is feeding me because he likes his women fat—too fat to run away, he adds with a laugh.

I was gratified to find myself as a character in her fantasy of captivity. I logged in as SAVR:

> SAVR:—I want to save you from this evil domain. Tell me where you are and I can be there in a day.
> PRZNR:—This island is near Isla Mujeres, the island of women, but too small to have an official name. Don Rey calls it Isla Niña. The castle where I'm kept is in the middle of the island, far from the shore and approachable only on horseback. Furthermore, Don Rey keeps me in a room within a room within a room, nestled like Russian dolls, seven rooms in all, with my bedroom a pink-and-lace boudoir at the center protected by seven locked doors. Only my handmaidens are allowed in—to serve me countless meals, to bathe me in rosewater, to massage me with hot sesame oil. Then Don Rey arrives to avail himself of my breasts, my mouth, my pussy, my ass.
> SAVR:—Lucky guy!!! I would like to be him, if only for a night.
> PRZNR:—You're a bonehead.

Pia had seen through SAVR.

> PRZNR:—Don Rey is a scrawny dirty smelly old man, about ninety years old. For twenty years he was not able to get an erection—not through Viagra or a penis pump or prostitutes flown in from around the world. He has a huge

thing. I've never measured, but it might be a foot long. Still, what good is a big dick, he says, if it refuses to stir from its wormy resting state? He had made a deal with himself that if ever his penis stopped working, he would kill himself. He didn't, unfortunately. And then he saw me one day on the beach at Cozumel. I was lying on the sand soaking up the rays when I felt his stare like a wet toad hopping on my back and legs. I turned to meet his gaze, and his dick uncoiled like a serpent until the head was peeking out from above his belt. Disgusting.

I heard Pia stir to wakefulness and quickly logged out, erased history, snapped down the screen. "Good morning, sunshine," I said, even though it was around midnight. By then, under my pharmaceutical ministrations, Pia was on a personal, variable clock with no regard for the normal rhythms of life.

She gazed out at the dark night. "What time is it anyway?"

"Time for breakfast," I said. I had set up a simple galley in a corner of my room with a heating coil for tea, a hot plate for grilling cheese sandwiches, and a variety of cookies, chips, candy. "Would you like a little fruit while your tea brews?" I put some jelly beans on a plate, ranging in color from purple grape to red cherry to lemon yellow.

She put a jelly bean in her mouth and sucked the flavor from it before spitting out the gummy center. Then she studied the remaining half dozen on the plate before picking a lime-green one. She was halfway into the process when I joked that she should finish her fruit.

"You sound like my mom," she said.

"Is that good?"

"It is now. I miss her. I'm also pissed at her for leaving me, thinking Dad would take care of me. After the fire he was barely taking care of himself."

"Parents are clueless."

"She's worried about me," Pia said. "I've seen her e-mails in my Yahoo in box. '*How* are you?' '*Where* are you?' "

"You shouldn't even be logging in."

"I want to know who's writing me."

"You can't answer them from my computer. You can't even open them. They'll find you in a heartbeat." At that time I still didn't know how much of my concern had to do with Pia's safety and how much with my fear of losing control of her. In any case I was growing more absorbed with the intricacies of being her keeper, a role that was growing increasingly complex the longer she stayed.

"I want to tell her not to worry about me."

"I can do that."

Later that morning I made Pia promise that she would be quiet while I went to log in with her name and password at a library in St. Paul, wanting to put as much random space as possible between my room and a public computer. I made her promise to stay inside, not use the phone, and stick to anonymous chat.

Fortunately the family was out of the house for the morning and I didn't have to deal with questions or explanations about the odd noises coming from my room. In any case, it helped that my strange behavior was preceded by years of purposeful eccentricity. No surprises there.

I took the first bus that came by our stop. The 22B turned out to be the express to downtown St. Paul. Perfect. As far as Pia was concerned, St. Paul was ten miles away but light-years distant in terms of where she was. St. Paul kids came to Minneapolis and sometimes stayed, not the other way around. I couldn't remember the last time I'd been there. Still, I found the library easily, a classic gray limestone building with a dozen marble steps leading to the portico over the carved oak door and Greek columns on either side.

I logged on at a computer and signed into Yahoo as Miss Entropia. By then I had lost track of most of Pia's names, settling on one as a way to keep her in focus in spite of her tendency to mutate from one persona to the next, each with its own quirks and wrinkles. Pia, Pia, Pia, I repeated to myself as I typed in her password, because I was sure if I let go of her name she might vanish from beneath my typing fingers.

The messages directed to Miss Entropia seemed remote and abstract, somehow disassociated from the girl I knew. It was a long list; it had been weeks since Pia had checked her e-mail. Some were laconic *what's up*s and *hey you*s from friends. One seemed a long lecture from her father, incorporating advice with a suggestions that she call someone he called "my buddy Frank," a lawyer friend of the family who would be glad to help her if she decided to talk to the insurance-company snoops. I deleted it. Several messages were junk, but a recent one from Felicia Timmins, her mother's maiden name, gave me a lurch, as if I myself were her daughter. It was dated ten days ago.

Subject: URGENT READ IMMEDIATELY!!!!!

Darling,

Your insane father, who has been living in his Range Rover for the past weeks, has finally heard from the insurance investigators on the burning down of our house. Everybody was suspicious about the huge insurance payoff. He always considered that monstrosity my house rather than ours. I wasn't going to be surprised if he ended up in jail. Still, they've officially decided it was an accident. I imagine he will send me my share soon. The check is in the mail, like they say.

I'm still in Elysium, Texas where, I have met a wonderful man. His name is Andres, and get this: we are pregnant!!! You will have a beautiful brown baby brother soon. You have a room in our house if you want to get away from those nasty Minnesota winters.

Tell your Father.

OOOXXX Mom.

I had to respond right away:

Subject: yeah!!!! whoopee!!! a baby?!

You tell your husband. I'm in Isla Mujeres, the captive of a rich drug lord. Nice and toasty here, too.

Are you sure you want to stay in Elysium? A deadly place, I'm told.

love,

P.

I erased both her mother's e-mail and my reply. Clearly, if the arson detectives were putting out the message that the investigation was over, it was only in order to smoke her out. I had grown to enjoy my power over her. She might walk away if she felt she was no longer an arson suspect.

It took forever to find the right bus to take me home, and I finally ran from the bus stop, slipped into the quiet house, and bounded up the stairs, worried about what Pia might have been up to. I opened the door to my room, expecting her to be asleep or reading or tapping away on the computer, only to find myself standing in silent, empty space, the ceiling globe, the nightstand light, and the desk lamp all burning brightly. It was the first time since I'd brought Pia home that she had wandered away.

I had no idea where to look first. I couldn't simply call out her name; the family seemed gone when I arrived, but I never knew when Ted had left work early or Iris was praying for the rapture behind closed doors. I ran down the hallway, checking the bathroom, peering through the open door of my parents' bedroom, finally rushing down the stairs from the living room to the foyer, checking the backyard until my racing ended abruptly at the kitchen.

Pia stood in a disaster zone, wearing my t-shirt with a picture of the original Al of Al's Breakfast wearing his tall chef's hat and holding the scepter of a wooden spoon dripping pancake batter. Around her were dripping eggshells, milk puddles, and random dustings of sugar and smearings of butter. I didn't have to ask what she'd been up to; from the oven came the beguiling scent of vanilla.

"I made flan," she exclaimed triumphantly. "I got hungry for something sweet and creamy, and I searched the house for ice cream. It was a serious craving, boyfriend. It will be ready in eight minutes. Yummy."

"Oh, Pia, what a mess you've made," I sighed, reaching for her arm to pull her out of the kitchen.

"That's very unappreciative," she sniffed. "I bet you've never had real flan."

"I would've brought you something sweet."

"Well, you were nowhere around, were you?"

"I was checking your e-mail."

"Any messages?"

"Later," I mumbled.

"So there is news for me?"

"Right now I have to deal with this chaos."

"Just the headlines," she pleaded. "Any news about my dad?"

"No." It was surprisingly easy to reply with a bland lie and then distract her with a piece of big news: "But your mom is pregnant."

Pia shrugged. "Now you know where I get my crazies."

"Speaking of which," I said. "I need to clean this kitchen up before the family gets home."

"I was just going to do that," she said. "I wanted to do something nice for you. Make you a nice dessert. I'll clean up quick as lightning."

"No, Pia," I said. "Just go to back to the room."

"I need to check the flan."

"No fucking time," I said, wincing at the shrill note in my own voice. "It's after five. The family will be home in the next few minutes."

"It's about ready," she said, opening the oven. Again the fragrance of the vanilla enveloped us like a magical cloud. She folded a dishcloth in her hand and pulled out the bowl, then flipped it onto a plate to reveal a golden wheel topped with burnt sugar.

"It's beautiful," I said.

"It's from *The Thelma and Louise Cookbook*."

"Who are Thelma and Louise?"

"The women who invented flan."

"Now, please go upstairs," I pleaded.

"Let me taste first," she said. "I need to know that it turned out okay."

"Go ahead."

"You taste it, too," she said after thoughtfully savoring a spoonful. She scooped out another corner and held it out to me.

I took the proffered spoon and tasted. It was a wonderful concoction, eggy and sweet, almost buttery, with the heady surge of vanilla.

"I put in a little extra love," she said. "Can you taste it?"

I savored thoughtfully but could discern nothing beyond the smooth richness. "No."

"Good." She smiled. "Added love is meant to work in subtle ways. Contributing to the whole effect without distracting."

"Time to go back to your room," I said firmly.

"Let's bring up the dish."

"Let's not," I said. "I need to show the family the results of the mess."

"Sharing is good." She beamed suddenly. Then she was gone, striding across the living room, up the stairs, and into my room just as Mother's car pulled in.

I was frantically washing the counters and stovetop when Mother walked into the kitchen and took a slow look at the situation. Ordinarily a place of harmony and meditative labor, the space appeared to have been the site of a toddlers' food war. "My, what happened here?"

"Hi Mom," I was quick to speak. "I made flan."

"You made flan," she echoed, as if trying to grasp some elusive truth in my statement.

"Yep, and I'll have the mess cleaned up in no time."

Her features softened as she saw the results of the surrounding chaos, a plate holding the golden sun.

"Why, thank you, Adam," she nearly sang. "That's a very sweet thing to do, just when I thought you were drifting away from us."

"Have a taste, Mom." I pushed the dish toward her.

"I am tempted." She smiled. "But I'd rather leave you to your cleanup and enjoy it with everybody after dinner."

Mom pushed me out as soon as I'd cleared the mess. We were having stir-fry with chicken, but with optional tofu "fingers" for me. I rushed upstairs to announce the menu to Pia. Sometimes, if she was feeling picky, I would have to go out and get her something from the deli counter at Lund's—marinated artichoke hearts, three-bean salad, tabouleh. Even in winter she liked salads. She was at my desk, turning away from the computer just long enough to announce that stir-fry sounded fine but that she would wait for more of her flan. She had tasted it and pronounced it delicious. She looked at me with a crooked smile and unfocused gaze, her eyelids fluttering until she rubbed her eyes and turned back to the computer screen.

"Are you okay, Pia?" This had become a frequent question. The answer was never particularly forthright. This time she ignored me, apparently absorbed by her web browsing.

"Are you okay?" I insisted.

She turned toward me with a sharp, impatient sigh. "Why do you keep asking that? I'm not okay. I'm a prisoner. I'm being kept all hushed up in the dungeon of some freak."

"Okay," I said amiably. "I'll bring up some stir-fry." I wanted to stay and keep an eye on her, but Mom called that dinner was ready.

Chapter Twenty-Four

It was my first leisurely dinner with the whole family after many days of rushing in and grabbing a bite before disappearing back into my room. There we were, gathered around the table while Mother dished out the stir-fry and Father popped open a beer and Ted passed around the Mighty Rooster hot sauce and Iris led us in a scary prayer: "Lord, in your mercy, sweep up every last one of us when the time comes!"

"The sooner the better," I exclaimed.

"Amen to that," added Ted.

"Boys, don't tease your cousin," Mother said. Then, turning to Iris, she added, "Thank you for including us in your prayer, dear."

"Let's eat," Father grumbled. "If the world is going to come to an end, I don't want it to happen while I'm hungry."

"We won't be hungry." Iris smiled her dreamy little smile. "We will all be filled with heaven's manna."

We fell silent as we feasted on veggies, tofu fingers, and brown rice. Mother had bragged to the family about my making the delicious dessert waiting for us at the center of the table. Father was skeptical, pointing out that he had never thought of me doing anything useful in the kitchen.

"It is my first attempt." I tried a bit of disarming modesty.

"Where did you learn to make flan?" Father insisted.

"One of the Mexican cooks at the 'Tute made flan. I watched."

By then I was a polished fraud. I had no doubt that I would be found out eventually; such is the way of truth. Meanwhile, I was enjoying the novelty of earnest goodwill being showered on me.

Finally Ted and Iris cleared the table, leaving only the plate in the middle and Mother's ancestral dessert dishes with the design of tea roses rimmed in gold. She delicately lifted each large, dense wedge of flan with a silver server. She wouldn't be making such a fuss if anyone other than the prodigal kid had baked it.

Ted started to take a bite when Mother stopped him with a look.

"What?" he asked, putting the spoon down.

"We will wait until everyone is served," she said. "Now, who wants coffee?" With that question the moment of communion was further postponed.

Then, at long last, flan! My first taste yielded a substantial satisfying texture, followed by the creamy molecules spreading like warm butter throughout my mouth, from the back of my tongue to the insides of my cheeks, so that I was tasting their deliciousness with every cell. This was the best dessert ever. I looked around the table, and sure enough, everyone's face indicated bliss. By the time I was halfway through, savoring slowly to make it last, the secret ingredients had made their presence felt. First a numbness spread over my tongue, as if the overwhelming sweetness had my taste buds recoiling. When I tried to speak my lips flapped thick and blubbery, my nose felt congested, my cheeks tingled, my skull sucked me inward so that I was being pulled into the quicksand that was my own brain.

I couldn't stop eating. Each spoonful led to the next. Whole minutes must've passed, with each succeeding bite pulling me deeper into the surrounding murk. I looked around the table. Ted was holding up his last spoonful and saying something to me, but I couldn't hear a word. He was grimacing as if speaking required a huge effort. Mother was smiling and nodding to some unheard rhythm. Father was sobbing. I had never seen him cry, and the sight startled me into a renewed alertness.

"War, war, war," he cried. "All I see on TV is things blowing up. Will there be no peace in my lifetime?"

"It's okay, darling," Mother said, putting her hand over his. "It's all happening far, far away."

Iris had stood up from the table and twirled around the kitchen, putting herself into a kind of trance as she surrendered to the impulse to whirl, soon turning so fast she seemed helpless to stop. "I'm ready, I'm ready, I'm ready," she repeated in a song that was both celebration and plea for release, until she landed on her butt and was suddenly silent.

And then, through the competing impressions of the family caroming in separate directions, I realized that we were all in the throes of a random psychotropic cocktail. I pushed my chair back, stood up, barely able to steady myself on the edge of the table, and begged to be excused. Then, with leaden feet, on legs that felt as if they were pushing through mud, I climbed the stairs, which were suddenly as steep as a mountain, methodically putting one foot on each succeeding step and pulling myself up by the banister.

It might have taken hours to climb up, and by the time I reached the hallway and started shuffling toward my room, I'd forgotten what all the urgency had been about. I opened the door, taking care not to open it any wider than I had to in order to push myself inside. Pia was sitting in her underwear, tapping away at my Mac, hardly giving me a glance as I slipped in.

Nothing seemed out of the ordinary until I spotted the pharmaceutical cigar box lying open, upside down on the floor, pills scattered. Pia must've sensed my bending down to pick it up because I heard a barely stifled snort as I lurched forward. Was she mocking me? Out of the corner of my eye I saw her smirk as I scooped the pills back into the box.

I sat on the edge of the bed and stared in disbelief at the box on my lap, knowing that I was in over my head thinking I could manage this sweet, destructive angel. Kali had been in seclusion, dormant in the confines of Pia's mind, but now the goddess, never far from ordinary life, had surged out of the dark ether into the light of my reality.

"Don't go anywhere, Pia," I said, confident that she would stay put for hours at my Mac.

It was easier to go down the stairs than it had been to climb them. Gravity helped. The biggest incentive was the need to make sure no one panicked. A call to 911 would bring a troop of police and medical types storming our mellow suburban house. What they would find once they barged in was an ensemble psychodrama. Father was sitting on the rug in front of the TV, his nose only inches from the screen, face flushed, eyes glinting as if from a fever. He was flipping from one channel to another with barely enough time to register the images. His weeping had been replaced by a muttered stream of commentary on the state of the world as seen on ninety-two cable channels. His screed was mostly unintelligible except for the occasional *bitch, asshole, crook, liar* that surfaced. He held the remote in one hand like a weapon, and with the other hand he kept picking at the buttons on his shirt, wanting to pull them out as if they were ticks attempting to burrow through the fabric to his skin.

Mother was sitting behind him, legs splayed around his hips so that she could reach to knead his shoulders, whispering in his ear words so soothing they distracted him from his anxiety and caused him to slump back into her embrace. He would rest a moment until an image on the TV pulled him back to the screen, upon which he would go on with the muttered curses and groans of despair at the hopelessness of the world. Mother caressed him, running her fingers over his hair and gently combing back the thin strands. She seemed more in control of herself than any of us, perhaps knowing that whatever madness had gripped the family would pass and all would be explained.

I'd been standing at the threshold of the living room for several seconds when Mother looked up and met my gaze. I had some explaining to do.

Iris broke the moment with a sudden whirling entrance, her dance to End Times unabated. Finally Mother looked away from me and snapped at her.

"Settle down, girl," she ordered. "Jesus is not going to come any sooner because you're spinning like a goddamn top."

Something in Mother's voice, her tone or the opportune yet unexpected curse, froze Iris in the middle of one of her turns, one hand aloft, the other reaching out to help her regain her balance. Then, her face growing pale, her eyes rolling upward, Iris slowly collapsed as her legs gave out, the impact of her fall cushioned by the thick carpet. A moment later she leaned back as if expecting a wall to support her only to end up supine, her eyes open to some point, perhaps beyond the ceiling.

Mother turned back to me. "She's scared," she said. "Tell her what's happening."

"How would I know?" My tongue was thick as fur inside my mouth, under the influence of either Pia's concoction or my mendacity.

"You made the flan," she said. "Did you forget what was in it?"

One thing about Mother that I had long admired was her ability to see through evasions and distractions.

"Relax, Cousin," I said gently, leaning down to speak to Iris. "The weirdness will pass."

"Apologize to her for intoxicating her."

Of course I wanted to apologize to everyone, even if the prank had been played by someone else and I was as much a victim as the rest of the family. Still, I could not plead innocence. "I'm sorry if there was something in the dessert that is not agreeing with you."

I was leaning down toward Iris, and I could see her gaze switch momentarily from the ceiling to look at me. The alarm seemed to dissipate; she closed her eyes, and her breathing became soft and easy. That is the nature of meds. They can be disturbing at first, but once you surrender to their spell, you can enjoy the experience.

"Where's Ted?" I asked Mother.

"Out—you know." She waved her hand vaguely. "Said he was going out to kick some ass."

Once I felt everyone's agitation had eased, I went back upstairs, shutting the bedroom door after me. I pulled Pia from the computer to the edge of the bed.

"You don't realize the havoc you've created downstairs. Are you irresponsible or criminally insane?"

'Why, yes," she answered sweetly, her eyebrows arching in surprise. "But you knew that already. What are you really asking me?"

"Did you want to poison my family? They're all downstairs floating around in a fog."

"You're the one who wanted to share. *We* ate the same flan," she pointed out. "We're doing fine."

"We dissect, disassociate, discriminate. It's taken us years to get to the stage where applied pharmacology is fun."

"Have them drink lots of water," she offered with shrug.

"Why did you do it?"

"I thought it would be fun *for us*. It was your idea to share dessert with everyone," she said. "But maybe if they all pass out we can run away."

"Jesus, Pia. You're already running away, remember?"

"Hiding is not quite running. I'd like to be running instead of hiding." She paused for a moment. "We could be like Bonnie and Clyde on some kind of a spree. Torching or shoplifting or driving until we ran out of gas. Please, Adam, let's just go."

Chapter Twenty-Five

The next morning, a Saturday, I was startled awake by knocking and jerking at the locked bedroom door. It was before 7:00, and Pia was still asleep, both of us having grown accustomed to sleeping late and rising only after the family had cleared out.

"Yeah?" I slurred, still punchy from the previous night's excesses. "What is it?"

"Open up, son," came Father's voice.

"What's going on?"

"I'm not going to shout from the hallway," he said.

I pulled myself out of bed, put on jeans, and bunched a blanket over Pia to disguise her form. "It's Saturday," I complained, cracking the door open.

"What difference does that make?" Father said. "You don't seem to have any pressing duties during the rest of the week."

"Is that what this is about?"

"Not exactly," he said. "Come downstairs. We need to have a family chat."

So that was the plan: one more intervention during which the unsuspecting victim could be berated and guilted by family and friends.

"And bring your guest." He tried to peer through the crack in the door. "We're all dying to meet her."

I could handle a family bullying session like in the old days, with my behavior examined, my proclivities questioned. But I was not ready to bring Pia into the circle. Her baking made for an awkward introduction; I wasn't sure how she would deal with the confused bunch still trying to get their bearings downstairs.

"Time to meet the folks!" I said cheerfully, pulling the blanket off her.

"You finally told them I was here?" she said.

"I think Marjorie and Albert have known for days," I said. "It's their style to wait and watch me. I'm a kind of lab rat to them."

"I can't wait to meet them all." She seemed glad to come out of hiding, as I was losing my hold on her.

"Here, try to look normal for everyone." I handed her a t-shirt.

I watched her, as always with delight, as she walked around the room, picking out clothes and running a comb through her hair. She could look pleasantly ordinary when she wasn't trying to goth herself up.

"Will they be okay with me staying on?" She took a breath before following me into the hallway.

"If you promise not to try to poison everyone again."

"They think I was out to kill them?"

"I wish I knew what they think."

"So they got some unintended thrills," she said. "Nothing wrong with that, is there?"

"The flan was tasty, and everyone loved it." I gave her shoulders a squeeze.

I expected a grim reception when we finally emerged. Instead the family had gathered at the dining table, with two place settings for Pia and me. Marjorie had made a batch of pancakes with pine nuts and lavender. She was passing the plates around the table when everyone stopped to look at us. The long-awaited mystery guest had finally emerged.

"Good morning," I said. "This is my friend Pia." I wanted normalcy. Sure, it might be awkward to reveal that I had harbored a girlfriend and fugitive at the ripe of age of seventeen. But I knew they would all love her and move beyond the business with the magic flan. Nobody was still sick. Nobody had gone crazy. Everybody was glad to be awake, smiling and nodding as I went through the introductions: Father, Mother, Brother Ted, Cousin Iris.

"Albert." Father smiled a toothy grin. "And Marjorie," he added, nodding toward Mother.

"Sit down, kids," she said. "There are fresh cakes coming off the griddle."

I poured coffee for us, and we sipped quietly. Everyone seemed too shy to speak, so they went back to eating. Except Iris, who was sitting next to Pia and spoke into her ear with a hushed urgency: "I hope we can be friends."

"I'm absolutely sure we will be," Pia said earnestly.

"Are you a person of faith?" Iris asked. "I sense you are."

"I have all kinds of faith," Pia said. She seemed about to enumerate when I pressed my knee against hers by way of warning her to be wary of Iris, who was apt to turn the most casual of conversations into a revival.

"I knew it," Iris said. "There is much work to be done in this family. And very little time in which to get it done."

"I'll be glad to help," Pia said with more poise than I could have mustered.

"Goody," said Iris. 'We'll talk." And she went back to her pancakes, happy that she had made a preemptive claim on Pia's spirit.

Meanwhile, oblivious to the attention focused on her, Pia ate hungrily, swirling the melting butter and ladling on more maple syrup; it was probably the first hot breakfast she'd had since the fire. I had to admire how smoothly she had gone from stowaway to guest. Meanwhile, Albert and Marjorie were all benign, unfocused smiles. They believed that certain conversations, fraught with suspicion and unease, had no place at the table.

That was not the case with Brother Ted. Ever since we'd sat down, he'd been stealing appraising glances at Pia and taunting me with smirks and raised eyebrows. I ignored him, so he focused on Pia.

"More coffee for you?" he asked, pushing the pot toward her.

"I still have coffee," she said, showing him her cup.

"Juice, milk?" he insisted.

"No, thanks." She smiled sweetly at him.

I could see his mind busily spinning in search of an opening. He scrunched his features into a semblance of deep thought, then blurted out what was probably inside everyone's head: "So, you sure do know how to make tasty desserts!"

"I'm glad you liked it."

"Loved it," he said. "Where did it come from?"

"The recipe is on the Internet."

"But you had a secret ingredient, didn't you?"

"Oh, more than one." She smiled. "But I can't tell you."

"Right, because they're secret," he exclaimed with a self-satisfied grin.

"Actually, because I forgot what all I put in the mix," she said.

"So you won't make flan again?"

"Of course I will, Ted," she said. "It will just be a different flan."

"With special ingredients?"

"For sure," Pia said seriously. "Great flan feeds the mind as well as the body."

By then Albert and Marjorie were showing some interest in Pia's promise to repeat her flan. Even if he hadn't been delighted by the added pharmaceuticals, Father seemed composed that morning; the sadness and despair of the night had been washed away by sleep.

Mother had a thoughtful look all through breakfast, as if she were trying to figure out this new domestic arrangement. If she remembered Pia from our clean-socks mission in the Stitchery, she didn't say. But both my parents were as gracious and hospitable as they could be, piling up our plates with more pancakes, puddling extra syrup, scattering a few more berries. They seemed relieved that I had a girlfriend and that my reclusive behavior of the past few weeks was not a sign of a relapse. Pia and I were basking in our new normalcy when, in the middle of the usual *hmm*s and *yummy*s of a happy breakfast, Albert leaned across the table and, raising his magnificent eyebrows, asked Pia, "So where did you come from?"

"From nowhere," Pia answered. "I just kind of appeared."

"Funny, actually." Albert nodded patiently.

Mother looked up with alarm. "Albert," she muttered. Then, explaining to Pia, "We'd like to know how you and Adam met."

I jumped in to deflect the question, afraid of what Pia was going to answer. "Oh, we met years ago. Then we lost track of each other. And now we met up again. You know, the give and take, the ebb and flow of fate."

"Did you meet at Loiseaux?" Father asked.

Iris and Ted were following the conversation as if it were a tennis match.

"Almost," Pia said.

"We were on our way to the 'Tute," I put in.

"And we took a detour," Pia added.

Albert and Marjorie exchanged a look of discovery.

"You're the girl who hijacked the van!" Albert said.

"Actually," Pia said modestly, "I was jacked *along* with the van. By your son here." I could swear that the memory of that night was as fond for Pia as for me when she turned to give me a not-so-private smile.

"And now you two have found each other again." Mother positively beamed.

"Does your family know you are here?" Father asked. "Are you expected home?"

"My house burned down while I was at school. We all left in different directions."

"They must be worried about you."

"They know I'm fine," she said. "Just not where, exactly."

"Still, parents worry," Mother insisted.

"They have problems of their own." Pia dismissed the subject with a shrug.

"We're hoping Pia can stay for a few days," I put in meekly.

Chapter Twenty-Six

I don't know that there was an official decision about Pia living with us, but she managed to fit smoothly into the household protocols— she was a ready volunteer for scouring, chopping, and dicing. Home life proved therapeutic after weeks of hiding. Pia enjoyed the attention, and she would find ways to amuse the family. One time at dinner she declared over the lasagna that half the world's cuisine was an excuse to eat melted cheese. A small competition ensued as to how many examples we could muster, with Ted offering to write down the results. From quesadillas to wontons to Welsh rarebit and finally, triumphantly, to fondue, he filled two sheets of notebook paper.

Another time she declared, after seeing how harmonious my parents were with each other, that she had figured out the secret of a happy relationship. By then Father was mumbling self-consciously while trying to hide behind the newspaper.

"You're pretty young to have such an insight," Mother teased.

"I've been watching you two," Pia said, "Especially compared to my parents, who were obviously miserable for years."

"We've taken in a spy," Father said.

"No spying needed. It's obvious what makes you two click."

"And that would be . . ." Mother coaxed her.

"Courtesy," Pia declared. "You speak to each other with attention to the niceties. You say 'please' and 'thank you,' and you're always considerate."

"Basic civility is the secret of a happy marriage?" Father shrugged, pleased with the discovery.

It was true, though I had never paused to remark on how my parents treated each other. Sometimes they did seem formal and never overly affectionate, but a brief touch or a light kiss seemed to communicate a depth of understanding and love that we all sensed was there. While they seemed to drift in different orbits, Father watching endless replays of the war or Mother out on her missions, there was an invisible thread connecting them. While Ted and I had grappled with our psyches and Iris badgered us over our unpreparedness for the End Times, Albert and Marjorie seemed to find in each other an island of sanity.

Pia celebrated her new freedom. She spent hours lounging in the den, browsing through Marjorie's library, playing Ted's CDs, snacking when she felt like it. Then, while going through the Sunday paper, she exclaimed, "Picasso is in town!"

"Who?"

"The great Pablo-man! The greatest artist of the twentieth century is here."

I'd been lying on the couch, diving into college brochures, seeing myself in a circle of multicolored students grinning and sunning on the lawn at Macalester, or squinting over a microscope at MIT, or cheering on the Tigers at Clemson, or dressed up like a soldier at West Point. So many seductive choices.

"Isn't he dead?"

"He's immortal," she said. "There's a show of his stuff at the Walker Art Center."

"Dumb to go anywhere, Pia." I tried to inject the note of caution into her fantasies. "There are men out there who want to talk with you."

"Yeah, and they're stalking the museums?"

"They're everywhere."

"Man, they let you out of the 'Tute too soon." She took a deep breath as if to process the fact that I was right about the risk of getting out in the world. "This is what we'll do," she finally said decisively. "I'll call the Walker and ask if they have a certain painting in the show. My all-time favorite Picasso. If they do, we go over there today because it's Thursday and it's free admission. We bask in the light of the masterpiece for ten minutes and dash back home."

An hour later we were in the Walker, standing before a skinny security guard too tall for the pants cuffs hovering above his ankles, who faced us with a look of profound indifference. His attitude was reassuring since heightened interest from people in uniforms made us uneasy.

"Can you direct us to the Picasso exhibit, sir?" Pia asked him.

"Galleries three and four," he said with a nod toward the stairs behind him.

Clearly Pia expected more. "What's your name?" she asked, as if she planned to lodge a complaint for his lack of enthusiasm.

"Ralph."

"Wow, short for Rafaello. A great artistic name. Art is in your DNA, Ralph. You are preordained for your profession."

He directed a look at her, then a quick glance in my direction to see if I was complicit in this exchange. I tried to convey with a slight shrug that I was simply a bystander.

"You must love your job," Pia said. "Spending your day surrounded by all this great art."

"Anything else I can do for you?" He gave Pia a blank stare designed to bring this odd conversation to its conclusion.

"I'm looking for *Girl Before a Mirror*," she said.

"I don't know her," he said, already dismissing us from his attention. "Check the ladies' room."

Pia took his answer at face value. "No, you wouldn't know her. She's Marie-Thérèse. She was Pablo's mistress back in the '30s."

I rushed to the rescue. "It's one of Picasso's paintings."

"Galleries three and four," he repeated mechanically.

"Thank you," I said, taking Pia by the arm and pulling her toward the stairs. "That is one guy who's going to remember you for the rest of his life, especially if someone shows him your picture."

"Crap," she snapped. "I was trying to amuse the man. Obviously he's bored out of his skull standing there hour after hour. What a waste of art."

I followed Pia through the galleries as she zeroed in on the painting she was searching for. At over six feet tall it was the dominant picture in the room, a double image of a woman—a girl, according to Picasso's title—standing in front of a mirror, more in confrontation than in reflection. The living face was divided into innocence and sexuality, purity and pollution coexisting, while the reflected image reconciled her conflicts with a steady gaze.

"What do you see?" I spoke softly into Pia's ear.

"The whole painting is a mirror," she said. "I see myself in it, to such depths that it scares me. It's the first time I've seen the real thing. And it just stands there, looking back at me with an unblinking eye. It's as if the great Pablo could see into every woman's soul."

"I guess I'm not seeing all that," I admitted.

"It's about being female, bonehead. Picasso understood women. You don't have a clue."

I knew better than to argue. "Let me know when you're ready to leave."

"Wait," she ordered. She had moved away from me and was standing very close to the painting, as if she were trying to see its every detail, the stroke of the brush, the cracks in the pigment, the black well of the girl's eyes. Then she turned partway toward the center of the gallery to face the skinny guard, who had followed us upstairs and was now staring at her. I moved close to Pia when she signaled as if to show me some detail in the painting. Instead she whispered that I was to go up to the guard and ask him for directions to somewhere, the gift store, the cafeteria, the restroom, anything that would turn his attention away from her.

"What are you up to?" I whispered in turn.

She turned away from the guard. "I'm trying to own this painting, and he is interfering. He has no right to stand there and ogle."

"Please stand back from the exhibit," the guard said, as if on cue.

Pia turned to him angrily. "I'm trying to analyze the brushstrokes. That's why it's here, you know, to be looked at."

"Sure," he said. "Just don't breathe on it. It will damage the pigment."

"Asshole," she muttered.

"It's his job," I muttered back.

"Tell him you have to piss. It's his job to show you where to go."

"I'd like to leave real soon, Pia. He's making me nervous. You're making me nervous."

"Go piss," she hissed.

I wasn't sure why I was supposed to distract the guard. Maybe he really was interfering with Pia's private immersion in the mysteries of *Girl Before a Mirror*, but knowing Pia, I feared there might be more to it than that. I stood between the guard and her, making him repeat his directions to the men's room. Suddenly Pia appeared at my side and, taking me by the arm, said it was time go, wasn't it? We would find the restroom on the way out.

"Now you want to leave?"

"Shut up," she said.

We found a secluded bench in the sculpture garden, and I breathed a sigh of relief. We sat staring at the bronze hare leaping over a bell. "What was that about?" I asked finally.

"I thought you had to piss," she said.

"No, that was your idea."

"The guy was all over me with his looks," she said. "What a creep."

"Tell me what you were up to back there," I insisted, having learned to be wary of Pia's dissembling.

"Nothing." She shrugged. "I just wanted to touch the canvas, put my finger on the actual paint Picasso had brushed on. Is that hard to understand?"

"So, happy now?"

"Happy," she said. "Time to go back into hiding." It was the first time we had left the house. Once she had reestablished her independence from me, she would want to venture out again.

have a treasure," Pia said once we were back in my room, the door closed. We were sitting together on the edge of the bed, and she held a neatly folded square of white tissue on her palm.

"What have you got?"

"A jewel." She unfolded the tissue carefully until I could see in the middle of the pristine white field, gleaming like a drop of blood, a red flake the size of a pinkie's fingernail.

"What is it?" I asked, hoping it was not what I thought it was.

"It's Picasso," she said. "It's a jewel."

"You scraped it off the painting?"

"No. I touched the reflection of the girl's face and the red from her skin came off on my finger. I was barely caressing her cheek, feeling the warm, rough surface of the paint, and a flake came unstuck on my finger." She made it sound like the paint had spontaneously jumped from the canvas to her hand.

"You stole part of a Picasso," I said, wavering between shock and admiration.

"I didn't steal it," she said. "It was a gift."

Chapter Twenty-Seven

One morning, when Ted did not show up for breakfast at his usual time, Mother knocked on his door a few minutes past 7:00. "Teddy, you're going to be late."

His only response was a muffled complaint that he was calling in sick.

"Can I get you something?"

"It's just a cold," he groaned. "I'm up, okay?"

"It's not a cold," Iris stated when Mother had returned to the kitchen. "I saw him come in last night."

We'd all been puttering about the kitchen getting breakfast together—toast and jam for Father, black coffee for Pia, an overripe banana for me. At that moment Ted wandered into the kitchen, dressed in the ratty terry-cloth robe he had worn for years. He looked terrible. One eye was nearly swollen shut, the other bruised to a deep purple, a puffy lip with crusted blood, a swollen nose. "Was someone calling for me?"

"Yes, Ted!" Iris gestured to him. "You heard the call. Come kneel with me so Jesus can heal you."

"I was hoping for coffee."

I pushed back from the table and offered him my seat. "Here, bro. Java coming up."

Ted's late-night forays into the fringes of the downtown bar scene, blank gray walls with steel doors, a name so opaque it screamed secrecy and anonymity, had left their mark. Inside, in the middle of a dance floor, was an octagonal enclosure of chain-link fencing where Ultimate Fighting pitted barefoot guys, with minimal gloves and no head protection beyond a teeth guard, letting loose at each other with feet and knees, heads and elbows.

He held the mug on the table to steady the tremor in his hand and looked up at us, seemingly embarrassed by all the attention.

"You look like hell, son," Father said, breaking the silence.

"Dear," Mother said, laying her fingers on Father's wrist, "tell him something he doesn't already know."

"I imagine it looks worse than it feels," Ted said thickly.

"So how do you feel?"

"Albert, the boy can hardly speak."

"Stuff hurts now," Ted said. "It didn't hurt at all when it happened." He shook his head as if in wonder.

"You got beat up pretty bad," I said.

"You should have seen the other guys." He tried a hoarse laugh but winced at a sudden stab of pain. He drank some coffee. "Actually,

I didn't even see them. It was after closing at the Spike. That's the last time I go there. I did okay with the official match and managed to beat one of last week's champs. Then his buddies decided I should be relieved of the hundred-dollar prize. I was walking out of the club feeling pleased with myself when someone slammed the back of my head so that I saw sparks. Such pretty fireworks in the night sky— mostly white but also yellow and red and orange. I remember being pushed around by the punches landing on my face and head. I knew I was being hit, but wondered why the blows felt so soft. All the time I heard these thudding sounds, as if I were underwater. I felt my legs buckle, and I sank to the ground, where I curled up with my knees against my chest and my arms around my head while they kicked and kicked until they must've gotten bored. After they stopped and I heard their footsteps running off, I felt as if I were lying on a sandy beach with the warm surf lapping at my body. Someone passing by helped me stand, and I realized I had pissed all over myself."

"My God," Mother exclaimed. "You poor boy. How on earth did you get home?"

"The guy that stopped to pull me up was driving a cab." Then, turning toward me, he said, "You could go for my car, little bro."

"Pia and I will go get it."

He finally turned to Pia as if he had not met her before. "So you're the secret girlfriend."

"You forget meeting Pia?" I asked.

"Oh, it's coming back to me." He nodded.

"A secret no more." Pia bestowed her most radiant smile on my wounded brother.

Father was the only discordant presence in this sweet moment as Mother and Pia and I clustered to comfort Ted. I think mothers are actually glad for their sons to be weird. I remember when I wore Mother's dresses, she would sometimes wear the same outfit I'd secretly tried on a few hours earlier, as if to let me know she was complicit.

Father looked at Ted with an expression of profound sadness, furrowing his brow and pressing his lips together to keep some hasty thought unspoken. "If you three will stop hovering over Ted, I'd like to get a word in," he said gruffly.

Ted looked up at Father, his beat-up face suddenly the naked proof of his weakness.

"Does this happen often?" Father asked, rubbing his head as if trying to figure out some deeper, darker question.

"I'm a thug magnet." Ted laughed through his swollen lip.

"No," Father snapped. "That's not good enough. You owe it to yourself and to all of us not to get beaten up."

"Okay," Ted murmured.

"Okay what?" Father insisted.

"I'll keep my anger at home," he said. "Can't be that difficult."

"Anger about what?" Father exclaimed.

Ted shrugged unhappily. "I'll let you know when I've figured it out."

Father rose and put on his suit jacket. His dour expression indicated that the topic had not been quite exhausted, that the discussion would continue. "Let me know what you need from us."

"It's nothing Jesus can't cure." Iris jumped at the opening.

"Please, Iris," Father insisted. "This is no time for your preaching."

"Not preaching. Praying," she said. "Oh, mighty Lord Jesus, bring your healing to bear on the soul of your servant Teddy. Listen to the pleas of his loving family."

Mother was the first to react. "You should not involve us in your deals, dear."

Iris went on, "And please cleanse this family of the sin of condonance."

Pia leaned close to me and whispered, "Is she always like this?"

Iris must've heard her. "And especially, Lord Jesus," she went on, "protect us from the alien being in our midst."

"That would be you," I whispered back.

"Gosh," Pia said. "I thought we were getting along."

"And protect the baby of the family from her influence."

"Your turn." Pia giggled in my ear.

"She wasn't always like this," I said. "Were you, Iris?" I added, loudly enough to break through her chatter.

"And please have pity on those about to be Left Behind."

Cousin Iris began disrupting the established harmony with a more strident level of zealotry. Until now her proselytizing had been a kind nagging that the Rapture was coming and she didn't want us to be left behind. But after Ted's assault she became a harridan of holiness. She refused even to be in the same room as Ted. Me she called the child pervert, Mother the facilitator of sodomy. But she reserved her special scorn for Pia, the devil worshipper, to whose presence she attributed the whole of our family's turmoil.

While Pia grew close to everyone, eager to help with the housework, sitting with Father to commiserate over the news, teasing Ted about his good looks gone black and blue and lumpy, Iris singled her out for pointed rejection. She refused to join the rest of us at the table, leaving the room as soon as Pia entered it, turning back if it appeared that the two women would cross paths in a hallway. Sometimes instead of fleeing Pia she would try to intimidate her with a glare of such profound contempt that it seemed to threaten a physical assault. At other times she would pause in the middle of a conversation to address Pia directly in some kind of mumbo jumbo, as if she had become possessed by the spirit and been commanded to deliver a message for Pia's ears alone.

"Damn, she's scary," Pia said breathlessly as she rushed into our room one night, locking the door behind her.

"Who?" I asked innocently, even though I knew whom she was talking about.

"Who? Who indeed," she shouted. "Your loving Christian cousin."

"She means well," I said. "She's trying to save all of us from being left behind when she is raised up."

Pia sat down on the bed with the meds box on her lap, idly running her fingers through the stash until she found a couple of our few remaining Zolofts. She placed the tablets on the tip of her tongue and swallowed them dry. "I don't think Iris wants me along when that big hand comes down to scoop up everyone else."

"Don't take her seriously," I said. "We all know she's nuts."

Pia shook her head, frustrated by her inability to fully describe

Iris's growing hold on her imagination. "You're not hearing me," she said.

Something in her eyes made me pause, drawing me to the edge of the bed to sit beside her. It seemed days since we had sat close to each other, the touch of my skin on hers reminding me of when we had been alone in the universe and she had been hiding beneath my wing.

"I need someone to listen," she insisted.

"What do you want to tell me?"

"I want to hurt her," she said. "She comes up behind me and whispers some hot and moist pig-Latin shit in my ear. And then she switches to real words just long enough to say, 'Jesus will send you to hell.' I can give *her* a taste of hell now, douse her in gasoline and strike a match."

"Go to sleep, Pia." I pulled her down on the bed, taking off her shoes, covering her with a blanket. "You are not going to hell. Everybody loves you."

"Man, I'm tired of being nice," she said. "I think I'm ready to take my chances with the law."

"I don't want you to go to jail," I said meekly.

"I'm not going to jail," she said. "I may have wished our home to burn down, but they can't prove I did it, can they?"

"The cops are not reasonable people, Pia."

"I'm tired of hiding." Pia was reclaiming her independence.

"Let's go for a drive. Scenery, speed, fresh air."

"Where to?"

"Anywhere. We'll have an adventure."

Part Three

Chapter Twenty-Eight

I needed Ted's car, but I did not want to invite his questions. I stepped into his room during dinner and made sure the Corolla's keys were hanging on a nail by the door. He did not go fighting that night. Sometime around 2:00 A.M., I told Pia to get dressed, that we were going out on a trip.

The anticipation of a small escapade brightened her mood to a giddy flush. She changed into jeans and my thick cable-knit sweater, which swamped her shoulders and hung below her hips. She looked beautiful. I stuffed some things into my backpack—underwear, socks, caps, the cigar box—in case we stopped somewhere. As we stole down the hall past Ted's room, I opened his door a crack and plucked his keys off the nail, closing my hand around them to silence their jingling.

We knew how to move as silently as ghosts. I grabbed our coats from the hall closet and led her by the hand to Ted's car, opened the door for her, and pushed it shut with a muffled thump.

I got behind the wheel and released the hand brake, and we coasted down the street. When we reached the corner, I switched on the ignition, picking up speed. The deserted street loomed ahead, drawing us toward the darkness beyond the reach of the headlights. When I stepped on the gas we were off with a screech of tires, and I felt as liberated as I ever had in my life. Pia exploded with a hoot and a surge of pent-up laughter. I'm not sure at what point in our escape I decided I would not return Ted's car anytime soon. For now I wanted to keep going and stop wherever the dawn found us. We had a good full day before Ted decided to report the car, and his brother, as missing. Winter was in full chill under a clear, starry sky.

I could only imagine Pia's delight in being free after all those days in hiding. Because our time together in the house had grown increasingly restless, I set out to re-create the excitement of our first meeting, regaining the sensation that only we two existed, sufficient unto ourselves like the night we'd jacked the 'Tute van and hidden under a blanket of snow.

The Corolla's full tank took us all the way to Lake Superior. We hit Duluth around 6:00 A.M. and kept going to Black Bear Inlet, a scruffy North Shore strip with a budget motel, a store with a gas pump, and a piece of rocky beach. We got pancakes at the café, my default food in times of stress. We were practically alone, out of sight behind the high back of a corner booth. I thought that seeing the sun rising over Lake Superior would fire Pia up.

She had grown somewhat sullen once we'd passed Duluth. She'd been in my care for almost a month, and nobody knew where she was. It wasn't that I expected to be thanked at every opportunity for keeping her out of the clutches of the arson investigation, but I was discovering a new side of her, a tendency to go from euphoria and unbridled passion to a chill of the mind and heart. Meds helped, but finding the right combination was a matter of luck. Basically she settled into a glum silence until some opportune event or pill shook her out of it. Earlier in the night it had been that first surge of power as the car had picked up speed along the northbound highway. Sitting across from me in the café, she chattered on and on about how the open road was an adventure and how I was her guide into the wilderness, but then she grew quiet and fell asleep, slumping into the booth against the wall.

In the end I finished her pancakes, drank her coffee, and had to coax her back to the car. We drove north on 61 a couple more hours and swung into a rest stop past Grand Marais.

"So where to now?" she finally said. We were belted in, with a full tank, and at the turn of the ignition key the engine sparked up with a reassuring hum. I had no idea where to go but automatically drove out of the rest area and continued north.

"Anyplace shy of Canada. We can't be on the road when word gets out that we are car thieves."

"Sure." She nodded, as if reluctant to admit I was making good sense. "But *where?*"

I was fumbling in my head to come up with something when I spotted a weathered wooden sign dangling from a pole well off the edge of the road: "Phil and Flo's Lakeshore Cabins."

"Phil and Flo's," I said, brimming with resolve, as if I had known all along that that was where we were headed. I turned onto a gravel road behind a thick stand of poplars and drove toward the shore.

I slowed down by a sturdy log building identifying itself as "Phil's Office." I wondered if Pia had noticed the sign by the road announcing that the cabins were closed for the season because Phil and Flo were warming their bones in Florida. She was about to get her adventure. Across a clearing bordered by evergreens, a couple of log cabins were visible among the trees. I drove the Corolla onto a rutted path and parked between a cabin and the surrounding woods so that the car was concealed. Pia was following our progress, but she was not yet asking any questions. It was hard enough to act as if I knew where I was going without having to spin my improvisation as it went along.

"Wait here," I said, more softly than I needed to considering we were quite alone. "I'll find the key." I went around to the cabin's door. Locked. I tried raising the window. Shut. I circled the hut, determined to avoid Pia's questions until I found a way inside. My feet crunched the layer of frost as I tried to peer into the cabin through the opaque windows; I could make out some simple furnishings, a floor lamp, a big chair, a galley kitchen. I went back to the front door and searched under the welcome mat, along the sill, finally under an upside-down flower pot. Key! The lock turned with a smooth unbolting.

In the gloom I stepped into a large room with an iron-frame bed at one end beneath a window. I drew the curtain and could see the shore about a hundred feet away, the big lake nicely framed by gingham curtains and stretching east to the horizon. There was a galley stove with three burners, a built-in fridge, a kettle. In the center of the room, a La-Z-Boy recliner, a card table with two chairs. No phone, TV, radio, computer.

Pia followed, leaning against me with a sudden shiver from the deepening chill. I tried turning on a floor lamp and the kitchen faucet without success. After flicking a couple of switches I noticed the circuit breaker to one side of the door. I pushed the lever and lights went on, a water pump hummed, baseboard heating started to glow.

A bathroom protruded from the back wall of the cabin, containing a shower and a sink. Through a small vent in the shower stall I could see an outhouse about twenty feet down a path and surrounded by trees. Not convenient but colorful. To one side of the bathroom was a closet with towels, sheets, and blankets. I turned on the water, and the icy stream numbed my hands.

We searched drawers, cabinets, and the fridge, marveling at the bounty—coffee, dehydrated soups, cans of beans, powdered milk, noodles, jars of tomato sauce, jalapeños, and olives, one open bottle of vodka and another half full of peach schnapps, generously left behind by previous guests.

A wooden box beside the bed served as an end table and contained a variety of tools, a flashlight, an ice pick, a couple of extension cords, light bulbs and fuses, jumper cables, a hammer, duct tape. All we needed to hunker down for a spell. Home! I couldn't believe our good luck.

"We might stay here forever," Pia said without much enthusiasm.

"Yes," I agreed cheerfully. Maybe through winter.

The energy from the pancakes at breakfast had been long exhausted, but ramen noodles and schnapps from the pantry made a comforting meal. We rubbed our teeth clean with baking soda and took a steamy shower together, soaping ourselves up with Dawn dish detergent, which was the only soap we found, emerging at last all pink-skinned and smelling of lemons.

We made up the bed, stretching the clean sheets, fragrant with the smells of laundry soap and pine boards. It was early, but the deepening evening outside quieted us. We lay stretched out side by side, and the initial silence of the place was enriched by the murmur of the surf lapping the rocky beach.

We made love for the first time in days, no longer gripped by the urgency of our initial embraces but moving together with a sweet melting into each other, an unhurried exploration of our bodies. We were artists playing unheard melodies on our skin, explorers probing where our tongues and fingers had not yet gone. In the end we made noise. We laughed and groaned and invoked God and all his mercies for the gift of our orgasms. Life was perfect.

Chapter Twenty-Nine

ia was already up when I awoke the next morning, sitting by the window, gazing out at the lake, coffee in a mug with a design of ducks in flight. She ignored me, studying the depths of the cup as if reading an oracle. I made a big deal out of stretching and yawning to get her attention, finally said a cheery good-morning and got barely a nod in response. I put on my jeans and shoes, draped a blanket over my shoulders, and headed to the outhouse. There was a commitment to trudging across the frozen ground for a bowel movement. Not an easy task with my skin bare to the frigid air of the dark shed. In the cold, bodily functions slow down, penis shrinks, asshole puckers. By the time I got back to the cabin, warming my hands happily in the glow of electric heat, Pia was curled up in the bed and had pulled the covers over her head.

"Hey," I said, pulling at her toes under the blanket, "I know you're under there."

"You don't know shit," came her muffled reply.

Sometime before dawn it must have occurred to her that she was once again captive, helpless under my care. We had come this far, and there was suddenly nowhere else to go.

"You're right," I said. "All I know is that I want you to feel safe."

"Then do something about the rat."

It took me a moment to figure out what she was talking about. Even in deep winter an occasional squirrel was still making last-minute forays. One had watched us curiously as we had walked to the cabin, stopping suddenly in the midst of its sprints to observe us before resuming its frantic hunt for the season's hoard.

"They're squirrels," I said.

"Please," she groaned, as if I were too stupid to converse sensibly. "I know what squirrels look like. They're disgusting, but it's the rat inside the cabin I'm worried about. Do you know how many diseases you could catch from its bite?"

"The black death?"

"Be funny, if that's how you want to deal with my concerns." She turned away from me. That simple gesture was a needle into my heart. I had to be in her favor all the time. If there was a rat inside the cabin, I would find it and banish it. The search was on. I opened the cabin door and made a show of looking under the bed (a great vantage point for haunting Pia's sleep), under the sink (dark and dank), behind the big La-Z-Boy (easy in and out), inside the shower stall (they love warm, wet places). I stabbed the broom into corners, ready to sweep the beast out.

"Close the fucking door," Pia said.

"It needs a way to escape," I explained, sounding as cool and methodical as if dealing with some engineering project. Rodent eradication was now one of my talents.

"It's outside," she snapped.

"Why are you so worried, then?"

"It was inside." She sighed heavily. "Then it left when you went to piss. Now you're inviting the thing back in."

I was suddenly slow and clumsy. I had been rushing around the cabin with the broom and was suddenly impressed by the futility of my efforts to please Pia when she was in no mood to be pleased. I leaned the broom against a wall and closed the door.

"It's nice out, Pia," I said. "You can get out of bed if the rat is outside. We can have lunch, walk to the lake, make a plan."

"What kind of plan?"

"We don't want to hunker down here forever, do we?"

"That's the story of our life, isn't it? Hunkering down in cars and rooms and cabins."

"No, we can take a walk."

"We can't," she said. "The rat's outside."

I turned in the direction she was pointing. On the other side of the small window above the sink, a squirrel with milky white fur and pink eyes sat on the ledge and peered inside the cabin.

"It's a squirrel," I said.

"It's white."

"An albino squirrel," I repeated. "Moby Dick."

She exploded with laughter, which sounded to me like a burst of relief. I grinned along with her, nodding my head in emphatic approval. Her laughter prolonged itself beyond the point where it seemed to be an expression of mirth. Its initial spontaneity was replaced by a harsh *ha ha ha* that went on and on, even as I stopped showing my approval and watched her with growing anxiety. I placed my hand on her shoulder to still the jerking in her body, but she angrily shook it off and continued with her mockery of a laugh.

I waited until she paused to breathe. "Pia. Stop!"

"It's a white rat," she screamed. "A fucking mutant rat." Then, finally, she stopped laughing. She gulped a couple of deep breaths, and for a moment I was confident that she would calm herself down. But she was only building her strength; she resumed her laughter in a listless, rhythmic panting. She seemed oblivious of me, watching the window where the white squirrel had appeared. There was nothing there, just a trail through the woods leading to the lake lapping the beach. The sky had clouded over and I had lost track of the time. It could've been late morning or afternoon; the slate-gray canopy above us hid the sun. In any case, I was feeling hungry, remembering that the previous night we had eaten mainly ramen noodles.

I opened two cans of cream-of-tomato soup, comfort food from days of childhood. I watched over a saucepan while the soup heated, thinking that if I could feed Pia, she might stop her goofy sham of a laugh. I set two places at the card table with two white-and-blue bowls, spoons, salt and pepper shakers, paper towels folded into triangles. I poured glasses of water and placed three pills—a white long one, a heart-shaped pink one, and a tiny yellow one—by her plate. One I knew had to be Zoloft. I didn't know what the other two were anymore, but together I hoped they would improve her mood.

I started eating by myself, making happy slurping sounds with every spoonful to get her to come to the table. She watched, no longer laughing, as I finished my bowl. Hers, meanwhile, had grown cold. I was not prepared to assume this odd parental role as caregiver to my unpredictable guest. She was usually so in control except when she unexpectedly slipped into an erratic, childish space. Every day it was something new, and I was not smart or patient or loving enough to handle her gyrations from normalcy to eccentricity and back. Now, as she watched me eat, I felt her ready to change gears again.

"Your soup is getting cold," I said.

"How sweet," she sighed. "You made lunch."

"Yes," I said as she sat at the table. "And be sure to take your vitamins."

"Oh, you're such a mommy," she said, leaning over to kiss me on the cheek. She took the pills and examined them on the palm of her hand, then, as if having reached a considered decision, gulped them down with water. "And you shooed the rat away," she added.

I would take whatever credit she granted me. I glanced at the window and was relieved that Moby Dick was still gone. Pia and I had hit some odd moments in our brief time together, and so far she had always regained her balance. There had been the day of the fires and the day of the ice-cream tantrum and the day of the family poisoning, and she'd always bounced back. I waited as she tasted the soup.

"I'm sorry I was such a baby," she said, smiling at me between sips. When she had finished it, she settled back in the chair, her face softening into a look of wan surrender. She went back to bed, and I waited for the pills to take hold and lull her to sleep. Meanwhile, I washed the dishes, feeling very much in control again, growing comfortable with our takeover of the cabin, confident that the search for Ted's car wouldn't lead to us anytime soon.

As Pia's breath settled into the rhythms of sleep, I made a mental note of the three pills, which in combination seemed to have sent her into a snooze. I had turned back to wiping the counter and drying dishes when I noticed that the white squirrel was standing on the window ledge, staring at me with its bloodshot gaze. I moved to the center of the room, and its stare stayed with me with a mixture of curiosity and amusement. I clutched the broom with both hands and stepped outside, sidling against the wall, thinking I must be out of its range. I circled the cabin, stepping carefully to mute the crunching of my feet on the hard snow. I wanted to get in one good whack, and even though I harbored little hope of actually incapacitating the thing, I figured if I swept it away with sufficient energy I would keep it from returning to its perch.

By the time I got to the kitchen window, Moby Dick was gone from the ledge. I should've known, of course, that the beast had guessed my intentions. I made a wide sweep of the surrounding forest, but I was no outdoorsman. The woods were something our family drove past on the occasional Sunday, the brilliant fall colors enlivening our spirits, the scents of winter warming our hearts, all the while keeping safely on the road. And now here I was, trying to hunt a squirrel with a broom, outsmarted before I was able to swing at shifting shadows and white streaks of flying fur.

Chapter Thirty

The sun had set early behind the treetops; evening's golden light had been a brief glimmer, and the sky was now darkening into a leaden gloom. I was still under the illusion that I was stalking my prey and would return a hero, Moby Dick hanging by its tail from my belt. Once off the path, progress in the snowy woods was a trudging, erratic thing, and I was soon disoriented. I had a vague idea of the cabin being somewhere behind me by the lakeshore. At night the woods teemed with the cracks and snaps of the frozen branches and the occasional squawks of the last remaining fowl in the midst of their southern migration, a kind of anxious anticipation of the deepening freeze. I realized with a shiver that my jeans and corduroy shirt were too thin.

My anxiety vanished at the sight of the main office at the entrance to the cabin grounds. It was a large two-story cabin in the same style as the one that sheltered us. I circled the building, running my fingers along the walls, feeling the blistered paint and dull, flat-tened nailheads, waiting for the sensation that would signal a way in. I tried the back door and side windows; I found one that rattled loose in its track.

It took a moment to pull off the storm window, push up the inner pane, wriggle inside, and land halfway up a staircase. There was a heavy, closed-in feeling throughout the house. The hallway felt dank and chilly. The walls, which at one time had glowed with earthy hues of peach mousse and cocoa silk, as the paint-can labels had probably put it, appeared dull and dusty. I climbed the stairs to the second story, where three doors faced an open sitting area.

I wandered through the bare rooms and entered a bedroom, where a flick of the switch lit up the wallpaper's pink and yellow flowers. Bedspreads and curtains extended the flower motif. Here and there the paper pattern was broken by bright yellow honeybees hovering above the flowers. Tiny holes in the wall marked where the child's pictures must have hung.

There was a line of scuff marks along the bottom edge of the door, flaking woodwork around the frame, and a key still in place. A couple of feet above the floor, I saw small handprints in faded maroon, the tiny palms and fingers pressed against the wallpaper, then extending into parallel streaks that ended abruptly at the edge of the door. The room looked un-lived-in, with toys and girl's clothes put away in the closet and in a wooden box. The only thing out of place was a plush bunny, neatly decapitated. The head, lying in a corner several feet away from its body, stared at me with black button eyes and a toothy grin. I picked it up by an ear and closed the door behind me.

B ack downstairs I sat at the cluttered manager's desk, held the phone, and listened to the solid absence of a dial tone. Service had been disconnected, and the computer would be dismally offline. The TV showed a grainy reception. I grabbed a small clock radio from the desk. In the hallway winter coats hung near the door; canned stews, chili, and soups were crammed into the pantry shelves; an assortment of liquor bottles glimmered invitingly in a closet. The medicine cabinets revealed an assortment of orange plastic bottles of mysterious prescription meds. I filled my pockets, intending to make an inventory later.

I hadn't planned for a long stay. I grabbed a backpack that sat next to the coats and filled it with sweaters and jeans and thick rag-wool socks from one of the bedroom closets, then took a couple of parkas from the mudroom hooks. I took a polished walking stick from a collection by the door and on impulse impaled the plush rabbit head on the end, from where it gazed out with a blank totemic look. As I marched to our sweet cabin, swinging the walking stick like a trophy, I was cheered by the lights glowing through the windows. Pia had awakened from her sedation, and I envisioned a happy reception. I felt securely at home already, especially with access to the main house, whose supply of warm clothes, food, and booze could sustain us through winter.

My expectations of a triumphant entrance were deflated by the locked door. I tried turning and jerking the doorknob, but it was clear that Pia had decided, for reasons that made sense only in her stormy brain, to shut me out. I felt exhausted. The trudge through the woods in the cold, preceded by the momentary panic at being lost, had numbed me. There had been something disturbing in my creeping around the empty house, even as I was cheered by all the stuff we could use. The child's room had reeked of lingering violence, the sensation that her life had grown anxious and unhappy. I needed Pia to welcome me and applaud my heroic hunt of the dreaded white squirrel, not to lock me out.

"Pia, let me in," I coaxed, rapping on the door. "I bear gifts and have adventures to relate."

She finally pulled the door open, acknowledging my presence with barely a glance. I walked in, awkwardly wielding my scepter. Pia turned away from me and plopped herself down on the big La-Z-Boy, where she sat gazing at the window on the opposite wall. I stood beside the chair, still holding the makeshift staff while we stared at our silent reflections in the window.

"Why didn't you tell me you were going?" she finally asked.

"I didn't want to wake you."

"I don't want that combination of meds again," she said. "My eyes itch. My head's shrinking. My mouth feels hairy."

I rushed to change her mood. "Hail the conquering hero!" I exclaimed, stepping in front of her and holding out the trophy.

"What the hell is that?"

I performed a bow. "I bring you the head of the white rat. We are free of the beast."

She seemed faintly amused. I felt lucky to be able to swing the polarity some degrees toward balance.

"Take it," I said, presenting the staff.

"It belongs to a plush toy!"

"A sacrificial bunny," I corrected. "A surrogate for the white rat that was haunting us. The white rabbit gave its head for the rat. The bunny dies, the rat vanishes. A classic sympathetic-magic tradeoff. The holy head of goodness vanquishes the evil creature." I felt like a priest delivering the sacrament to the goddess. Without planning it, I had set in motion the ancient alchemy of guilt and expiation. "The bunny is dead. The bunny has risen. You know, Easter!"

"What a bonehead." There was a hint that things might be returning to normal.

"Here," I said, handing her the stick. "Receive your scepter."

She played along, as I knew she would. For the moment she rose back to her queenly dimension, shades of Kali and Nefertiti and Tonantzin, the qualities that I had first imagined in her. There was no questioning her authority; if she wanted the white rat hunted down, then that was what I would do. No matter that there was no white rat in the first place. I sat at her feet and gazed up at her. I had made Pia my goddess, and as long as she was happy in that position, she was free to rule our little castle. Only when she forgot herself and became a tangle of fears and furies would I maintain control.

"Stop staring at me like that," she said.

"I adore you," I said.

She didn't call me a bonehead. Or disagree. Or reject me. We both knew we could be very happy if she would give in to my love.

"I guess I can't do anything about that." She let out a long sigh.

"You can let yourself be loved."

"Okay," she said. "Now what?"

"What do you mean, now what?"

"Yes. Does it mean we are going to be married and be together all our lives, that you will grow up to be my little hubby and I will be your wifey?"

"You make me sound stupid."

"Tell me, then, what does it mean to be loved by you?"

"It means I will do anything to make you happy."

"That's crap. Unless you think owning me will make me happy."

"I want you to be with me because it's what's best for you," I argued weakly.

"And if leaving will make me happy?"

"But you can't go yet," I said. "You have to stay out of sight because of the investigation."

"I'm in prison in order to keep from going to prison?"

"You should consider being with me a space of your own. A place you rule."

"And my realm is this hole?"

"You can will it into anything you want. It's your pleasure dome, your shelter, your island of sanity."

"It's a shack," she said. "And I'm not your goddess."

"You don't know what you are."

"And you're going to tell me?"

"Maybe you're not there yet. But you are rising into goddess-hood. Once you claim your natural power, you'll be free no matter where you are. Like Hamlet said, 'Assume a virtue if you have it not.' In the play lies the truth. You're an apprentice deity."

"And what are you?"

What could I say to her? I was her lover, her devotee, her pal. I was also her creator. Would God exist if humankind had not invented Him? Someone decided that God created the world in seven days, and we have been creating Him ever since. Was Jesus a geek with a girly face and limpid blue eyes? After two thousand years of artistic consensus, I would recognize him if he appeared on my doorstep. In any case he would take on the look that was expected of him. As I watched Pia sitting in the La-Z-Boy, the ceremonial rabbit-head staff in hand, I realized she would be the perfect deity of the North Shore of Lake Superior, a mix of the native and the Valkyrian, if she would only place her head just so, to the left, so that she might gaze at me from a properly aloof angle, with contempt and indulgence, and, yes, with affection, granting me the specialness of the favored disciple. I waited for the slight motion of her head, the look that singled me out for her mockery.

"I'm your bonehead," I said.

And then it happened. She beamed me a quizzical smile, and, as if she hadn't quite understood what I'd said, she tilted her head to the right, just so, with that special angle that drew a line from her ear across her breast to her heart.

"Hold it," I blurted.

"Hold what?"

"Your head," I snapped. "Put it back to where it was, tilted to the right."

She sighed and let her head flop lifelessly onto her shoulder. I rose from the ground and stood behind the chair so that I could hold her head between my hands and pull it up and to the side to its proper angle. It was heavy and unwieldy in my hands.

"Just keep your head tilted like that," I said. "Don't move." I walked around the chair and stood in front of Pia, inspecting her pose as a photographer might. I reached toward her and placed my finger delicately under her chin to further adjust the angle. She rolled her eyes; it was the goddess's right to mock me.

I stepped back and sat on my heels. Pia looked perfect. One hand held the rabbit head at her side, the other lay on the armrest in a regal pose, ready to lift the palm in blessing or flick the fingers in dismissal. I shut my eyes so as not to embarrass her with my adoring gaze, yet her image remained, a purple silhouette pulsing to the thump of my heart. It had grown quiet inside the cabin; even the woods outside, once darkness had fallen, sank into a thick silence. At first I could hear only my own breathing, a silken thread warming the edges of my nostrils, and then Pia's breath falling heavily in a series of sighs, our two streams merging into a shared rhythm, released and inhaled, creating a kind of completeness, an equilibrium of forces, male and female, yin and yang, goddess and devotee.

Pia's breath grew rhythmical, a labored murmur at the back of her throat. I opened my eyes and saw that she had slumped down, the staff leaning on her arm, her head no longer tilted at the provocative angle I had so carefully sought. My goddess had fallen asleep. I had been breathing in the force of her consciousness, and now she had gone unconscious on me.

I turned on the lights, nudged the thermostat, and waited for the heater to warm the cabin. The kettle was on the stove, and when the water boiled I let its whistle shriek until Pia was startled awake.

"Jesus," she exclaimed. "What was that about?"

"You fell asleep on me." I turned off the burner.

"Well, excuse me."

"I didn't mean that you don't have a right to fall asleep." I tried to soften my tone. "I felt abandoned is all."

"Well, I'm awake now," she said with a shiver.

I took a blanket from the bed and laid it on her lap. She looked up at me curiously but accepted the wrap with a nod, pulling it close around her.

"Some tea would be nice," she said. "Is there any of the cinnamon clove we had this morning?"

"Yes," I said and stood expectantly.

"Could we have some?" she said.

"Tell me to make you some tea."

"I did already." She shook her head in confusion.

"No," I said. "You asked. The goddess does not suggest, hint, or request."

"I'm fucking bored, Adam," she said. "But it would be nice to have some tea."

I waited. Of course I couldn't actually put the words in her mouth. But the words were important. The tone was crucial. The quality of her gaze, the angle of her head, the position of her hand. If she could not read my mind, I could spell it out, guide her through the details, take her hands and head and position them just right. But

that would not further the need I had for Pia to assume her authority. So I stood there as if I hadn't heard her and was still waiting for
her to tell me what she wanted.

"Make . . . tea," she said.

And there it was, the edge in her voice, terse like the snap of a
finger, that sent me scurrying to the pantry for the tea boxes and to
the cabinet for the mugs. My heart was beating like crazy, for in that
brief moment I had heard the true voice of the goddess. I poured the
hot water into a mug with a snowflake design, then added a shot of
schnapps.

I presented her with the cup and a couple of pills for her to pop;
she had grown to trust my offerings. She sipped tea and swallowed
pills while I sat back on my heels in front of her and waited for the
magic of tea, booze, and pharma to work though her system. I took
her feet and rested them on my thigh, massaging one through the
thick rag-wool sock. I kneaded my thumbs into the fleshy pad just
behind the toes, dug into the sole with my knuckles, paying attention to her breath, which, as she relaxed with the toddy, lengthened
into sighs of contentment. At that moment I was as happy as I had
ever been with Pia, knowing I could somehow enable her to rise to
her true stature by giving her a taste of her power. I didn't want to
admit that she was not by temperament a true goddess, that I would
have to bring her along slowly, somehow draw out of her complex
moods a kind of easy, confident authority. The drugs were a mixed
blessing. They toned down her psychic flare-ups, but I didn't much
like her usual feistiness being replaced by a glum passivity, her wit
reduced to dull shrugs. I resisted the urge to kiss her feet, to pull off

her socks and take her toes into my mouth, to nuzzle my way up between her thighs and worship her center. It would not do to scare her off. I wanted her to discover the possibilities of my love by herself, to feel the rush of my adoration. There was no hurry. We had all winter as long as we remained undiscovered inside the cabin. With the lights on, I was afraid the place was a beacon in the middle of the dark woods.

Chapter Thirty-One

lowered Pia's feet to the floor and walked around the room, pulling the drapes shut and turning off most of the lights. Then I stepped out of the cabin and got into the car. I was gratified by the sudden rumble of the engine in the quiet night as I pulled out of the driveway and circled our cabin, lurching over the uneven ground, sliding to a stop in a small clearing among the pines. In the morning I would lay branches over the car's roof and hood. They would provide sufficient camouflage until it snowed again, and then the whole thing would be blanketed out of sight.

The moon cast a cool glow through the trees, and their shadows made a lacy pattern on the cabin walls. I marveled at the shimmering texture of the Milky Way, so resplendent that I felt I had never really seen the sky before. The bracing clean air, the starry night, the presence of Pia inside the cabin blended into a sense of utter well-being.

"Where were you?" Pia complained softly as soon as I stepped inside. In the gloom I located her dim figure standing by the bed and embraced her. She was trembling.

"I had to do a couple of things to protect us."

"From what?"

"From being found," I said patiently. I had grown used to Pia pretending to forget that we were hiding, trespassing on private property, that we had stolen Ted's car, that she was suspected of arson. The combinations of meds, including Haldol and Serenace for her mood spikes, Ritalin to help her focus, and a nice antidepressant combo of Zoloft and Prozac for good measure, fogged her awareness in a chemical mist. I had a couple of others in reserve—Klonopin for sleep and the anticonvulsant Lamictal. I saved them all for Pia.

As for me, the pills had perhaps been too effective back at the 'Tute. Give me Prozac and I would become emotionally counterfeit. Phony cheer combined with torpid equanimity, leavened by gushes of sentimental affection toward strangers, family, the whole fucking world. I would become stupidly optimistic about everything—my own psyche, the state of the planet, my plans for Harvard or Stanford when I left the 'Tute. I could do anything: get a couple of PhDs, become a brain surgeon, master the guitar and join a band, write a screenplay and direct the movie, marry Miss Entropia. I cheated on the pills, made up new symptoms so I could accumulate greater variety. I even swiped paper cups of cocktails from the nurses' trays. This was my capital at the 'Tute. I traded with certain clients, collecting the pills they had secreted without swallowing. I could identify most of my inventory except the pink triangles and violet disks and the capsules striped black and yellow like plump bum-blebees.

"Yes, I remember now," she said after a moment's hesitation. "I'm supposed to be an arsonist."

"Right."

"Except that I was in school at the time. No point setting the fire if I couldn't watch it. Right?"

"Ever try to explain anything to cops?"

"I was in English class," she insisted.

"They're going to have to blame somebody, if not you." I added, "Maybe your father. He's the one who will cash in on the insurance."

"Poor Dad." She shrugged as if to say his situation was beyond hope.

We had that in common, Pia and I, intrigued by the vulnerabilities of our parents. In the years since I had left for the 'Tute, I had grown to think of Albert and Marjorie as fuzzy-headed romantics, haplessly in love, firm believers in the rightness of their destiny. From their perspective Cousin Iris was not obsessed with the rapture fantasies of Pastor Bob and his menagerie of fundies; Brother Ted was not headed for more beatings; I had not ingeniously become a kidnapper. Our aberrations were bumps on the road to normal.

"How parents survive in today's world," I said, "is one of the great mysteries of our time. They are like children."

"I don't worry about Mom," Pia said. "She has always found a way to get others to take care of her. First my grandparents, until they blew all their money and died. Then Dad, until he lost his. Now she has run off to Elysium, Texas."

"I thought you had to be Greek and dead to go to Elysium."

"No, she's living with some cowboy."

Of course I knew that, and more than Pia suspected. I made a note to find an Internet connection and e-mail Mrs. Cowboy that Pia was fine and happy and staying out of trouble.

"Dad is another story."

I didn't want to tell her that I had met her father when he'd been sleeping in his van and spending his days at the mall food court. He looked okay until you smelled his socks. Knowing all this about Pia gave me a sense of power. Not power for its own sake but the power to create a goddess. She would become Kali without realizing that I, the unmoved mover, had set her divine nature in motion.

"I get my crazy genes from him," she said casually, as if describing his blond hair or plump earlobes. "From the time I was a girl I could recognize myself in his eyes. I got a kick seeing which of us had the louder tantrums. I was four and he was thirty-four. I would usually start it in a store because I wanted the cereal box with Count Chocula. Father would explain that it was garbage food that would rot my teeth. I would be perched on the grocery cart, and he would lean his head close to me, his face just inches from mine, and go through a measured analysis of the evils of sugar and its devastation on young bodies. Did I care?"

"Let me guess."

"He would be smiling all the time, a tight grin that he would occasionally flash at shoppers pausing in the aisle to catch the developing drama. 'Now you see, little girl?' He'd emphasize 'little' and 'girl' as if being young and female were problems. 'The amino acids in Tony the Tiger eat at the enamel on your teeth and worm their way inside, rotting the hell out of them, so they fall out and you go around like a toothless hag by the time you're six.' Then he'd cover his teeth with his lips and go *mhmhmhm* at me. This was supposed to be amusing, and the hope was that I would forget about the box and laugh at his performance."

"So you screamed."

"Let me show you." Pia tilted her head back, took a breath, and let out a scream that might have been heard all the way to the road. It was an unworldly shriek, full of anger and anguish, that she sustained for half a minute, its trill unwavering, a pure, piercing note.

"I think I get it," I said when she paused to breathe.

"It was louder when I was a kid. Dad could tell when I was cranking up to deliver the Call of the Banshee, as he called it. I would be sitting in the cart, stewing in my frustration, face turning red, lower lip trembling. He would smile wider, murmuring that I was his little girl, his treasure, his darling child. Offering, finally, to buy sugary cereal, holding it out to me like a peace offering. It was too late. I would slap the box from his hand, send it clumping to the aisle, and unleash the Banshee."

By that time Pia and I had slipped under the covers, facing each other, so that as we spoke our breath caressed our faces, our voices barely above a whisper. Life had never seemed more harmonious to me. I welcomed the surrender to the moment brought on by the pills, oh, sacramental pills, all glory to Pfizer and Warner-Lambert and Glaxo, the holy trinity of pharma-fun.

"I'm sleepy. I'll go on later."

"Now," I pleaded. "You were screaming in the grocery store . . ."

"It's my earliest memory. Out of the dark I hear my cry, and I see my father's eyes glinting with fury. He shakes me by the shoulders, making my head bob from side to side, all the time shouting at me to *Shut the fuck up*. I remember going limp as a doll, and then, as people in the store rushed to us, a woman's strong hands pulled me from Father's grip and nestled me against her bosom. By then I had grown quiet, my anger exhausted, Count Chocula forgotten."

"Your father calmed down eventually?"

"The cops took him away. I was put in the manager's office with boxes of Cocoa Puffs and Froot Loops, which I ate one piece at a time. They kept me happy until my mother showed up. She didn't like being inconvenienced, had most likely been on one of her dates. She couldn't stop bitching about what an ape my dad was, how he couldn't be trusted to do a simple grocery trip with the baby. That started me bawling all over again."

"So the furies run in the family."

"Shut up."

"Good night."

Night was an edgy time for us. Perhaps because we had snoozed through the day, sleep did not come readily, and we would both lie flat on our backs, our eyes shut to the bright moonlight pouring in through the window. The room would not darken completely until the moon had traveled to the upper reaches of the sky. As the night grew colder, the woods would grow still, without a whisper of traffic from the distant road. Even the murmur from the lake faded to silence as the tide receded. With the deep cold in the air, the creatures outside burrowed into the forest, and the silence lay like a blanket on our minds. Then the walls and roof of the cabin came alive with sudden creaks and snaps, and in the middle of this utter stillness the occasional crack in the wall joints would ring like a pistol shot. These moments went on indefinitely, the silence broken by smaller sounds, picked out of the darkness by our fears and imaginings. The noises signaled an intruder testing the door locks and window jamb, perhaps some vagrant seeking shelter from the cold or a hostile neighbor who had spotted our presence.

"Somebody's out there," Pia whispered one night, her voice tight with fear. It was 2:00 A.M., according to my glowing Timex, the perfect hour for mayhem. I wondered how long she had been awake beside me, conjuring up the same images that haunted me.

"Houses are noisy when it gets cold at night."

"Well, go see."

"There's nothing out there," I insisted.

"You're afraid," she whispered.

"There's nothing to be afraid of."

"Then why aren't you checking that there's nobody out there?" she said.

"Because it's freezing out there."

"Christ, I'll go." She kicked off the bedcovers and walked resolutely to the door. A blast of cold air streamed around her and rushed into the cabin. I imagined her trying to see into the dark night until she was seized by a series of shivers. I could see her pushing hard

271

against the door, her long legs planted firmly at an angle to provide the leverage to shove it shut.

"I couldn't see a thing out there." She climbed back inside the covers.

"I would have gone, you know," I said as she sought my body for warmth.

"Next time I'll let you," she said. "If you're really, really up to it."

Clearly she had seen through me. I was a coward with a fervid imagination, a troublesome pair of qualities. I had visions of our secluded hideaway being invaded by psychos. I saw the two of us raped, tortured, killed, filleted, and eaten. All in great detail, the chafing of ropes and duct tape, colors rich in the reds of blood, the whites of proud flesh and bone, and the stink of sweat and semen.

Chapter Thirty-Two

We settled into a sodden domesticity, sleeping until the winter sun blazed through the window out of a clear blue sky. I got up first, stepping into my cold jeans and making my way to the outhouse, turning my head often to keep the cabin in sight, afraid that Pia might decide to go off on her own. Sometimes I dispensed with the latrine and pissed against the back wall, a territorial mark to keep bears and wolves at bay.

Eventually, when Pia stirred from the warm bed, I accompanied her to the outhouse, all the time denying that I was her jailer. I was here for her protection, I insisted.

"Protect me from what?"

"Anything. Wildlife."

"I would like some privacy." She stopped on the path until I walked a few yards away. Usually she would let out a shriek as soon as she sat on the frigid board. On such moments was our intimacy built.

I made tea and we crawled back into bed with our mugs. As our topics for conversation wore out, the mornings became increasingly quiet, and I waited for some comment from her on the weather or our food supply or a complaint about our seclusion. Depending on Pia's mood in the morning, I would come up with a med cocktail for her to swallow with her tea. "Thank you, Dr. Bonehead," she'd say.

We had sex under the covers still warm from the night unless a bad combo sent Pia into a torpid indifference to my efforts. Whether we fucked or not, we slept for another hour or so. Eating was postponed in order to manage with one meal a day. Later we played games—Scrabble, hearts, rock-scissors-paper, thumb wrestling, slappy hands—anything to help us shake off the sloth. I tried to coax her into playing goddess from the big chair, even if her heart was not in it. She would tilt her head just so, and lift her hand the way I liked her to, and cross her legs and dangle her toes and suffer me to rub her feet. But the process bored her, and she complained that it made her feel stupid, especially when I asked her to hold the rabbit-head staff.

No matter; I could get off on her boredom. I took off my clothes for the rush it gave me to be naked and vulnerable, shivering in the cabin's tepid heat while she remained clothed. It dramatized her stature without her having to do anything. If I was lucky she might make some small, telling gesture on her own—a yawn, a rolling of her eyes, a smirk. But I suffered stabs of frustration that she would not be exactly who I wanted her to be. I was kneeling on the rug and looking up at her, as if expecting some visionary utterance or divine gesture. If I played my role, she would assume hers.

I pushed her knees apart, trying to contain her squirming, my arms wrapped around her legs to hold them still as I buried my face between her thighs. For a moment in her contortions she appeared about to wriggle out of my hold. Then she stopped suddenly, as if exhausted by the effort, and lay beneath me, a wooden stillness. It was my role to be the worshipper of the goddess, to teach Pia the ways of the superior being she was destined to be. Once she accepted being worshipped, she would rise to the occasion; how could any sane woman resist the call of the divine? My claim on her destiny was inexpressible; it would have to be something she experienced. And because I loved Pia beyond my love for any human being in my life, the purity and innocence of my adoration would lift her from this world into spheres she had not yet imagined.

"Get away from me."

At some point in my struggle to burrow at her center, her voice reached me through a kind of fog, I became aware of her low, muffled cries by an unexpected knee to my balls. Her renewed efforts to escape from under my weight surprised me.

"Let go. Now."

I scrambled to hold her kicking feet, tightening my hold around her ankles until I felt her strength ebb. "Pia? Do you want to hurt me? It's your right to inflict pain on me if that's what you'd like."

"Adam, stop doing this," she said.

I pulled her off the chair by her feet, her body sliding until she landed heavily on the floor. I gazed down at her for a moment, then fell on her with the whole weight of my body. I wrestled with the elastic band of her panties until I managed to jerk them past her ankles. I had never wanted to be closer to her than at that moment.

"No," she said.

I pried her legs open with my knees and held her wrists to the floor. She struggled briefly to slide out from under me, then seemed purposefully to yield and go softly inert.

"No."

It was over in seconds. Unlike other times when we had messed around for hours, my intention had been not to satisfy my lust but to offer a tribute, as if the whole of my being, every fiber of cells and consciousness, could be distilled into semen, the alchemy of spirit and life force. I let out a small, exultant cry as I lost myself within her.

Feeling Pia still motionless beneath me, her eyes closed, her expression a blank, I rose on my elbows and stared at her face, trying to move her with the force of my attention into some kind of response.

Then I rolled off her body and straightened out her clothes, wadded up the torn panties, and laid a blanket over her.

"You had your fun," she murmured.

I couldn't think of a reply.

I hurried back into my jeans and shirt, bewildered by the strange space I had just left. I had allowed some alternate personality, held captive for my own protection, to emerge and unleash itself for a spell, only to shrink back into its hole, leaving behind sadness and unease. After the intense pleasure of a few minutes earlier, I was now paying a price for that moment of astonishing violence. I couldn't remember when I had last experienced the deep sadness that colored every thought with inky despair. My first impulse was to swallow a couple of Paxils, but I decided it would be better to keep my stash well stocked for Pia.

An hour later we were sitting on the bed, having cereal for supper. "This granola needs more raisins," I said, examining the bowl.

"You ever done that with a girl before?" she asked.

"Eat granola?"

"Rape her."

I tried to resist a sour taste at the back of my throat as I spoke. "I don't think it was like that. We've been doing this every night for weeks."

"You think we had sex."

"No. It was something different, purer."

She looked stunned. "What kind of world do you live in, anyway?"

"I'm not sure I can find the words, you know, to talk about it."

"Don't bother. Talk is overrated."

I had to agree with her. With all the confession therapy with Auntie and Dr. Clara at the 'Tute, I'd been able to talk myself into being declared fit for family, school, friends, work, love. I knew the formulas for remorse and conviction, the ways of the reasonable and adaptable client.

And now I could not find language that would allow me to push us back to a time when violence was unrealized. There were no words that would repair the damage I knew I had done. I said, finally, that I was sorry, sounding somewhere between a plaint and a whine. Her response was to hand me her unfinished bowl of cereal and to retreat deeper into the far side of the bed until the covers were over her head.

Chapter Thirty-Three

It must've started snowing after we fell asleep around midnight, and the sudden gusts shearing through the trees startled me awake before dawn. Pia's breath, marked by long exhalations, sounded exhausted, as if she had spent the whole night struggling against her dreams. I scraped the frost from the window and could see, illuminated by the moon, bunched flakes landing on the glass. Wet snow swirled in the wind, the first sign of the coming storm. I decided to make a run to the main house for more provisions; there was no telling how the blizzard might develop.

Pia was aroused from her slumber by my clumping around the cabin getting ready for my foraging expedition. She kicked down the covers and stretched her body, swamped in a set of borrowed sweats.

"What time is it?" Then, seeing that I was standing by the door, dressed for the outside, she asked where was I going. Ever since my first foray to the main house, she had grown insecure and greedy for my presence, fearful that I might leave her.

"We need more food," I said, opening the door.

"Snow!" she exclaimed as flurries swirled into the room.

"I know," I agreed warily. "We'd better stock up before we're snowed in."

"I think we should get the hell out before that happens."

"We're safe here."

"I don't like being here with you." There were clearly limits to the meds; Pia had not forgiven me.

"We should think of where we want to go," I said.

"I don't care *where* we go, Adam."

"Sure, we'll go somewhere. Meanwhile, you'll need warmer clothes." I had dressed quickly in Phil's jeans with flannel lining, a sweatshirt, and a parka. The pants were way too big for me; I had to cinch them in with a belt and roll them up before I put on a pair of duck boots, also too big, my sockless feet swimming inside them. I completed my expedition getup with a thick wool cap.

"I'd better go," I said quickly. "The snow's blowing in." A sudden gust slammed the door shut with a bang. I cracked it open and shouted to make myself heard above the roar outside. "It was the wind."

"Now I'm really trapped."

"I'll get you some boots from the house."

"Don't slam the door again."

"It was the wind," I insisted meekly. I knew there was more that I needed to explain, but it felt fitting that the goddess should withhold her forgiveness. Even as I insisted on hanging on to the image of the idealized object, she was gazing at me with a look of detachment, her eyes clouded with indifference. She knew before I did that there was nothing I could say to regain her trust.

I was about to leave when I sensed that leaving Pia alone was not a good thing. I turned around and faced her cold gaze, as if I had caught her in an unguarded moment, and her face was rigid with anger, without expression except for a hardening of her mouth and a tautness across her cheekbones. She was transformed, looking older, her body as she sat on the edge of the bed rigid, shoulders hunched forward as if to protect her chest, tight fists on her thighs, knees tightly pressed together.

"What's the matter?" I asked.

She said nothing but looked at me curiously, as if perplexed that I would ask such a question. I was immediately sorry I had blundered into one of her dangerous moods.

"Want me to heat some water for tea?" I said. "We still have some chamomile."

"No."

"Well, I'll bring some other teas from the big house. Any requests?"

"No."

I went to the sink and filled a glass of water. I sat beside her on the bed and handed it to her, and she took it in her hand without a word. Then I pulled out the cigar box with the meds and picked out a couple of Paxils and a Xanax, just the ticket, I thought, to mellow her mood and maybe send her back to sleep until I came back.

"No," she said when I offered her the pills.

"Come on, Pia." I tried to coax her, holding the pills out to her on the palm of my hand. "They'll help. Remember me, Dr. Bonehead?"

"No," she said. And then, in a motion as quick as a slap to my face, she knocked the pills out of my hand and sent them flying across the room. "No. No. No," she said, slapping my hands and arms in a beat to her every utterance. Then she reached behind me and grabbed the cigar box. For a moment I thought she was going to pick out some other meds, but instead she opened the lid and flung its contents to the far reaches of the cabin, scattering pills to every corner, under furniture, into the piles of clothes we had stuffed inside the narrow closet.

"*No,*" she shouted. I rose quickly to retrieve the pills I could see, but she started pushing me off balance, hitting my hands and arms so I had to drop whatever I picked up.

"Okay," I said. "I'm going to the house. Settle down. Please. And if you want to pick up the pills, that would be really great, Pia. Really cool. I mean, that's our stash."

"Just go."

It was a relief to escape into the storm. Wet flakes landed on my face, clinging to my eyebrows, melting on my skin and running down my cheeks and into my mouth. The way to the main house was covered with snow in a milky twilight, smoothing out the shape of the land so that I had to continually watch the position of the tree stands in order to stay on the path. Meanwhile, the word *No*, a hoarse moan coming from deep inside her chest, kept following me even as I walked away from the cabin and finally into the woods, its sound barely muffled by the falling snow but still loud in my head as if all the distance in the world could not get me away from her cry.

I felt clumsy in Phil's jacket and pants. Once at the main house I would pick out some clothes and load up with as much food as I could hoard under the pressure of the blizzard. We needed powdered milk, crackers, soups, more granola, pasta, sugar, coffee, candles, and matches. I had given up any attempt to make our stay imperceptible. We would be long gone before the owners returned and needed only to make sure we left no evidence that might identify us. I sympathized with Phil and Flo, who would return to a plundered house and a trashed cabin. I would leave a note and the promise of cash by mail. I didn't want them to think they had been invaded by ordinary criminals. I was eager to rationalize how Pia and I were spontaneous rather than premeditated in our stealing, for personal use rather than commerce and with every intention to repay once our adventure was concluded. All that made us fairly extraordinary, I thought. Foragers rather than burglars.

I loaded up the food in a backpack and extra clothes and boots for Pia in two pillowcases. I was about to leave the house when, on a whim, I set the bags down and decided to take one last look, like a hotel guest who checks the drawers for forgotten items before departing.

I started in the bathroom. I had already emptied the medicine cabinet, but I was attracted to the array of hair and skin stuff, the lotions and fragrances and cosmetics that signaled the room as the woman's domain. The bath looked inviting, a deep turquoise tub with a handheld shower. I started up the water heater and continued my exploration of the house.

The owners of the cabins were Phil and Florence and their kid, Emily, the three currently wintering in Daytona Beach, where, for six months out of the year, they managed the Sandpiper Motel. There were photos of them in their Florida mode—shorts, Hawaiian shirts, t-shirts, and even one of Florence in a bathing suit, showing off a decent figure for a forty-something. There were Florida pictures all over the house, as if they needed a reminder of the other half of their life. Unlike his wife and daughter, Phil showed a certain joy at being photographed. In one shot, placed prominently in a frame on his desk, he grinned with obvious enthusiasm as he hugged his wife and daughter tightly around the shoulders, more in ownership than affection. The girl had turned to her mother with a tense, questioning look while the woman gazed straight ahead with bland impassivity, as if daring the viewer to doubt the perfection of that moment.

I lifted the cover of the rolltop and peered inside the drawers, picking out green hanging files with bank statements, utility bills, tax returns, all neatly arranged by date and subject. The top cubbyholes held a variety of curious objects—a Las Vegas key chain, a variety of ballpoints with different motel logos, a Lake Superior engagement calendar showing advance reservations. I opened the book to that day's date and wrote in, *Two strange ones, Cabin #4*. I thought with some satisfaction that this was a clever gesture, much like taggers spraying their presence at the scenes of their mischief.

The bottom drawer held a mostly full bottle of peach schnapps, stress medication while working. I took the bottle to the kitchen and poured myself a taste. It was sweet and sticky, like melted ice cream, and tasted intensely of a jammy confection. Under the sweetness, a warming goodness traveled down my throat and chest, settling with a nice glow in my belly.

I told myself I was going upstairs for a last look, but I had already, without deliberation, decided to take a bath. Burglars have a tradition of taking a dump on a bed or a tabletop to mark the territory they have violated. I would do the opposite.

I turned on the faucet, and hot water gushed out. I had some huge clean underwear and socks from Phil's closet, and by the time I got back to the bathroom, the tub was filling fast. I threw my dirty clothes in a hamper (another surprise for Phil and Flo) and tested the water with my hand. I couldn't remember the last time I had bathed in a tub, maybe when I was little and Mother would decide that enough time had gone by between showers that I needed a thorough soak. I had brought the schnapps, and this time I took a sip right from the bottle. I set it on the floor and climbed in, my hands on the side to help me lower my butt. The sensation of the scalding water gradually covering my ass and genitals came back from my childhood episodes of self-torture as I moved my feet forward, allowing the delicious pain to inch up my legs. Steam rose all around me, bringing on a bright blush and beads of sweat. I took another drink of schnapps.

I rested the back of my head on the edge of the tub, and the water reached up to my neck. Then I plunged the showerhead into the water, letting the spray send streams of heat all over my body, a delicious tickling along my back, under my arms, between my legs. I poured half a bottle of bath salts into the water and lathered up my hair with lavender shampoo. Oh, thank you, Flo!

My days with Pia were precarious with the certainty that a crisis was always one breath away. Now, even as I felt a needle of guilt at enjoying such delights while Pia was stuck in the cabin, I wallowed in the riot of bubbles, drank more schnapps, and resolved that I would bring her for a bath as soon as the storm passed.

I closed my eyes and felt myself floating in a cosmic amniotic broth, a live, simmering brew stirring all about me, waking up hidden corners and forgotten cells. The effect was one of such fine sensuality and fleshly pleasure that I could feel a kind of sexual tension building, not localized in my genitals but in the totality of my body so that when an orgasm came, it spread in waves starting at the center of my chest and traveling in delicious shivers just beneath the skin on my back, arms, legs, and shoulders, then up my neck to the top of my head. I hoped that the violence of the previous night might be ritually washed away.

I might have started to doze off inside the tub when, under the scents of lavender bath salts and rosemary shampoo, I had a thought that bread was toasting in the kitchen. A moment later that first domestic image of breakfast back home was seared by the distinct smell of something burning nearby.

I leaped out of the tub and, dripping wet, ran, half slipping on the wet bathroom floor, into Phil and Flo's bedroom. Smoke was seeping out from under the closet door, and when I opened it small flames were licking one of Flo's dresses. I pulled it down to the floor and took some heavier clothes off the bar to smother the fire.

I'd sensed from the first reek of smoke that Pia was in the house. She had probably seen me in the tub and decided to ruin my bath. "Pia," I kept shouting as I ran out the bedroom and down the hall. The stink of smoke led me to the kid's bedroom, where the pillow on the bed was smoldering. I beat it down and realized that smoke was also coming out of the chest against the wall. I pulled one of the drawers out and put out a fire of pajamas and socks with a blanket from the bed.

I was running naked all over the house, shouting Pia's name, expecting her at every turn. I imagined she had already gone, leaving me with fires burning in corners, inside closets and wastebaskets, and finally in the office a furious blaze from a desk drawer stuffed with file folders.

I was yelping and shouting for Pia and cursing helplessly, dancing about the room, looking for something to use on the fire, when I saw the fire extinguisher on the office wall. I grabbed it, pulled the chain, and started spraying foam all over the house. I ran around in a panic, afraid that Pia had decided to torch the house with me in it. I was now the firefighter hero, wielding the extinguisher like a super-weapon, sending the white whoosh of chemicals into corners, drawers, closets, and cabinets.

The spout finally gasped to a white dribble from the end of the hose. I stood back in the hallway and felt the chill of the empty, smelly house. I dropped the extinguisher on the floor and ran back to the bedroom for the clothes I'd left on the bed. Once I was dressed I walked through all the rooms in the house, making sure there were no fires lingering to burn it down.

Chapter Thirty-Four

I put on the parka downstairs, pulled the thick cap to below my ears, and strapped on the backpack. I pushed my way out the door. A massive snow dump was on.

"Come on, blizzard!" I shouted. I didn't think anyone would be within range. The isolation freed me of accountability. Over a foot of snow had accumulated against the stoop, but I could still make out a fresh set of prints, Pia's, I guessed, leading away from the house. My own tracks had already been snowed over, and the path back to the cabin had drifted over in gentle waves. I pushed on, quickening the pace by lifting my knees high, making my way back by memory and guesswork, walking blindly until I could see, through the swirling fog, the faint outlines of cabin 4 somewhere to my right. I had, without realizing it, already strayed from the path and was heading deeper into the woods when I saw deep footprints straying from the cabin and meandering in a wide trench to the outhouse and then, as if having lost their way, through the woods toward the lake. What timid light had been present earlier in the day had disappeared behind dense cloud cover above the swirling flakes. The air was colder, and my face quickly numbed, ice crystals freezing on my lashes and turning the world into a fragmented fog.

The door to the dark cabin was cracked open where ice had compacted against the jamb. Inside, the air was frigid with air blowing in through the open door and snow dusting the floor, counters, and tabletop. Pia was not inside. I stepped out to shout her name several times, straining to hear a reply through the wind. When none came, I held on to a pillowcase containing the boots, thick socks, and hooded parka for Pia.

In the time I had taken to check the cabin, the drifts had further obscured Pia's trail. I shouted her name again but felt my voice swallowed by the roar of the wind. I wondered if she had intended to meet me at the main house, a half-mile stroll, then strayed from the path as she became disoriented in the storm. I expected to find her nearby since the accumulating snow made for slow progress. I would wrap her in the warm clothes and boots and lead her back. The clarity of the plan, the perfect rightness of my good intentions, eased the pangs of remorse that continued to nag me.

I cheerfully shouted out her name when I saw her standing motionless where the woods stopped at the edge of the rocky beach. I hadn't gone even a hundred yards from the cabin, but I was breathing hard from the labored march. Pia was facing the lake's rough surface, just a few feet away from where the waves broke against the rocks.

She was bareheaded, wearing only sweats, her shoulders hunched forward, her arms hugging her chest. It was only when I was close enough to touch her that I realized she was shaking violently, her whole body, from head to toe as if possessed by a current that rattled her to her bones. I tried to still her tremors by holding her close to me. Even when she stopped shaking under my embrace, I could still feel a faint vibration surging inside her.

"What are you doing here?" I spoke into her ear.

She managed to mutter, "Nothing," through her chattering teeth.

"Nothing?" I shouted. "Nothing? You just decided to stand out here in the middle of a blizzard for no fucking reason?" My words seemed to back up into my mouth almost as I spoke them.

Pia was trying to make herself heard through the quaver in her voice. "Hurt," she said.

"What hurts?"

I stepped back and felt her arms and legs and chest, thinking that maybe she had fallen. Her clothes had grown stiff and icy, but she did not cry out as I felt her body for an injury. She was still hugging her chest, and as soon as I let go, her knees buckled and she sank into the snow. I took out Flo's cap, cheerfully pink and white with a pompom on top, and pulled it onto Pia's head down to her ears. Then I tried to separate the arms from her chest so I could get the parka on her, but she held them locked.

"Please let go," I coaxed. "You need to put something warm on."

She had resumed shaking once I was no longer holding her close. The wind kept blowing the coat around until I managed to pull it over her shoulders and zip it part of the way up. I had started to shake, too, and my fingers were numb and unwieldy, overgrown mitts trying to tie the sleeves close to her chest.

I knelt in the snow, pulled my gloves off, and dropped them beside me to zip her into the parka. When I bent down for my gloves, I could only find the left one. I used my gloved hand to dig around the snow for the missing one, feeling as stupid as a drunk who has dropped his keys in the dark.

"Where the fuck's my glove?" I shouted at Pia, who was hunched over, her head tucked into her chest. Her only reply was to shake her head back and forth. It kept moving until I placed my hand on top of the cap's pompom and the motion ceased as if I'd hit a switch.

I went back to digging. I was convinced that finding that glove was a matter of survival. Without it my fingers would freeze, fall off, blood would drain. I needed that glove in order to help Pia. I was no use if all I could think of was my hand, frozen into a claw. I was shaking violently now, and all the time I was convinced that if I could just find that glove and put it on, then all would be well and I would warm up, starting with the tips of my fingers. Then blood would course along my veins and arteries, comforting the whole of my body from the inside out. And I would be able to rest, cozied up next to Pia, our bodies drawing heat from each other, our breathing slowing into the rhythms of sleep. The reverie was so vivid that it took a leap of consciousness to realize that for several minutes we had been sitting on the frozen beach, facing the white tundra of Lake Superior.

Chapter Thirty-Five

took off Pia's stiff sneakers and socks and tried to rub some warmth into her feet. Then I put on the winter boots I had found at the house, big, heavy things that reached above her ankle and which I laced up so they might stay on when she tried to walk. My fingers, as thick and lifeless as sausages, could hardly grip the laces, even when I took my gloves off. That's when I realized that I'd had gloves on both hands and had somehow found the missing one. I thought back to the moment, which seemed hours ago, when I was down to one glove and frantically rooting through the blowing snow. I managed to get the bootlaces tied and gratefully slipped the gloves back on. I clapped my hands to get them warm again, calling to Pia that it was time to get up and go. My mental gears seemed to be turning in sludge, but I knew we had to move to the warmth of the cabin.

"Come on, Pia," I coaxed. "We've got to get indoors."

Her only reply was a whimper of pain and anxiety, as if my pulling her to her feet was meant to hurt her. Her fists punched at the inside of the jacket. "Get me out of this thing. I can't breathe." Her teeth chattered as she spoke, and when I coaxed her to take a first step, she could only complain that she couldn't walk.

"It hurts to move," she moaned.

"Where's the pain?" I worried that she might have injured herself.

"Everywhere. In my chest, when I breathe."

I was holding her by the shoulders, hoping the closeness of our bodies would subdue the shivering that shook us down to our boots. "Come on," I coaxed her. "We can't stay here. It will be dark soon."

"It's already night." She forced out a laugh so filled with hopelessness and futility that it startled me. "I can't see a thing."

I turned her back to the lake, facing a mass of fog and swirling snow that had long ago erased any signs of a path and had reduced the woods to a looming phalanx of ghostly giants. I told Pia to lift her knees, to stride with purpose, like a horse, confident that we would be walking toward the cabin, away from the lake.

We couldn't help stumbling, the snow tripping our feet, our legs heavy and stiff so that we reeled like drunks, clownish at first but soon exhausting. "*Oh, show me the way to go home,*" I bellowed.

I decided I would help Pia by marching in front, making her hold on to me with my belt as a tether. I'd plow through the snow so that she could place her feet in my tracks, moving easily one step at a time. I looped the belt to the front of Pia's pants and wrapped it around my hand, pulling her onward whenever I sensed her flagging.

I missed the touch of our bodies but expected that the strenuous marching would warm us. Pia kept up with me for the first few minutes as I searched out the way to the cabin. For a time I had the satisfaction of movement, always forward into the woods, the certainty that the way to the cabin would reveal itself as we approached it. Even without a visible path, the groupings of trees created obvious directions where the way straightened out among them. I had a memory of having turned slightly right upon leaving the cabin, so I veered left, but always forward, no turns that might take us back to the lake.

Whenever Pia stumbled or paused, the strap tightened in my hand. Then I would either insist she continue by pulling the belt, or, for a brief rest, I would stop and retreat a couple of steps to help her along. Pia would simply stand flat-footed, her body swaying slightly with the wind. A quick yank served to wake her up, and she would resume the march, putting one foot after the other, her face in a frown as she concentrated on staying upright, and would manage to stumble along a dozen steps before stopping again.

Finally I felt the tug of the belt hard and low, and I turned to see that Pia had fallen back, sinking in the snow to her waist. I crouched before her, my face close to hers, willing her eyes to open and look at me. She had managed to push down the big parka, which was now draped around her waist. "You've got to cover up," I whispered.

"I'm hot. This thing is cooking me inside."

I knelt in front of her and pulled the coat up. "You can't take clothes off, Pia. It's freezing. Keep your hands in the pockets."

"I told you, I'm fucking hot," she slurred.

"It's not hot, Pia," I whispered, my face close to hers. "It's really, really cold."

I walked around behind her and circled her waist with my arms, then, clasping my hands at the wrists, I stood up with her, her weight then pushing me back. As I stumbled a couple of steps to regain my balance, I felt myself bumping into a hard surface. I turned to face a white boulder in a clearing among the trees. I ran my hands over it, energized by a surge of excitement, and brushed off the snow to reveal the smooth contours of Ted's blue Toyota. We'd been sitting in front of the car. I tried to announce the cheerful news to Pia, but all I could muster was a rattling laugh from the center of my chest. I scraped off more snow until I found the door handle. It took some effort to pry it open because it had been iced shut along the edges, but it finally swung out with a crack to reveal the inside, all velvety plush and free of snow.

"My God, we're safe," I yelled at Pia, who was nodding off again. This time I pulled her upright, though her legs, as rigid as logs, would not move. In the end I was able to lift her by the waist and in a couple of steps managed to push her into the backseat. I crawled in after her and pulled the door shut. The inside of the car was a freezer, but we were sheltered from the wind and the falling snow. It felt good to know that we weren't hopelessly lost, that the cabin was close by.

For a moment I pictured myself leaving the safety of the car and going to get the keys. It would be nice to start the engine and get some heat flowing. The thought came and went; I didn't have it in me to find the cabin. In any case our body heat would warm the car up. And Pia required close attention. I pulled off her icy boots to warm her feet with my hands. Then I stretched her along the backseat and laid her head and shoulders on my lap. I took off a glove and brushed the back of my hand across her face, which was white and dry as paper. I leaned over her chest and tried to offer her whatever warmth I still retained. She had fallen asleep again. I put my face close to her mouth and could feel her breath, now quiet and shallow, matching my own. Outside, it kept snowing, but the wind had stopped and the night had grown silent.

For the first time since setting off to find Pia, I was able to rest in the relative safety of the car to wait out the storm. I took off Pia's soaking wool cap and squeezed the melted snow into her mouth. She swallowed eagerly. Then I pulled the cap back onto her head, remembering that even wet wool will provide warmth. I felt that my fate was now out of my hands, and I could simply surrender. I didn't think to pray or hope for safety. I was content to let go of all effort and fall into slow-churning mental torpor. Tears welled up and rolled down my face, which I was helpless to understand or will away. Waves of relief washed over me, as if my weeping were dissolving my profound exhaustion, the draining of all strength from my arms and legs. The pain that had seized my head dulled as I gave up my struggle to stay awake.

Chapter Thirty-Six

I awoke to sunshine casting jeweled refractions through the ice crusted on the windshield, blue and red and yellow spots mottling the inside of the car, my chest, Pia's face. I shook her shoulders to awaken her to the good news, lowering my face to her mouth in expectation of a word or a sigh. I pressed my lips to her cheek, trying to breathe warmth on her dry skin. I kissed her repeatedly on the lips to get them to speak, on her eyelids to get them to open. She remained still as I nestled her in my arms, and after a moment I knew that she had not stirred during the night. She had been fading even before we'd found the car, and now, the rescue from the cold and the wind having come too late, her stillness was profound and unshakable. I imagined that she had slipped into sleep beyond the pain that had gripped her. Her face had settled into a distant serenity, reminiscent of some of her more aloof moments when I would fuss about, trying for her attention.

"Please." I heard myself choke on a sob. And for only a moment I was filled with a kind of desperation and rage that sent a sour bile burning into my throat. I tried to will a reversal of the last hours, the last days, a retreat to a time when we might have been outside the sway of the fates.

The turmoil in my guts that had threatened my ability to keep from vomiting, from shitting myself, subsided and was replaced by an ache at the center of my chest. In those minutes I grew out of blind adolescent faith in the entitlement of a full and happy destiny into the realization that a part of my life had been sliced out and would be forever cheated out of my experience. A cloud of mourning came over me, as much for my own partial death as for the loss of Pia. I would be awake to my own incompleteness for as long as I lived.

I rolled down the window, and a surge of frigid air made me gasp. It was so much colder than the bright sunshine had predicted. I estimated it might be close to noon. From all directions came the sounds of the forest emerging from its withdrawal, wings flapping overhead, creatures scurrying in the brush, ice-sheathed branches chiming in the wind.

I stepped out onto the deep snow and was amazed at the transparency in the air. Everything shimmered with new clarity: the trees around me, the silvery surface of the lake, the cabin no more than a few feet away. It was hard to believe what a short distance we had traveled through the blizzard for what had felt like hours of moving about aimlessly. I leaned inside and stretched Pia out on the backseat, bending her legs at the knee so that she looked relaxed, yet as if she were considering getting up at any moment. I covered her with my coat. I was not ready to let go of her face and allowed it to emerge between the parka collar and the wool cap. I shut the door and marched toward the cabin.

I was back at the car in a few minutes, armed with the ignition key and a shovel. I cleared the snow behind the back wheels and swept off the branches I had laid over the roof and hood. I scraped the ice off the windows and side mirrors and started the engine, letting the defroster blow warm air on the windshield. After days of lingering around the cabin with no purpose, I was filled with a sense of urgency. It was time to lay Pia to rest. And to go home.

I was so focused on following some kind of orderly sequence, moment by moment, that practical considerations did not occur to me. I had started up the car; I could easily have followed the driveway out to the road and gone to the nearest phone to call for help, to hand over Pia to someone who would know how to deal with her body. Instead I decided to back the car to the side of the cabin in a straight line along the ruts made a few days before. I got it there in stages. The first, amid much wheel spinning, took me off the trench I had created around the car. I shoveled the back tires clear again and pushed back a few more feet. Then, after more rocking and wheel spinning, I slid to a stop beside the cabin door.

The lurching had caused Pia to fall off the backseat onto the floor, and for a moment I felt ashamed for her rag-doll helplessness. I hurried to the cabin and shoved the big chair out of the way to clear a space in the middle of the room. Then I went back to the car, hooked my hands around Pia's chest, and pulled her out of the car, wincing as her feet dropped to the ground, then dragging her through the snow and into the cabin. I laid her supine on the braided rug, stretched her arms to her sides, straightened her legs, and aligned her head along the center of her body.

The bright sunlight of earlier in the day had been blanketed by clouds, leaving the inside of the cabin suffused in a gray light. I clicked on a switch, and nothing happened. Ice and falling branches had crashed the power supply. The baseboard heating panels were cold to the touch, and the refrigerator's groaning hum had gone silent. I had expected to spend another night in the cabin, in a vigil with Pia, while I figured out what to do next. I didn't have the heart to wrestle her back into the car.

I spread a clean sheet over Pia's body, observing her for a moment to fix the image in my memory, then finally pulling the end over her face. I gathered a dozen candle stubs and held a match to their ends to melt the wax, then placed them on the floor at Pia's head and feet and around her body. I thought she would appreciate the ritual formality of the flame points burning for her. I pulled the sheet down to see her face one more time; she appeared to be in deep repose, not quite absent, as if the flickering lights might cause in her eyelids a tremor of wakefulness.

It would be determined eventually that Pia had died from hypothermia. With no evidence of a crime, there might not be much of an investigation or a search for witnesses. Still, I wasn't ready to tell the whole story of our misadventure to the police or her parents. My first thought was to clear the cabin of anything that might be traced to me. We had not brought much, so I was able to fit our things into the backpack. I thoroughly searched through drawers and shelves. We'd had with us little more than the clothes we were wearing. In a few minutes there would be nothing to identify who had been here.

I found it difficult to pull myself away from Pia, as if finally leaving her behind would bring me to the full realization of our separation. I thought I should speak a few words. Could I ask forgiveness for having loved her, adored her, wanted to possess her? It's as if I had known that our time together would be brief and that losing her for even an hour in the storm would cost us a lifetime. In the end, as I opened my mouth to utter some declaration of love, all I could muster was a sob that seemed to have been lodged in my chest and was now exploding full blown in a blubbering, sniffling jag. And still I couldn't leave.

Once I stopped moving around the cabin, I felt the chill of the room hardening its grip, numbing the pain in my heart, confusing my mind. I thought to leave a note apologizing for the mess, explaining that the beautiful young woman surrounded by lights had died in the forest. It took me about an hour to find a pencil. I seemed to be looking in the same cabinets and drawers over and over again while the pencil was in a drawer I had rummaged through twice. Finally I tore a page out of the spiral notebook I kept in my backpack. *I'm sorry*, I scribbled. *I'm sorry, I'm sorry, I'm sorry.* And then I couldn't think of anything else to say, so I folded the piece of paper, intending to put it in her hand, which had balled up into a fist. I pulled open her index and middle fingers and slipped the note beneath them.

I took one last look, marveling again at Pia's stillness, surrounded by the candles casting a honeyed glow inside the room. I shut the door, letting it lock behind me. Ted's Toyota was parked in the middle of the clearing, aimed roughly in the direction of the driveway. I figured as long as I steered a middle course between the trees I would be guided by the track under the snow. I started the engine, and as the heater blew warm air on my face and chest, my new bout of shivering subsided. After a momentary spin on the snow, I was able to rock out of a deep rut and with a lurch found the traction to leave the cabin behind and aim for the main house, somewhere to my right, which luckily had not burned to the ground, and then onto the main road, turning south and heading for home.

Chapter Thirty-Seven

It was night when I reached Minneapolis. In contrast with the shadow darkening my mood, the city lights bouncing off the dense cloud cover gave the sky a festive glow. I drove aimlessly, rolling slowly through our neighborhood, marveling at the prevailing warmth of bright windows, TV sets flickering, the occasional Christmas display promising the stuff of storybook cheer in a world that I was reentering with a sense of loss and alienation. I drove past our house three times, slowing only to see that everyone seemed awake, the windows buzzing with light, teasing me with the imagined smells and sounds of the family's routines.

It was past midnight by the time the house finally settled into darkness. I approached the driveway, cutting the engine and coasting to Ted's spot in front of the garage.

I circled around to the kitchen door, which was open, as I had expected. I managed to slip into my room and shut the door without attracting any attention in spite of the snaps of the door latch shutting, the clatter of the car keys landing on the kitchen table, the creak of my footsteps. I took off Phil's clothes and pushed them deep into a corner of my closet. As I looked around for something clean to wear, I gathered Pia's clothes from around the room and held them closely, her presence a weightless cloud in my arms. I folded them back inside a drawer,.

I stole out of the room and down the hallway to the bathroom. I must've been under the spray for five minutes before I saw through the shower curtain the blurred figure of Ted sitting on the toilet. Please, Ted, I pleaded inside my head, go away.

"I think you're clean enough, little brother," he shouted through the rush of the shower.

I shut off the water. "I want to know where the hell you've been with my car."

"Your car is fine," I said, still hiding behind the shower curtain.

"That's good to know," he said. "But that's not what I asked."

One thing I learned at the 'Tute is that you don't want to be having a confrontational conversation with someone when you're naked and they're not. So I didn't say anything while I stepped out of the shower and toweled myself dry. I put on my jeans and sweatshirt as Ted, wearing his dragon red-and-black kimono, continued to sit on the toilet like some lordly samurai.

"I'm surprised you weren't stopped by the cops," he said. "I reported it stolen before I realized you were the culprit."

"I didn't mean to borrow it for so long."

303

"And then Albert and Marjorie reported you and your girlfriend as missing persons. You will be glad to know that the police worried more about my rusted Toyota than about you two fine human beings."

"We're all back here safe and sound," I said. "Well, not Pia," I added, catching the shadow in my mind again. "Just me. And your car."

"And your girl?"

I found myself squirming under his gaze.

"She'd been talking about going to see her mom in Texas, in a hole called Elysium." I added with sudden conviction, "In fact, we started to drive down there together."

"Jesus! You were taking my car to Texas?"

Ted left the bathroom, shaking his head

t took me a long time to fall asleep. I was exhausted, but my bed was a foreign, inhospitable rack, riddled with lumps and gaps. It was the first time in weeks that I had not spent the night with the press of Pia's body against mine, the sound of her breathing close by, the touch of skin on skin giving off moist heat. Even when our day had been shadowed by impatience and malaise, once we were in bed we clung to each other. If during the night our skin became sticky or the weight of a leg grew cumbersome, we shifted easily into a new position, perhaps my arm around her waist, her hips against my groin, then me holding on to her the whole of the night like a drowning man clinging to his rescuer.

When I finally fell asleep I was out until the following afternoon. My first waking thought was for Pia. It would be that way, I expected, for the rest of my life; I would fall asleep thinking of Pia, and I would awaken with the hollow of her absence haunting my first thoughts. I felt a transformation had taken place in my head and that I now understood life to be a state of constant mourning. We never stop thinking of our dead. Mother and Father would never get over the passing of their own parents, the death of their ambitions, the loss of Ted's and my childhoods, their expectations for our lives betrayed.

I ventured down the stairs to the kitchen, where I found Mother nursing a cup of tea, looking up as soon as I came in, clearly waiting for me.

"You must be hungry," she said, rising from the table and opening the fridge. "I could fix you some eggs or a sandwich."

I hadn't eaten since the previous day, when I'd rummaged around Phil and Flo's pantry for chips and cookies, but I felt a total lack of appetite.

"Just tea," I said,.

Mother poured and I wrapped my hands around the cup, comforted by its heat after the chill of the previous days. Mother had the ability to be in the moment with any of us without a need for chatter to fill the void.

"Do you think she will come back?"

I shrugged.

"You can't give her up."

"I suppose not." I sipped my tea in silence, and Mother stopped questioning me.

I had a history of not giving up on Pia. After we'd lost track of each other on my way to the 'Tute, I had thought of her every day. Then, once I'd been certified no longer a nuisance to myself or my family, I had set off on the search for Miss Entropia, scouring the web until I tracked her down.

Now I logged on several times a day, as if I could will my in box to show a message from Pia. I started a game with myself. I began to e-mail her in the mornings. And then in the afternoons, I would log on as *miss entropia* and read the messages from *adambomb*. I would reply, then log on to pick them up the following morning.

> adambomb@gmx.com
> oh goddess!!!!
> everyone here misses you! ted thinks you are really special and forgives you for your part in jacking his car. can you believe that they had an APB ("all-points bulletin" in police talk) and we weren't spotted during our joyride? LOL!!!! also, he has gone two weeks without a beating! his face is back to normal, but he's prowling that scene again. i wish he'd find another hobby. i know my life changed after i found you. there! i can hear you calling me a "bonehead"!
> latergator,
> a.

> missentropia@rocketmail.com
> Greetings from Elysium, Texas. I miss you all, too. Tell Albert and Marjorie that they are my favorite parents. Mom

here is a berserker, and her hubby, Tex (not his real name), is a number one a-hole. I do like the baby, Twinkletoes. I dyed her diapers black to make her really goth when I babysit. A high point. I get high and blow smoke in her face—she loves it!!!!!

P.

P.S. You should use uppercase. All lowercase makes you sound immature.

adambomb@gmx.com

you are insane. lucky baby twinkletoes!!!!

everybody keeps asking about you. iris doesn't think you are in texas. she says she may have been wrong about you. that you were probably spirited aloft in a preview of the rapture. HAHAHAHAHAHA. (see? uppercase!!!)

a.

missentropia@rocketmail.com

I never thought Texas could be so quiet at night. I can actually hear my hair and nails growing. It is true, you know, the nails make squeaking sounds. Hair sounds like a silky stirring of grass in the wind. You can only hear this when the body has become so quiet—no breath, no digestion, no blood flowing.

P.

adambomb@gmx.com

i keep thinking of you, down there in texas, surrounded by candles flickering in the night.

a.

missentropia@rocketmail.com

The candles have burned down to little frozen puddles of wax. It's cold and dark here. By the way, pretty clever of you to put me in Texas.

P.

adambomb@gmx.com

i didn't put you there. you took a bus.

a.

missentropia@rocketmail.com

Ha! So you say.

P.

adambomb@gmx.com

will you be back in the spring?

a.

missentropia@rocketmail.com

Why would you ask such a dumb question? I'm not looking forward to Phil and Flo coming back to reopen the cabins. They will freak!!!!!!

P.

I'd been home a week, and I still felt tired. I got winded walking upstairs, pulling a chair from the table, sticking a bag of Movietime Real Buttered Golden Kernels in the microwave. All I wanted to do was sleep and watch reruns of *Laugh-In*. I could identify with the slapstick and frenzied humor, Goldie Hawn grinning manically, the old man falling off the bench, all from before I was born but relevant to my current state. I ate crunchy, salty things washed down with beer. I was reluctant to leave the house for even a breath of air in the backyard. I was afraid of being seen. As if even a casual glance would open me for the world to look into the depths of my heart. The most I could handle was to look out a window, through a sliver in the blinds, and watch the leaden sky for signs of snow, for a glimmer of sun, for the occasional V of geese flapping south. The world's palette had gone gray and dun, and every surface exuded exhaustion.

missentropia@rocketmail.com
You can't go around in a funk. It puts the blame on me. Like I'm the bitch who left you—to go to Texas. Keep it up and you'll be on meds again, all sappy-happy and full of manic-panic. My advice: get out of bed by seven. Shower before you smell. Eat your veggies.
P.

missentropia@rocketmail.com
Of course I can give you advice now. I've got perspective. Besides, you're the one that's coming to me with your lame loser lamentations. Want me to shut up? Stop e-mailing me!!!! Easy. I DON'T need to be entertained. And don't get all self-tormented with guilt. You are not that important.
P.

missentropia@rocketmail.com
I think it's time you get on with your life. Get a job. Anything to make you clean up, eat regularly, get out of the house. The money will be nice, too.
P.

missentropia@rocketmail.com

You're not a criminal. But you are a bonehead, and that is its own kind of crime. Even if you don't go to jail for it.

P.

missentropia@rocketmail.com

Okay, time to snap out of it. The less you think, the less you will blab. This is your secret to hoard like a tumor. But if you insist on moping around looking suicidal, you will definitely attract more attention than you want. You know what Kali would say—you can't fight pain, sorrow, decay, death. They are part of the fabric of life. Kali gives you the freedom of the child after you accept death. You think we live forever? The goddess is LOL!

P.

It was the longest winter of my life. My good intentions about getting a job, getting into college, getting in touch with other kids from the 'Tute had withered. January was a gray shroud over the city, which lifted in February with a brilliant blue sky and −5 for the high. Weeping burned the edges of my eyelids; the tears crusted over and felt like sand so that in the morning I could hardly open my eyes. Every few days I would log on as *miss entropia* and follow my words into a frozen stillness in my head. No matter how avidly I wanted to hear her voice, read her thoughts, she was growing distant and elusive.

adambomb@gmx.com

why aren't you writing back? one e-mail after another and all i get is silence. please, one more word from you. and then, i'll stop bugging you. one more word, okay?

a

No? *No?* I could not accept that. There had to be more from Pia than a final, definitive, slamming rejection. I sought comfort in her things, her clothes. Anything that she had touched brought her closer, made her a presence in my room. I opened her books and inhaled the faint scent of her skin as it mixed with the notes of paper and ink. I rubbed her underwear on my face. I poured the contents of her black-beaded sack and jiggled her keys, struck matches from souvenir matchbooks, I looked at the world through her D&G sunglasses, I smelled her dark cherry lipstick and was instantly tumescent. Flipping through her address book, I stopped at her mother's name:

Felicia Timmins (Mom)
436 Boynton St.
Elysium, TX 39877
936-269-3290

I thought about it for days until I had to dial the number; everything that was Pia brought her closer to me. I pulled the phone into my room and shut the door. Even as I held the receiver to my ear and listened for the dial tone, I wasn't sure what I expected to happen. On the other hand, I decided that I would punch in one number at a time, and if I didn't change my mind and hit all ten digits, then whatever happened happened. I was curious, as if I were watching someone else go through this exercise. I heard the line ringing on the other end, and I knew that I could disconnect with the quick press of my thumb. The low, resonant voice speaking into my ear startled me, as if I hadn't expected an answer.

Hello.

Hello.

Who is this?

Its tone was so familiar that I feared I would not be able to keep myself from blurting out Pia's name. Instead I said nothing.

And then, abruptly, there was nothing on the other end.

I punched in the numbers again. This time the ringing went on longer than before, but I held on, intent on hearing that voice again, marveling that it could be so similar to Pia's.

"Hello?"

This time I would not give her cause to hang up. "Yes, hello," I stammered. "That was me just a second ago. I'm sorry we were disconnected."

"So, who is this?"

"I'd like to speak to Pia."

"You mean my daughter, Francine."

"Yes, that's right, Francine."

"And who are you?"

"I'm a friend of hers."

"Do you have a name?"

"She called me Bonehead."

"So you expect me to tell her that Bonehead is calling?"

"Yes, she'll know who it is."

"And you're a friend of hers."

"Yes."

"And how did you get this number?"

"She gave it to me before she left."

"She left Minnesota?"

"Yes, she said she was coming to stay with you."

"When did Francine take off?"

"Oh, some days ago. Maybe longer."

"Francine is not here. I haven't heard from her in weeks. And I want to know how you got this number."

"Ma'am, I told you. She gave it to me. I'm her friend. I know all about you and your burned house and your cowboy husband and your baby Twinkletoes."

"I don't believe you. I want to know what's going on with my daughter."

"Well, *I* don't believe *you*. How's *that?* I think she's in her room and you won't tell her I'm calling for her. I think you have her prisoner."

"You're nuts."

"Pia!" I yelled, even after the phone had died in my ear.

In the evening, when the family gathered for dinner, Father asked, "So who were you talking to this morning?"

"Nobody."

Ted was not about to let me off the hook. "You had the phone tied up forever. You were practically screaming someone's head off."

"Oh, that," I said. "I was trying to talk to Pia. But her mother said she didn't want to talk to me. She just kept saying no. 'Mrs. No'

313

is what Pia used to call her. And now Pia was also saying no, that she didn't want to talk to me."

"So what are you going to do?"

"I could kill myself," I said. And then, when I saw everyone's face go pale, I let out a silly laugh. "Just kidding, guys!"

Father cleared his throat and took a sip of coffee, a ritual of his whenever he was about to make a pronouncement. "Well, the best thing is for you to get on with the business of life. I hope your slacking days are over."

"Yes, I believe they are," I said as earnestly as I could.

"So what on earth do you do with yourself all day?" he insisted.

"I pray," I said, which pretty much shut everybody up, including Iris, who had a hard time picturing me in prayer. What do they know? I actually had a history of praying for all kinds of things and to all kinds of deities at the 'Tute, where a little extra magic could result in better meds and happier therapies. I used to pray to Kali, to Tonantzin, and to Isis. And now, in the middle of the darkest winter of my life, I was about to start praying again in earnest. I would pray for Marjorie and Albert to stay cool once the truth of my adventure with Pia came out. This was going to happen soon. Once March came the weather would moderate, Phil and Flo would return from Florida, and shit would rain.

"What do you pray for, son?" Mother asked.

"For the living and the dead, and everyone in between."

"That's nice." She forced a smile.

At the time I was actually praying that Pia would vanish before she was found. I had fantasies of the cabin going up in flames. She would be eaten by wolves. Her body would be washed out to the lake by a freak tsunami. All violent ends, to be sure, but more dignified than Phil and Flo walking in and confronting her frozen body. And that would be just the start of the indignities. There would be forensic poking and scraping to establish her identity and time of death, to seek evidence of foul play. Then the search would be on for whoever saw her last. Eventually, after a month or two, the story of her last days would be reconstructed—from the original break-in to the fires in the main house to our trudge in the blizzard to my frenzied departure.

Eventually they would know my name.

Epilogue

'Ve returned to the North Shore for the first time in the ten years since Pia and I came here together. Once I was past Duluth and on 61, the rush of the landscape took on a kind of inevitability. I pushed the rental car without stopping for gas or food, as if any delay might cause me to change my mind. This time it's March; the landscape is bleaker than when I was last here. The skeletal woods bare of foliage, the road shoulders packed with dirty snow, the sky a low gray slate. The exuberance and sense of adventure I felt in my long-ago trip with Pia have been replaced by a sense of obligation, with the need for reflection and cleansing, to close the chapter on those distant events.

I almost missed the turnoff to Phil and Flo's Lakeshore Cabins by Lake Superior. I was looking for the faded billboard I had seen the last time, but now I was alerted to the turnoff by a neutral highway sign, white Helvetica on blue. No promise of fishing, canoeing, and campfire sing-alongs.

Little had changed in the approach along the dirt road, its ruts smoothed over by a fresh scattering of gravel. About a mile into the woods I recognized the main house, still flaking green, with a sagging porch and broken concrete steps leading to the front door marked by a wooden "Office" sign. I parked beside the house and waited for a surge of anxiety to pass, then took a deep breath and walked up the steps. The door gave way to a slight push, and I found myself in the familiar front room facing the pine counter with the registration book, pen on a chain, and bell to announce my presence. I slapped the bell, and Phil, recognizable from the family pictures placed around the house, looking rumpled in corduroys and a flannel shirt, emerged from the back office.

"Welcome," he said amiably, using a corner of his shirt to clean his glasses. He hooked them back around his ears and peered at me through the foggy lenses. "Jack Adams?"

"That's right." I smiled blandly back at him, secure that he wouldn't know my face, despite all the publicity, unless he and Flo had attended any of the hearings or happened to look me up on some public records website. He would certainly have remembered the name "Adam." In any case I'd been seventeen then and now, at twenty-seven, I'm no longer the clean-living youth I once was. I have a pale complexion and a pudgy shape from too much time indoors, too much starchy food, too many meds, and too little sleep.

I filled out a registration card with the first things that came to mind, a fanciful phone number and address, and my name for the occasion, Jackson K. Adams.

"You'll be checking out on Friday," he said as he scanned the calendar on the counter. "That's three nights, one ninety total. We take Visa and MasterCard. Even checks."

"I can give you cash." I pulled out my wallet and handed him a sheaf of twenties from my recent visit to the ATM.

"Oh, sure, we take money, too." He pocketed the bills without counting and handed me a ten in change. Peering into my empty wallet, he added, "I don't want to clean you out."

"I brought tea and sandwich makings," I said. "I need to hunker down to finish some work. Deadlines, you know."

"Are you a writer?" he asked, willing to be impressed.

"Of a dissertation on the Hindu goddess Kali." I tried what I hoped was a modest smile.

"Can't say I know much about that."

"Obscure stuff."

"Well, we can offer you peace and quiet," he said. "No other guests; it's too soon for spring break, even. So it's just us bachelors."

"The sign says, *Phil and Flo.*"

"Well, a while back Flo cut me loose, as we say in fishing. It got to be a hassle keeping up the place, what with winter maintenance and the occasional vandalism." He gave a rueful smile. "Take it from me, you don't know what you had until you lose it."

I tried a sympathetic shrug. "It's been years since I had a girlfriend."

He placed three keys on the counter. "You can have your pick of cabins 6, 4, or 2."

"I don't need much," I said, reaching for number 4 as if at random.

"Fine. You will want to switch on the thermostat by the door. It'll be toasty in no time."

I walked gingerly toward the cabin, pausing at the threshold to allow a sudden lurch of queasiness to settle down in my gut. I closed the door behind me and, with the rustle and chirping in the woods shut off behind me, was taken in by the room's profound silence.

Once I've set my laptop on the table by the kitchen, plugged it in, and opened this document, I sit back on the familiar dinette chair and finally take a look around me. I'm pleased that little seems to have changed. The same La-Z-Boy from which Pia ruled my heart. The beat-up wooden table where I'm writing this has been spruced up with a plastic tablecloth in a pattern of pinecones and acorns. A couple of new prints of the fall woods, a sunrise over Lake Superior, an elk staring straight at the camera with sad, dewy eyes enliven the knotty-pine walls. And in the middle of the room is the same oval braided rug in reds and oranges and blacks on which I laid Pia to rest. I notice the evenly placed wax stains, round as quarters, where the candle stubs burned down.

I haven't jacked up the thermostat, but the lights are on, and they provide a measure of warmth and cheer. I've set water to boil for tea and cracked open a new bottle of peach schnapps.

The whistle from the kettle brings me back to the moment. I'm pleased that Phil is still providing the basics to his guests—I find teas, sugar, powdered milk, and the familiar mugs with flying ducks. I drop a bag of chamomile tea into the largest mug and half fill it with boiling water, then top it to the rim with the schnapps.

Finally, as I type these words I settle down to the task at hand. I scroll back to the beginning of the document and am happy to reread my story of how I met Pia, how I lost her and found her again. How we loved each other and how we weren't able to claim a life together.

It's a story that through the years has come out in bits and pieces. I was relieved when Father came home one evening in the early spring, almost ten years ago to the day, with the newspaper rolled in his hands. He sat heavily on the chair and waited for me to come into the room, as if he had been silently ordering my presence.

We seemed to be alone in the house, and I felt that he had come home early to speak with me. In any case I could wait for the small talk about job searches and weather and baseball to run through its paces like an athlete warming up for a hard run at truth and consequence. We'd never been particularly easy in each other's company, so I could sympathize with Father stumbling around for an angle to guide his conversation.

"Any news from your girlfriend lately?" he asked.

"No."

"So you haven't heard anything?"

"No."

I realized he was edging into what he really wanted to talk about. He gestured at the newspaper in his lap. "The things one reads about," he said. "Sad, terrible things right in our backyard."

"What happened?"

"Read it for yourself," he said, reaching across to me and handing me the newspaper folded to a brief inside article. I didn't have to read its four paragraphs word for word; it was enough to take in the mass of gray print in one visual gulp, swallowing the essence of the story about an unknown female found dead, her body arranged as if in some kind of ritual in a North Shore cabin. Phrases jumped out in disjointed sequence. Signs of vandalism and burglary. Dead for months. Cause unknown. Frozen. No sign of foul play. Autopsy and identification in the works. Cabin owners Florence and Phillip Benson have no idea who she is or what she was doing there while the resort was closed for the season.

I handed the paper back to Father. He took it and looked at me in his steady, inquisitorial style.

I shook my head in response to his gaze, a shared moment of wordless horror.

"You know something about this, don't you."

It was not a question. I nodded and searched for some place to begin, but I could not figure out how to tell the rest of the story.

Whatever I did say eventually came out haltingly, extracted first by a lawyer my family hired, then by a couple of detectives, a district attorney, a judge, and a psychiatrist. I answered questions with absolute precision, bit by bit, yet everyone shook their heads in disbelief, incomprehension, confusion, and finally pity. The facts I dispersed gave ground to different narratives of those six days, tailored to the questions each asked, yet as far removed from the story of my relationship with Pia as a map from the road. By the time it was all over, even my

321

family thought they had heard the complete story. When Mother asked me one morning what I knew before I was to turn myself in, all I could say was the truth, that I didn't know where to begin.

In the end I was convicted of reckless endangerment resulting in death, but rather than prison time I was paroled to the care of The Cedars, a kind of postgraduate facility for the 'Tute. I did miss my family, but by then I had become an alien, bewildering appendage to their lives. No problem; I've always thrived in institutions. I did okay at The Cedars. I liked the social life, the games, the jokes, the meds, the time to think.

Along with all that came the urge, more of a desperate need, as I recall, to write down the complete story of the two brief times when my life intersected with Pia's, in total no more than a few weeks but with such shattering consequences.

As I look back on these pages, I realize there is little left to add. These past ten years have been an exercise in memory, the search inside my mind for the shadings of emotion that color my every thought of Pia. And always the residual regret and speculation that if I had not raped her that last day we were together, she might not have gone on a torching binge in the house and then wandered off in the blizzard. I never revealed this ugly fact during the questioning and subsequent therapy sessions, but I am now obliged to face it.

This evening, being back in Phil and Flo's cabin 4 allows me to shake off the past and be in the present. There is something liberating about having no future, no hopes or expectations to be dashed, no fears to be realized. The truth is that the path to this moment has been straight and unencumbered. I was not sidetracked by the hours of therapy or the years of pretending to be free of guilt and grief and love. And what an actor I've been—polite and docile, usually cheerful. Meanwhile, I was building up my stash, and the more pills I collected, the more secure I felt, like a miser who counts his money every night, afraid that the slightest drain on the bankbook could expose him to penury and hardship. No matter how tempting it was to swallow a dose now and then, I exercised great willpower by lodging the pill behind my lip and then transferring it to my secret box. I tailored my symptoms to my growing inventory. A year of insomnia produced a ton of Snoozers; agitation brought me Zippers; depression, my number-one symptom, gave me dozens of Zonkers.

I've unpacked the small suitcase I brought. There was not much in it, some books I want to have close to me—*Don Quixote*, *The Bhagavad Gita*, *Das Kapital*. Interesting what a short distance my reading has traveled since I was thirteen. From the bottom of the case I pulled out Pia's turquoise prom dress. I unfolded it and laid it over the oval braided rug where Pia had lain ten years ago. It's the first time I've looked at it since stashing it away before checking into The Cedars. Already the empty dress calls me.

I poured all the pink and blue and green and purple pills out on the table like confetti, sorted them in piles by color, subdivided them by shape: rounds, triangles, capsules, and caplets. I took a dozen Zippers and swallowed them down with half a cup of schnapps tea.

Even the few steps to the kettle to refill the mug and add more schnapps took a long, slow time as I picked up my feet one after the other. Not a bad start as I waited for the distinctive heaviness, my hands leaden on the keyboard, my shoes sinking down as if the floor had turned into a swamp.

decided to take the kettle back to the table, as having to make the trip to the stove again seemed way too big an effort.

Next a handful of Zonkers. So far I'm not even queasy.

After about fifteen minutes this mellowness grows into a separation of skin from flesh, hair from head, bone from marrow, thoughts from mind.

The hand that reaches for the kettle and pours is not the hand that reaches for the first handful of Snoozers.

This is the definitive action, the moment of truth.

Until now simple preliminaries, warm-up exercises, stretches for the sprint.

I feel the pills are settling and another handful goes down i'm staying awake so far so good concentrate on my two fingers poking away at the keyboard on my thoughts fuzzy like dreams i have to keep my stomach from churning then stand at the table and fill my mouth with Snoozers of different colors and shapes moons and stars and cosmic dust the tea has cooled enough to be chugged down with gulps of the sweet peachy liquor mix to flood the pills all the way into my stomach yes where they stay i am so focused to think of Pia but she's only a vague idea a faint presence at the other end of the room.

Okay now i will circle the table and lie down on the rug my face to the stars my thoughts on elysium pia's prom dress covering me

here I go . . .

to whoever finds me forgive

Acknowledgments

The genesis of this novel was a short story, "Feast," which was published in *Eclipse*, a national literary journal from Glendale College edited by Bart Edelman. Ordinarily the publication of a piece of fiction would have put the idea to rest.

In this case, however, the characters continued to grow in my imagination, and one action led to another. Along the way, as the initial story became this novel, I was fortunate to receive comments and observations from friends and colleagues.

Andrew Proctor critiqued an early draft with uncommon clarity and sensitivity to the needs of the story.

Robert Warde's generous reading left no inconsistencies, malaprops, danglers, or splits unchallenged.

Bart Schneider has been a valued adviser and friend for many years, and his reading of my fiction always opens windows to add both sheen and substance.

It has been my enormous good fortune to enjoy Fred Ramey's editorial vision. I'm grateful to him and all the Unbridled stalwarts for their embrace of my work.

Juanita Garciagodoy nourishes my writing with her intelligence and love. She is present in every story I tell.

To all of you: *Mil gracias*.